Matter of Time

J E Nice

Book One
of the
Last War Trilogy

Copyright © J E Nice 2016
All rights reserved.

J E Nice has asserted her right to be identified as the author of this work in accordance with the Copyright, Designs and Patents Act 1988.

First published in Great Britain in 2016 by
Write Into The Woods Publishing.

ISBN 978-0-9955326-1-8

Cover design by BioBlossom Creative.

www.jenice.co.uk
www.writeintothewoods.com

*To me mam
who gave me the gift of storytelling
and is my support, idea bouncer-off-er and
cheerleader.*

*My dad
who supports me endlessly without question and
always gives the best advice at the right time.*

*And my Chris
who allowed my dreams to take flight.*

One

Between the vast fields separated by stone walls and small homes, and the cold water's edge of the murky ocean, sits the disjointed city of Drummbek, populated with humans and dragons. In the centre sits the castle, as if grown from the rock upon which it sits, overlooking the buildings of the rich and poor which spill across the land in all directions, joined by bridges over what was once a large lake. And from this castle, on this particular afternoon, there came a horrendous, but muffled, scream.

*

It was just loud enough to make the kitchen staff all pause in their stirring, chopping, cleaning and chatting to listen, but not quite loud enough to move them into helping. Tabitha had just poised the cheese cutter over a large block of dark yellow, foul smelling cheese, when the scream sounded. She lowered the device and stared into the centre of the kitchens, listening with the others.

'It's the Drummbek Witch,' muttered one of the cooks. He seemed too old to believe in such superstition, thought Tabitha.

'Don't be ridiculous,' called Agnes. Her large, scaled body moved through the kitchen, glittering yellow, her swinging tail artfully missing every pot, knife and pan. 'No such thing as witches.' She heaved in her breath, making her chest bulge, and then moved up onto her hind legs to glare over her kitchen. 'Everyone back to work!'

The noise level in the kitchen immediately increased as the staff returned to their jobs. Tabitha eased the cutter through the cheese.

'There is such a thing as a witch,' said the cook who Tabitha deemed too old for such fairy tales. He was slicing vegetables at speed and seemingly talking to himself. 'Mark my words. They'll be another missing body before the sun has set.'

'Shouldn't we find out who screamed?' asked a boy with a mop. The man gave him a sympathetic look. The boy was new.

'There're always screams,' said a woman nearby, polishing cutlery. 'They come from the dungeons. 'Tis prisoners being bitten by the rats or cryin' about their starving bellies. Nothin' to worry your young 'ead about.'

Tabitha stared out of the nearest window, into a small courtyard that overlooked the hills towering over a corner of the city, and sighed. It was a perfectly logical argument, if only the scream hadn't come from the opposite side of the castle to the prison.

'And the witch lives in the prisons,' pointed out the man, scooping up a handful of finely diced carrot and throwing them into a pan of boiling water.

'She kills prisoners?' asked the boy. The man stared at him.

''Course not. She's flies out and steals someone. Makes them do her bidding, eats them or sacrifices them to her gods, or peels their skin from-'

'Kelvin!' Agnes glided through the workstations.

The man snapped to attention. 'Did I hear you right? They'll be no more talk of witches. Certainly no talk of peeling human or dragon skins. My word, man, this is a kitchen. Food is present. Watch your mouth.' Then the chef was gone, on the other side of the kitchen remarking on some well baked apple turnovers.

After a short pause, the boy asked, 'How does she escape the dungeon?'

Kelvin the cook rolled his eyes, returning to his vegetables.

'She's a witch. She uses magic.'

Tabitha stopped listening. The cheese now suitably cut into small cubes, she wiped her hands and stared at the plate as her mind wandered. What if someone did go missing tonight? It wouldn't be the first time. Often there were screams, at all times of the day and night, heard from the castle. From the prisons, they said. The walls and tunnels of the castle creating echoes, transplanting noise to other areas. Those who went missing didn't turn up in the prison and, so far, no one had returned.

'Tabitha?' Agnes barked from behind. Tabitha jumped and looked sheepishly at the small dragon. 'Are you finished, girl?'

'Yes, Ma'am.'

'Good. On with you then. I'll need you for serving, be back dressed and preened in an hour. Don't be late.' Agnes grinned as Tabitha nodded and walked past. Despite the mouth of sharp teeth, Agnes' smile was friendly and warm. Tabitha was never late.

But there was a first for everything. Yes, Tabitha had mopping to do but there was also a mystery to solve. There was no reason for her to go outside. The castle was one large building of corridors, one labyrinth for servants and vast, grand hallways for those of higher standing. The only staff seen in those hallways were those who were hard at work, cleaning or rushing to fulfil the king's orders.

Tabitha's duties that day included helping in the kitchens and serving the evening meal, as well as cleaning a part of the servants' corridor. If anyone had spotted Tabitha stood in the doorway, looking out at one of the courtyards that separated the buildings in the castle grounds, and asked her what she was doing, she would have struggled to come up with a story. That made her pause. With a shake of her head, she stepped outside and into a sharp breeze. Hugging herself, Tabitha scurried over to the building covered in shadows off to the side.

The dungeons were not a welcoming place; almost hanging over the edge of the rock upon which the castle sat. The breeze strengthened and whistled down the steps, cut into the rock, leading to the single door entrance. One guard stood at the top of the stairs, his eyes half closed, rocking as the wind caught him. It was getting dark, one or two early stars blinking in the navy sky, so it took him a while to notice the small figure of Tabitha stood before him.

'Uh!' He straightened, his cheeks puffing out. 'Who goes?'

'Where?'

'What?'

Tabitha blinked up at the guard.

'Did you hear the scream?' she asked. He bent a little to give her a proper look, and then his expression softened and he laughed.

'Tabitha?'

'What?' Tabitha didn't recognise him.

'You're little Tabby Dunn, ain't ya? Yeah, my mam

knows your mam. They work together. Richie.' He held out his hand. Tabitha took it, his hand consuming hers, and they shook. His touch was gentle and for a moment she was lost for words. 'Now then, what's this about a scream?'

Tabitha stood with her mouth open.

'A scream,' she said. 'Yes. Did you hear it?'

A scream sounded from below them.

'That's a tricky one,' said Richie. 'You hear a lot of screams when you're stood here for hours. Just standing. Listening.' He sighed.

'Oh. Well, do you mind if I take a look?' She moved to go down the stairs.

'Woah!' Richie stood in front of her with his hand held out. He thought that made him look more official. 'You can't go down there. Little girl like you.'

Tabitha bristled.

'I'm not a little girl.'

'You're little from where I'm standing.' Richie winked at her. Tabitha bit down on her tongue, clenching her hands into fists.

'I'm short. I'm not a child.'

Richie laughed.

'Ain't you got work to do, little Tabby Dunn?'

Another scream sounded from below. It wasn't the same pitch as the earlier scream heard in the kitchens. Tabitha looked up at Richie and decided to play along.

'You ever seen the Witch of Drummbek?'

Richie hesitated.

'No.'

'Do you believe she exists?'

He shrugged.

'Explains where all those people went, don't it.'

'Does it? Where did they go then?'

Richie frowned.

'Pretty sure you got work that needs doing, Miss Dunn. And I'm pretty sure that it don't include annoying the prison guards.'

Richie became tall and quiet, signalling the end of the conversation. Tabitha took one last look down the stairwell, listening carefully to the cries and grunts. With a shiver, she returned to the castle. It was quiet back inside those walls and she wondered where that scream could have come from. The throne room perhaps, where the King met with visitors. Or the grand hall where he took his meals.

Tabitha swore loudly. If her mother had heard her she would have reminded her that ladies employed within the earshot of aristocracy swore only under their breath where people wouldn't hear. That was her mother's logic, Tabitha thought with a smile. She faced the long servants' corridor. It had to be cleaned before the king took his evening meal and she knew by the shadows stretching across the walls that she wouldn't have enough time.

*

Rupert reread his message, written in scrawled handwriting, one last time. With a nod, he rolled up the letter and sealed it with melted wax. The messenger, a small bronze dragon who kept his gaze to the ground, bowed as Rupert passed the scroll to him.

'Fly swift,' the king told the small dragon. The messenger bowed again and backed out of the room, using a wing to close the door behind him.

King Rupert sat back in his chair and smiled. Everything was coming together. Perhaps a little slow for his liking, but finally his plans were falling into place. It wouldn't be long now.

There came a knock at the door.

'Enter,' the king called.

'Your Majesty, your dinner is due to be served.'

'Already? I'm sure I just ate.'

The servant hesitated.

'Your Majesty. Lunch was six hours ago.'

Rupert cocked his head at the man and watched the human grow pale. The king stood, pushing back his chair.

'Was it now? My, how the time flies when you are reading.' He glanced at the books that surrounded him. 'Very well. I'm sure I have room for something tasty.' Smiling as the trembling servant moved out of the way, Rupert left his library and headed towards his chambers to prepare for his next meal.

*

The muscles in Markkus's right thigh were twitching again. He rubbed at them, trying to soothe the movement. His right leg began to bounce. Placing his palms down on his thighs, he inhaled and held it before letting the breath escape through his mouth. His legs fell still. The large table at which he sat in the grand hall had two place settings, one large and one small, befitting the king and his taster. It was the same routine three times a day, every day, and it had been so for the last four years. Markkus swallowed a laugh. Four years.

His fingers drummed on his thighs as noise beyond the doors heralded the arrival of the king. The doors opened and King Rupert entered, flanked by guards and staff. Markkus stood, tall and straight, his legs now strong. This was the moment when he could forget where he was and give in to the instinct that decades of training had instilled in him.

King Rupert made his way through the hall and took his place next to Markkus. After bowing and taking his seat once more, the muscles in Markkus's thigh again began to twitch. He tried to ignore them.

'Good evening, Markkus,' rumbled the King. 'I hope we are still well since we last met?' There was a flash of teeth as Rupert smiled.

'Very well, Your Majesty, thank you. And I do hope that you are also still well?'

'I've had an excellent afternoon, Markkus.' The King chuckled. 'Most productive. I spent most of the hours in my library, reading.'

'What are you reading, Your Majesty?'

King Rupert looked down at Markkus from his great height. Something in the gleam of his green eye made Markkus nauseated.

'"*The Art of War Strategy*." Have you read it? You were a commander in the last war, were you not?'

'I was, Your Majesty, and I have read that book. Are you enjoying it?'

'I find it boring at times.'

Markkus gave a wry smile and then felt the King's keen gaze upon him. 'Did you find it boring, Markkus?'

'No, Sire. But I believe it is a book that may have to be read in context.'

King Rupert nodded.

'Indeed. Perhaps you are right. Well, we wouldn't want another war, would we? So let's hope I continue to find it boring.'

Markkus considered suggesting that the king try reading something else, when the doors opened and three maids entered carrying the first course. The first he recognised; she was young with non-descript brown hair tied tightly in a bun although wisps still escaped around her ears. Her eyes were soft and although she kept her head bowed, her gaze flitted around the room. He smiled as it landed on him and, much to his surprise, she held the eye contact. She was pushing a large golden bowl of soup on a trolley. The maid behind her helped to transfer the bowl onto the table, before the king. As she stepped back, hands folded in front of her, she once again lifted her eyes and met Markkus.

The third maid placed a bowl in front of him and ladled a small helping of soup from the king's bowl into Markkus's. He thanked her and lifted his spoon, waiting for the king's order.

Tabitha was sure that the royal taster looked at the other two girls just as much as he looked at her. He smiled and thanked Daisy as she served him his portion of soup. Markkus was a good man, Tabitha thought. A polite man. Was that his training, she wondered. Was that the military that had given him good manners, or was that him?

At the king's signal, Markkus dipped his spoon into the soup and sipped at it. A pregnant pause fell in the grand hall as everyone waited. It was silly. Tabitha had never heard a bad word said about Markkus, and no one would dare put poison into the king's food for fear of killing him.

He had been handsome once in his youth. Over the years his hair had fallen out and his blue eyes had become flecked with grey. The deep lines on his face were the first giveaway of his past, his iron leg was the second. It was rumoured that during his time in the army Markkus had built up his immune system by tasting a different poison every day.

He fascinated Tabitha.

Markkus gave his approval to the king, who grunted

and began to feast upon his own serving. The three maids bowed and Tabitha couldn't resist one last glance at the taster before she turned to leave. Her cheeks burned as her eyes caught Markkus's once again and she turned sharply as he gave her quick smile.

The evening meal was long. There would be plenty of time for Tabitha to study the taster. As she waited patiently to be called back into the grand hall to clear the bowls, she thought back to the scream. Had Markkus heard it? She couldn't imagine him believing in the Witch of Drummbek.

'The ghost is walking again tonight.' One of the guards stood near them sniffed. 'Heard its screams earlier.'

'That weren't a ghost,' said the other guard. Tabitha didn't look up, but she pricked her ears.

'What else screams like that?'

The second guard shrugged.

'It was a cat or somethin'. No such thin' as ghosts.'

'My little boy says it's the Witch of Drummbek.'

The second guard seemed to consider this.

'Aye, well, maybe there's such a thin' as witches. But what would a witch be doin' in the castle? Witches live in little cottages in woods. Everyone knows that.'

'In stories they do. This is real life,' the first guard pointed out.

'If we're talking about real life, it were probably one of those poor bastards down in the prisons. There's all sorts down there. Rats that gnaw off yer toes, drips that eat through yer skin, and that's before you start thinkin' about those what're in there with yer.' The second guard shuddered.

''Course. Probably the prisons. I didn't think of that.'

'Ghosts and witches. My, my. You and your

imagination,' the second guard laughed. Tabitha frowned. Could the castle be haunted? She looked up, towards the end of the long, wide hallway and imagined hearing the screams of the dead.

*

In a small, loved house down Black Bull Lane in Old Town, Tabitha collapsed into the small wooden chair that her father had made for her when she was a child. The chair creaked but it didn't break. Tabitha's mother glanced over her shoulder from where she stood at the stove.

'Tough day, love?'

Tabitha stared up at the cracked ceiling.

'No, normal day,' she murmured.

Her mother held out a plate. 'Here, set the table. Your father'll be home soon.'

Tabitha sighed as quietly as possible, stood and took the plate. She laid the table in silence, glancing up at her mother intermittently.

Compared to the king's three course feast, their evening meal was a meagre sight. Thin chicken boiled with small potatoes and carrots, the remains of which made a broth for tomorrow's supper. Tabitha's mother grew her own vegetables but the weather had been cruel. Money was, as always, lacking, even more so since the king had raised the taxes for the sixth time during his reign.

'Good evening!'

Tabitha's father swept through the front door and into the kitchen, his arms outstretched wide, bending a little as he walked through door frames. Tabitha's mother smiled and gave him a kiss. He turned to Tabitha and offered her his cheek. She kissed him. She loved her father, there was nothing not to love.

Every family has one, the mad one, the eccentric one, the loud one. Usually it's an uncle and indeed Tabitha's cousins called her father Mad Uncle Erik. According to Erik, he had travelled to the very edge of the world as a salesman. When she was little he told Tabitha that he had sold spells to wizards and hexes to witches. Her mother told her one day that he had actually sold utensils and pots and pans, door to door. It was true that he had travelled far although she did not comment on the edge of the world. He had knocked on her father's door one morning and she had opened it. Unlike any other man she had met, she had promptly fallen in love and married him.

Erik sat next to Tabitha at the table and pulled his plate of food towards him.

'Mmm. So, how is the castle? Still snooping?'

Tabitha cringed. She slowly looked up at her mother who glared down at her.

'You told me you'd stopped snooping.'

'I have,' Tabitha said, hoping she sounded believable.

'Nothing wrong with a bit of snooping.' Erik wagged his fork at Tabitha. 'It could lead to a promotion if you find anything juicy.'

Tabitha swallowed.

'That's blackmail.' Tabitha's mother swiped her husband round the head. He ducked playfully.

'But what about that young fella? The one that's gone missing.'

'Sammy Updike?' said her mother. 'Have they found him?'

'Nope.' Erik shook his head. 'But I heard today about his last known whereabouts.' He leaned towards Tabitha conspiratorially. 'According to Mikey's friend's brother's son, young Mr Updike was on his way to the castle.' He pointed his fork at his daughter, as if he was proving something. Both women stared at him.

'So?' asked her mother. Erik rolled his eyes.

'So, he went to the castle and vanished. Just like that last fella. And wasn't there a woman a few months ago or so who went for a job interview at the castle and wasn't seen again?'

'Yes she was. She took a job in a tavern down by the docks.'

'Did she? I don't remember that. It wasn't in the paper.'

No, thought Tabitha. It hadn't been in the paper. And the girls at the castle were still talking about that woman, wondering where she could have got to. And even if she did take a different job, what of the others?

'One of the boys has been off sick for two weeks now,' she murmured. Erik's eyes flashed.

'What with?'

'Poor lad,' murmured her mother.

'I don't know. No one will say. They've stopped talking about him.' Tabitha was about to mention the scream in the castle, but she snapped her mouth shut before the words could escape.

'Maybe Tab shouldn't be working with royalty. Sounds like a dangerous place to be working, that castle. Plus it's haunted. Everyone knows that. And what if there are riots again, like when good old King Tobyias kicked the bucket? Especially with King Rupert being so greedy.' Erik looked at his wife.

'Don't say things like that. It does Tabitha good to work there. Don't listen to those rumours,' her mother whispered to Tabitha.

'Which rumours?' said Tabitha. There were so

many, and adding those to the ghost and witch explanations gave Tabitha a headache.

'Well, I heard word down the market today that the king is taking people and selling them.'

'Who to?' said Erik, aghast.

Now Tabitha's mother leaned forward, lowering her voice. 'Other dragons,' she hissed.

'What would dragons wants with humans?' Tabitha asked before she could think.

Her mother shuffled in her seat uncomfortably.

'Never you mind.'

'For food?' blurted Erik. His wife shot him a deadly look but he grinned into it. 'Greedy bastard.'

'Erik!' Tabitha's mother leaned back, glancing around the small kitchen. 'Someone might hear you.'

'Round here? I doubt anyone cares, love. Anyway, I didn't know about them rumours.' Erik grinned at his daughter. 'I was talking about the taxes. Here we sit struggling to put food on the table while the king bathes in our hard earned money.'

'There are those worse off than us.'

'And don't you forget it,' Erik said to his wife who smiled despite herself. He turned back to Tabitha. 'So?'

Tabitha again considered telling them but just shrugged.

'Nothing. Today was like any other day.'

Erik looked disappointed as he chewed.

'Ah well, maybe tomorrow then.'

'Stop encouraging her.' Her mother sat down at the table. 'She should be working hard so that she gets noticed by a good man.'

'A nobleman is not going to notice a cleaning maid, Milly,' Erik said with all the seriousness of sanity. He glanced at Tabitha, not wishing to hurt her. Tabitha almost laughed. As if she wanted to marry a nobleman.

'Well, perhaps not. But if you work your way up…' Milly looked at her daughter. 'There must be some nice men in the castle?'

Tabitha's mind instantly conjured up an image of Markkus. She blushed and felt a ball of guilt settle in her churning stomach. Milly saw the blush and smiled.

'Yes, a nice handsome young man. Money would be nice,' she said, dreamily. 'But it's not of great importance, I suppose. As long as he treats you right.'

Tabitha stared at her food. Yes, young and handsome. Those were the qualities that should make her blush, certainly not an old, bald, crippled war veteran. She stirred the food around her plate. Her father watched her thoughtfully.

'Don't matter who he is, Milly. Long as he has a good heart and loves our little girl. That'll be enough for me.'

Tabitha looked up at her father and he winked at her. 'Anyway, if all these rumours about the king are true then I want to know about it and Tabitha's in just the right place to get the information. Ain't you, my girl.'

'Well, if I find anything dad, I'll let you know.' Tabitha smiled and took a mouthful of food.

Two

It was raining. Sheets of water, bouncing off the ground and roof of the ruined mansion house with a roar. The house was silent, the thick stone walls blocking out the noise. The rooms Del had adopted were peaceful except for the constant tapping as raindrops pattered off the large windows.

Del was missing this, however, because she was outside in the stable block. It was a grand building and had once been home to up to thirty horses, but that had been the same time that the house had a complete roof, a dry cellar and much less ivy growing up the inside walls. Del ran a brush over her horse's rich black coat, watching him listening to the rain thundering above their heads. His pricked ears turning this way and that. Del gave his back one last brush and left his stable, sitting just outside his door to face the rain and clean her sword. Normally she would do this in the house where she could light a fire but she didn't fancy braving the rain.

That was one reason.

The other reason was the smell. The scent of fresh rain filled the stables but it came with a heaviness. Del breathed it in trying to discern whether a storm was approaching and if so, what kind. In Del's experience there were three different types of storm. The light ones with a dash of rain and a flash of lightning. The heavy ones when the sky near fell to the ground and thunder boomed. And the storms defined by blood. The latter of these was the reason that Del sharpened her sword, staring out from her vantage point at the soaking countryside.

The ruins of the house, its outbuildings and stable block sat on a hill. Once a nobleman had been able to look out from his house over his land and the peasants who worked it. That had been a long time ago but Del knew her history. It was all about power and who has it.

The land that had once belonged to the peasants was now scrubland and marked on modern maps as the Wastelands. It had been a battleground during the Great War. Del hardly recognised it without the array of tents, dragons and men sat around fires. Without the lingering smell of cooking meat and sweat and fear. No one would have known that there had been battles fought here so recently, were it not for the odd piece of armour or weapon, missed by the looters and half buried beneath the earth by the weather and animals. Del imagined somewhere there was an old map which showed that this land belonged to one of the nearby cities or towns. For now, the land was not fertile, so no one saw fit to claim it. That would change one day. Perhaps there would be another battle. Another war. More lives lost just so that someone, somewhere could say they ruled this piece of earth. But that was nothing new. Del leaned back and looked at her sword, seeing the world in its gleam.

Over a nearby hill a group of people were riding towards Del and her little horse. Not that they knew Del and her horse existed at that moment in time. At the front was a woman walking, taking care to guide her horse around every hole and drop in the ground. She reached the top of the hill, her horse trotting a few paces to keep up, and stopped to stare at the large abandoned building. Wiping the rain from her eyes, she turned back to her men.

'We could camp there for the night,' she shouted over the roar of the weather. One or two looked to where she pointed, the rest kept their eyes down, avoiding the sting of the heavy raindrops.

Del stood as she spotted the movement, her sword by her side. As the company began to approach the stables, Del turned away. She lent her sword against the wall before blending into the shadows in the corner of the block, the wall cold against her back. Slowly, she slid a knife from its sheath in her belt.

The leader of the group walked cautiously into the block, out of the rain. The others followed, dripping on the cracked pave stones and glancing into the stables as they went. The leader stopped and held up her hand as she spotted the small black horse stood in his stable. The company stopped behind her.

'There's someone here,' said one of the men. They began peering into the nearby shadows and searching around them. Those at the back mumbled their opinions about still being stood in the drenching rain. Del flattened herself against the wall and slowed her breathing. The leader moved closer, watching Del's horse. There was a ring as she unsheathed her sword, holding it up as she moved forward, dropping her horse's reins. The mare nodded her head for more freedom and moved over to Del's little mount, snuffling at some stray hay. Del's horse continued munching, unperplexed. The leader walked around the stable and past the hidden Del. She was short with a ruddy complexion. Her blue eyes were set off against her blonde hair shorn close to her head. Del watched as she studied the polished sword against the wall, her eyes narrowing. Del wrapped her arm around the leader's neck, spinning her and pulling her close. Holding the knife to her throat, she pushed the blade against her skin. All attention turned to Del. Two of the closer horses lifted their heads high, their eyes wide as they struggled backwards. Del's horse continued munching; he had seen worse.

'Hello,' the woman in Del's grasp croaked. Del scanned the people stood before her. One man with olive skin had unhooked a crossbow from a saddle and aimed it at her. 'We didn't realise the house had inhabitants,' the woman continued with a smile. Del glanced at her. It wasn't often that she met someone who could hold a decent conversation with a knife to their jugular. 'Please excuse us,' she continued. 'Allow us to introduce ourselves. We're not a threat, I assure you.'

'You'd be amazed how often I've heard that,' Del hissed.

'I'm sure. My name is Andra. Captain Andra Ferrer. These are my company. We're Dragonslayers,' Andra said gruffly, her hand pulling a little on Del's grip as she strained to look at her.

Del blinked.

'Where are you headed?' she asked.

'Drummbek. And you are? If you would be so kind.'

'My name's Jude.' Del let Andra go, pushing her away. Andra turned to face her, studying her and rubbing at her neck.

'Jude. And what are you doing in an old abandoned house in the middle of nowhere, if you don't mind my asking? Are you alone?'

'I'm just stopping.' Del squared off to her.

'And where are you headed?'

Del thought quickly as doubt dropped into her thoughts. She wondered if now was the time. After all, she was only a few miles from the city, a company of Dragonslayers had arrived on her doorstep and there was a smell of blood on the air.

'Drummbek. I've come from Peacedown, outside of Arisdon. I need the work,' she told them. Andra searched her eyes.

'What do you do?'

'I'm a blacksmith,' said Del, without hesitation. Andra looked down to Del's knife and then to her sword. It was a believable story, many tradesfolk travelled between cities searching for work, especially in these unsettled times. She nodded to the men behind her and her company began to settle their horses and remove harnesses.

'What are you doing?'

'You don't own this house. We have as much right as you to squat here for the night. We need shelter, our horses are tired.' Andra turned to her own mare still eating from Del's hay. 'Perhaps you could grace them with some new shoes.'

Del searched Andra's eyes for mistrust or perhaps even familiarity. She found the former in abundance but did not recognise the woman. Unfortunately, that didn't mean that Andra didn't recognise her. It would only take one person.

'Is the house habitable?' Andra pushed past her men and back out to face the rain. Del hurried after her, fingers tight around the hilt of her knife.

'Parts of it. I can show you which rooms are dry,' she submitted.

'Good and perhaps in return for your hospitality you would like to join us for tonight's meal?'

Del made a non-committal noise as she led Andra up a damp staircase and away from her own adopted rooms.

*

Andra lit a fire in the huge range of the largest of the rooms Del had showed her. She stood with her back to the flames as she watched her company enter the room and collapse onto the floor.

'Did you scout the area?'

A little man with sharp eyes nodded.

'Nothing, sir. No sign of dragon or man. I suggest look outs, however sir, as always.'

'As always.' Andra nodded. 'Two hour shifts throughout the night. Volunteer for the first?'

The short man snapped to attention and saluted.

'I volunteer, sir.'

'Good man, Peking.'

Peking spun on his heel and marched out of the room, picking up his pistol from an antique but worm eaten table as he went.

'Where's the woman?' Venkell asked. He rested his crossbow against the wall and sat by the fire. He was a tall man with silver scars across his face and short hair that curled when he allowed it to grow. He pulled his knees up to his chest and pulled off a worn boot to inspect a sodden sock.

Andra shrugged, glancing down at him, absently noticing the flecks of grey in his hair.

'Outside I imagine, hammering some metal.'

'You don't think she's a blacksmith?'

'She's handy with a knife.' Andra rubbed her throat

as she turned to face the fire. 'But she's no blacksmith.'

'Well, you would know.'

'Yes.' Andra glanced at Venkell once more over her shoulder, wondering how much he knew, before walking from the room. Her men watched her, knowing well enough not to question where she was going, and began to unpack provisions.

*

Del stood under the shelter of the stable block staring out at the bleak hills. The rain had stopped but the clouds had not lifted, giving everything a washed out, grey appearance. She watched one of Andra's men setting up a perimeter around the grounds.

'Will you join us?'

Del jumped, jerking her head round and cracking her neck in the process. She did her best to pretend it hadn't happened. Andra moved to stand beside her, watching Peking. 'For a meal.' Del relaxed, rubbing the back of her neck. 'We have some beef that we collected only two days ago. Makes a lovely stew.'

Del's stomach grumbled in response. She hadn't eaten a good meal in days.

'Where did you get beef from?'

There were no large animals in this part of the Wastelands, if there were Del would have been hunting them. There were no cattle. The nearest farm was a good half days ride away.

'A cow. Found a group of five near here walking on the road towards Arisdon. Strangest thing, don't you think?'

Del nodded.

'Only five?'

'Only five. No one herding them. I suppose they

were either lost or stolen. We had run out of food so we slaughtered one. Makes me wonder who would have brought them onto the Wastelands. Not much grazing in these parts.'

'They can eat the bushes,' Del said absent-mindedly. She was staring at the horizon, all forms of explanations playing out in her mind. 'But any cow would choose grass over bush. You say you are dragonslayers? Were you on a job?'

'A few actually, yes. In Arisdon and some villages on the edge of the Wastelands. We've come from a rogue that had been killing sheep in a village some forty miles from here. Last week she took a little girl. There was no dragon near the cattle, if that's what you're wondering.'

'But you ran out of food? I would have thought the king of Drummbek would give you more than enough to last you.'

There was a silence.

Del felt Andra's stare on her. She shifted her weight from one foot to the other.

'When do we eat?' she asked. Andra smiled.

'That's a nice necklace.'

Del looked down sharply, her hand rising to cover the jewellery. It was too late, it had been seen. 'Some charming dragonslayer give it to you? A token of his affection, maybe?'

Del looked up and searched Andra's eyes.

'Yes,' she said finally, her fingers brushing over the worn dragon tooth hanging from a silver chain. 'It must be very exciting, being a dragonslayer.'

Andra's eyes flickered.

'Yes.' She smiled. 'Yes it is. Lots of travel and fraught with danger. Tell me, what happened to your young gentleman?'

'Oh, he was killed.' Del shrugged, remembering the faces of past lovers.

'I'm sorry.' Andra studied her. Del was staring hard at the horizon. Andra followed her gaze. There was a distant roar which echoed up the hill. Andra glanced at Del out of the corner of her eye as she remained fixed on the horizon.

*

Del stopped at the doorway. The room was a bustle of noise. A big pot was hanging in the fireplace, the yellow and orange flames licking at its bottom. Andra stirred the stew, nodding to the tall, olive skinned man talking with her. Del imagined the right thing to do would be to sit down and join in. She remained standing, distant from the group. Andra began to pass around the stew until everyone cupped their hands around a steaming bowl. Spoons were produced from saddle bags and pockets. Del's stomach growled as she watched one man lift a spoonful of meat to his mouth. Andra smiled at her, holding out a bowl brimming with meat and water.

'Here. Come and sit.'

Del took the bowl. Her fingers delighted in the warmth and she breathed it in. Andra gestured for her to sit beside her as the others shuffled around to create room. She sat cross-legged. Andra passed her a wooden spoon from her pack and produced a second for herself. Del managed a smile of gratitude. She dipped the spoon into the thin stew and drew it to her lips, blowing gently to cool it. The others were already half way through their own meals. The chatter had died down and only whispers amongst those on the edge of the group remained. Del placed the spoon in her mouth.

'How is it?'

'Good. Thank you.' She swallowed the tender piece of meat.

'It's good to have some fresh meat. Shame about the lack of vegetables. What have you been eating out here?' Andra asked.

'I have some dried meat but not much. Tastes like wood and some of it could break your teeth.'

'We should thank the gods for sending cattle our way,' said one man on the right of the circle.

'And the dragon that ate the herders.'

The whispers stopped.

'Corporal Lawrence. You'd do well to keep your mouth shut,' Andra warned. Del looked at the boy who had spoken, he looked barely fourteen despite an attempt at a beard.

'You think a dragon killed the cattle herders?' Del tested. The corporal met her eyes.

'A dragon prob'bly just stole the cows.' His eyes flicked to Andra, waiting for his scolding.

'You'd think a dragon would know better than to go rogue. Was only recently that dragon's treated their rogues the way we treat ours. Doesn't bear thinking about, turning rogue. Bloody death sentence,' said another man.

'What about Del Thorburn? She isn't dead. Is she?' Corporal Lawrence leaned forward, as if this was a story he had enjoyed before.

'Probably is, Lawrie. Rogue slayers don't stay alive long,' said someone.

'How would you know? Del was the only rogue we've had in a long time. Rules get forgotten when they're not practised. Probably why more dragons are turning rogue. They've just forgotten what happens to them.'

'And it's our job to remind them,' the olive skinned man sat next to Andra pointed out.

Del fancied she could feel Andra's gaze on her.

'Del weren't no usual rogue, though,' came another voice from the circle. 'She was different. She was fighting for something she believed in. She didn't just get power hungry or turn mad. And she didn't kill anyone she shouldn't have.'

'She threatened the king's life,' said the olive skinned man. 'She committed treason.'

There was a murmur from the circle that lifted Del's heart.

'Everything okay, Jude?' Andra asked. Del realized she'd stopped eating. Her stew was going cold. Piling another spoonful into her mouth, she nodded. There was an awkward silence as the company looked at her, remembering she was there.

'Who was this Del?' Del asked after swallowing hard. The company relaxed, some leaning back, scratching at their full bellies or beards.

'One of the greats,' said someone. 'Led us into war under King Tobyias. Led us to victory. She had a knack, did Del Thorburn. She never lost.'

'Never lost a battle, no. But she did her own kind of damage, I heard. Shared a bed with the king and then lost his baby. And the princess blamed her for the death of her son. Can't blame the queen, of course. Must've been hard. Seeing the woman your husband loved lead your only son to his death.'

'People die in war. Wasn't Del's fault.'

Del had stopped listening. So that was what people remembered. The supposed affair, the lost baby, the death of the prince. If only they knew. Del remembered King Tobyias vividly; his kind eyes in his hard face, just as she remembered the Queen Consort Natalia's keen gaze and the pain that had replaced their softness. It made her feel sick.

A barking laugh broke into Del's thoughts. The heat in the room was overbearing and the men were enjoying themselves.

'No such thing as the Drummbek Witch, Lawrie,' laughed the barking man.

'Then how do you explain it? All these people going missing? No dragons, mind. No one's mentioned that.' Corporal Lawrence raised an eyebrow. A few men rolled their eyes.

'People are going missing in Drummbek?' Del turned to Andra. The captain gave a non-committal shrug.

'It's all just rumours that have spread outside the city and become twisted.'

Del heard the doubt in Andra's voice, a slight waiver.

'What would a witch want with people?' Del asked.

'For her spells,' said Lawrie. The men laughed again. 'Well, who else is taking 'em then?' the boy near shouted.

Del knew, and from the silence that followed she realised that others knew too. Things had obviously changed. Had they changed enough?

One of the men broke the silence with a new subject. Soon the dragonslayers were discussing their families left behind four months ago. Del sat quietly through the descriptions of children, of how others met their partners, of how Grandma Bun fell in the pond. At first she searched her memories for a shareable funny story to continue the charade. She attempted to recall a loved one's face. She remembered her mother and father, but they were blurred images worn at the edges. The memories of the women of her village and their harsh tones were clearer. Even more so where those of her peers and colleagues. Of the Great War, the battlefield, what happened in the tents. The memories of life in the royal castle, of aristocrats and underpaid servants, were clearer still. She remembered King Tobyias and his faith, his Queen Consort Natalia and her gentleness, King Rupert and his sharpness.

After a while, Del blocked her ears to the others and stared at the fire. She listened to the white noise inside her head growing louder before mellowing and reaching out, over the heads of the dragonslayers, through the walls of the house and out into the darkness. Del heard her horse whinny to his neighbour. She listened to his slow breathing and moved past him out to the scrub of the hills. There was a loud thud which shattered through Del. A low growl and Del was back in the house. She blinked a few times and took a deep breath before standing and walking, mostly unnoticed, from the room and out of the house.

*

'I know who you are.'

Del didn't turn at Andra's voice. She continued to stroke her horse's nose as his eyes drifted closed, his ears flopping to the sides.

'Will you return to Drummbek?' Andra continued.

'I said I was heading that way.'

'You're really going back?'

Del looked up at Andra and gave a small smile.

'Will you arrest me?'

Andra immediately shook her head.

'Why not? You have oaths and tradition to keep, Captain. The order was created when dragons and humans warred. They still teach about the Old War, I hope? When the slayers protected the rulers and their kingdoms from the dragons. And when peace came, the Dragonslayer Order continued to serve under the First Law of dragons and men. And so it continues.'

'The teachings haven't changed,' Andra murmured.

'The Dragonslayer Order ended in all cities apart from Drummbek. I would have thought something in the Order would have shifted by now. Time has a way of changing things.'

'It does. It has.' Andra's mouth twisted. 'Perhaps it would be better if they didn't teach the history. To concentrate on what really matters.'

'And what's that?'

Andra hesitated.

'To fight,' she said. Del raised an eyebrow. 'There are too many of them,' Andra murmured.

'Is something going on?'

Andra didn't reply and in that pause Del made up her mind.

'I'm coming back. With you.'

Andra looked up in surprise.

'With us?'

Del nodded, patting her horse on the neck and walking back into the house before Andra could find the words to respond.

*

As dawn reached over the horizon, the company were saddling their horses. Andra found Del bent over inspecting her horse's hooves.

'Farrier work?' Andra said finally, glancing at the men around them.

Del didn't look up or acknowledge her although she smiled to herself, falling back into character. She gave the hoof a quick brush, dropped it and moved to a hind leg.

'I was wondering if you would be so kind as to escort me to Drummbek?' She ran a hand down the horse's leg and he obediently lifted his foot. She caught it and inspected it for nicks and grazes.

'Going to find work in the city?'

Del lowered the hoof.

'Yes. I'd appreciate the protection of dragonslayers.'

Andra gave a curt nod.

'We can't have you getting in our way.'

'If you have work to do I will stand aside.'

'Fine.' Andra nodded. 'We leave in an hour.' She left the stable block, checking on the company's progress as she passed. Del ran a hand over her horse's small black ears.

'What do you think, Shadow?'

Shadow pricked his ears forward at the sound of her voice. She had never liked the name but it had been his when she'd bought him as a starved carthorse from a young farmer unable to find the pennies for his feed. Six months of good food and rest had turned him into a stocky little horse. The fact that he had turned out to be brave and sure footed was a wonderful bonus. 'Time to go home,' she whispered to him, running a hand down his neck.

*

She listened to the dragonslayers from inside the house as they prepared to leave with the odd shout of instruction or whoop of an inside joke. Del squeezed her spare pair of thick woollen socks into the last empty space of her saddlebags. Tying the bags closed, she tested their weight. Standing back, she looked around the room and considered what she had packed. The socks and a clean shirt, her only spare clothes. Her trusted penknife lived in a sheath on her belt in preparation for the worse. Until the worse happened it came in handy when Shadow caught a stone in his hoof. The equipment she used to clean and sharpen her sword, knife and pistol. The pistol lay on top of her folded shirt in the first saddlebag, hidden but within easy reach. The shots and powder were in a leather pouch beside the pistol. In the second saddlebag was another leather pouch filled with herbal ointment and wraps of cloth for use as bandage. Giving the room another once over, she sighed. She was missing a lot of her possessions, lost or broken during the last year. The most important being her rifle, broken beyond repair three months before. It niggled at her that she was returning to Drummbek without it. She could buy a new rifle when she arrived. With what money, she would have to figure out along the way. She bent to look under the bed. The floor was clear except for a four-inch layer of dust and a touch of green from the ivy pushing its way through the floorboards. Of course, she may need a rifle on the journey. No, she was travelling with bona fide dragonslayers, she should have no need for a rifle. She struggled to convince herself. It wasn't that she didn't trust them. It was more that, well, it didn't matter if she had no rifle. A pistol would have to do. She could only use the pistol as a last resort, as soon as the company laid eyes on it their suspicions would grow. Many dangers waited for her in Drummbek, she wanted the journey there to be safe at least. She would have to remain calm and quiet, she decided, no matter what happened.

Del looked down at herself, at her mucky hands and torn clothes. She remembered a time when her skin had been clean, well-scrubbed even. When her hair was always brushed and tied back without a wisp coming loose. Back when she had owned a full uniform. Now dirt smudged her skin and her black hair was grimy with grease, the silver ring in the top of her right ear would be a small shine peeking through. At least she looked like a travelling blacksmith. She might have to neaten herself up when she got to the city, but for now the dirt served a purpose.

*

The company left within the hour as Andra had promised. They travelled for twelve companionable hours that first day without incident.

As the sun began to dip below the horizon, the company set up camp. Del led Shadow away from the others to a large patch of grass and the shelter of a tree, and dropped his reins to the ground. He immediately lowered his head and began to graze on the near yellow grass underfoot. He knew this routine well. Del placed her bags under the tree. She lifted the saddle from Shadow's back, propping it up against the tree trunk. Taking an old rag from one of her packs, she rubbed down Shadow's back, belly and legs. Satisfied that he was clean, she removed his bridle and faced the newly made camp, leaving Shadow to pull at the grass. Rough tents already scattered the ground surrounding a large pile of twigs and branches. Del approached Andra who stood in the centre, watching her company work. The tethered horses stood on one side of the camp, slightly along from Shadow, under a row of trees. Three men were working on removing the harnesses, replacing bridles with collars and rubbing each horse down. Andra turned to Del as she approached and looked back towards Shadow.

'You'd better tether him. You don't want to have to walk the rest of the way.'

'He'll be fine.'

'Fine. Do you have a tent?'

Del shook her head.

'There may be room in one of ours.'

Del almost laughed.

'No, thanks. I'll be fine over there with my horse.'

'Nonsense, it'll be freezing.'

'With a fire that size burning? I doubt if anyone in a five mile radius will be cold.' Del flashed a smile at Andra before wandering back to Shadow and seating herself, cross-legged, under the tree where she continued to watch the fire lighting efforts.

Andra watched Del momentarily before approaching the large unlit fire.

'Trouble?'

Venkell looked up at Andra's distracted voice and glanced back to Del.

'Just a bit damp,' he said by way of explanation. 'Something troubling you?'

'Night is drawing in.' She wrapped her long coat around her as emphasis. Venkell nodded.

'And something about that woman troubles you too.'

'Oh. Nothing new.'

'She's no blacksmith. So what is she?' Andra met Venkell's gaze. 'Why not ask her? Woman to woman.'

Andra looked into his dark narrowed eyes and gave a small sigh. Hands on her hips, she strolled over and stood looking at Shadow. Del kept her eyes fixed on the small flame which now licked at the insides of the large pile of wood.

'Back so soon,' she murmured.

Andra sucked on her front teeth as she gave Del a long sideways look. She carefully sat beside Del on the limp grass.

'You've had dealings with a farmer, by the looks of things.'

'He was a farm horse, yes.' Andra waited for more but Del wasn't forthcoming.

'They'll find out who you are eventually,' Andra said after a long pause.

'Maybe.' Del nodded. 'We'll see.'

Three

Markkus woke with a start, the sound of gunfire and screams easing from his ears. He stared up at the dark ceiling, breathing hard. Once his heart beat had calmed he sat up and unclenched his fists from his bed sheets. Swinging out of bed, he picked up the prosthetic leg from where it leaned against a chair. Placing the limb beside him, Markkus rubbed his hand over the stump just below his right knee. He looked at where his right foot should have been and wiggled invisible toes. Lifting cloth from the nearby chair, he pulled the material over the stump, fastening a leather harness over his right thigh which twitched painfully in response. Pummeling his fist into the damaged muscle, he reached for the leg beside him. It had once taken him an hour just to fit the leg to his knee, now it took only minutes. He could do it with his eyes closed. The limb's weight uncomfortably familiar in his hand. One of the royal blacksmiths had designed a limb of iron for him but it had proved unwieldy. Markkus had gone to Mister Ferrer, the blacksmith of Old Town, who had tutted and taken it away. He had replaced it with a thinner leg of beaten iron to produce a lighter limb, bound in a soft cloth so that it wouldn't cause injury. Now Markkus pulled this old friend onto the stump of his right leg and fastened the leather buckles. He stood, caught his balance and moved to study his reflection in the mirror.

Surrounded by dark bronze hammered into twirls, the glass shone back at him. He stared into his grey eyes, looking past the colour and back to his nightmares. The battle cries and wounded men, the uniforms, the swords and crossbows, the gun shots, the feeling of a knife as it plunged into his leg. The pain, the numbness, the numbing sound of the explosion, the roar of the dragons in the darkness. He saw the faces of the boys he had fought with and against. Swallowing, he felt the memory of the first time he had let a drop of poison fall down his throat, of the fear and burning. He inadvertently touched his bare chest, his fingers running over the wisps of dark hair, the slight definition of muscle, stroking the scar. Thick and purple, it ran diagonally from his right shoulder across his chest and stomach, stopping just short of his left hip. The skin on his left arm rippled with burn scars, the flesh hanging loosely compared to his thick, tanned right arm.

He glanced out of the window. It was early, or late, depending on how you looked at it. Not quite morning. He stared at his bed but decided against returning to it. After pulling on clothes, he made his way out of his large house, provided by the king for his duteous service to the crown, and down the street towards the city centre.

*

Tabitha walked into the servants' quarters. The rooms were cold. It was always cold. The walls were stone, the floor was stone and the chairs may as well have been stone. There was a large fireplace to her right, the chimney allowing in every gust of cold air in the winter. Five chairs and a table surrounded the fireplace and up two steps was a small kitchenette. On either side of the kitchenette were two pokey rooms with small hard beds inside. They were rarely slept in but came in handy for any member of staff who needed a nap or had been kicked from his house by an angry wife. Tabitha was alone but she made sure of this fact by checking every corner and every shadow, including the sparse kitchen cupboards and under each bed. Once satisfied, she lowered herself into a chair facing the empty, cold fireplace and sat in quiet contemplation. She was thinking about the king, as was common of late. Not all of Drummbek's rulers had acted like King Rupert, she was sure. None of the recent kings had treated the people in the city in such a way, and Tabitha felt certain that the castle had not echoed with screams under the rule of the old royalty. The king who had ruled before Rupert had been honest and even handed. King Tobyias had inherited the Great War from his predecessor. He had been a visionary, although Tabitha had heard it mentioned that a lot of this was down to his wife, Natalia. It was said that the war would not have been won without King Tobyias leading them. She was too young to fully appreciate what he had done, what he had changed. The king before Tobyias had been a dragon, and a kind and just ruler. She had learned in her schooling days that King George had refrained from entering the Great War for as long as possible, fighting to keep his people safe. But the war saw such atrocities he just couldn't ignore. He had died at an old age after a successful hundred and four-year reign. Neither king had been anything like King Rupert.

Back when she was new to the castle, she had watched two men taken into King Rupert's chambers and she had watched as they hadn't come back. She had told her mother and, as would become routine, her mother dismissed Tabitha's worries and told her to knuckle down and work hard. Her father was right, cleaning the castle and working in the kitchen was not going to attract a husband as her mother wanted. Unless he was a young and desperate kitchen porter. Perhaps by the time she was ready to marry she would have worked her way up to be worthy of a chef. The idea of that made her stomach turn. It wasn't that she didn't want to get married. It was the thought of being stuck, still in the same castle, in the same city, with the same people.

Tabitha jumped as someone walked in. She turned, wide-eyed, and stared.

Markkus never came down to the servants' quarters. Did he? She had never seen him down here before. She turned sharply back to the dull fireplace. Markkus walked past her and up the steps into the kitchenette. There were some rummaging noises and then he sat in a chair next to Tabitha. She stole a glance in his direction. He had an apple and a chunk of cheese on a plate. He looked up at Tabitha, his eyes sending a shock through her but she found herself unable to turn away. He took a bite out of the apple.

'On the early shift?' he asked, chewing. Tabitha nodded. 'Tabitha, right?'

Again, she nodded, wondering who had told him her name. He studied the apple in his hand. Tabitha blinked out of her daze and looked at the apple.

'Is it poisoned?'

Markkus smiled gently at her and took another bite. 'No.'

Tabitha felt that he was about to elaborate but he appeared to change his mind, swallowed and took another bite. She wanted to ask him more questions, about his past, about his job, about the king. Her mouth opened and closed as she decided upon the right words.

'I don't understand.'

Markkus watched her as he chewed. 'If you are immune to poison, how can you tell if someone is trying to poison the king?'

'The theory is that I will be able to taste the poison, rather than it hurting me. Who said I was immune?' Tabitha looked down at the floor. 'I hear there are a lot of rumours about me floating around the castle.'

Tabitha went to nod but stopped herself. Markkus laughed. It was low and deep and it made Tabitha's insides rumble pleasantly. Markkus studied her.

'How long have you been working here?'

'Four years.' Tabitha cleared her throat.

'How old are you?'

'Nineteen.'

Markkus nodded.

'I'd already been in the army for seven years when I was nineteen Well, this isn't a bad place to work. I guess it's not bad money?'

'My mother is glad of it.' Tabitha nodded.

'A king's castle is a good place for a young girl to work,' he said slowly. Tabitha met his gaze.

'Tabitha!'

Tabitha leapt to her feet and turned to Doris, the head maid stood filling the doorway.

'Have you been sat here doing nothing?' Doris narrowed her eyes, allowing Markkus a fleeting glance.

'No,' Tabitha told her. 'I've...been dusting.'

'I'm afraid I interrupted her and made her talk to me,' Markkus said. Doris turned to him.

'Oh. Well, if it pleases sir, she is required for the king's breakfast.'

'Excuse me?' Tabitha almost took a step back.

'His breakfast, my girl,' Doris blustered. 'He needs you to serve his breakfast.'

'Oh.' Tabitha enjoyed a moments relief before giving a small curtsey to the room and running past Doris. The head maid turned to Markkus. 'I believe His Grace will be requesting your company also. Sir.' She made an effort of a small curtsey before swirling and gliding after Tabitha.

Markkus watched Tabitha as she left the room, ignoring Doris' curtsey. A pain had ripped through his chest at the mention of Tabitha's presence for the king's meal. He was too old for this. His right thigh twitched in response and he rubbed it before pulling himself out of his chair.

*

That evening Markkus thanked Bobby, stood behind the bar, and raised his pint of ale to a roar of good cheer. He supped at it as the man beside him downed his entire pint in one go. The Old Boot tavern had been his local since the day he'd left the army. It was warm, close and familiar, filled with friendly faces and the stale scent of men and ale. He smiled. Cassie, one of the serving girls, returned his smile as she walked past carrying two full jugs of ale.

'Here.' One of his old friends brushed a hand on Markkus's shoulder. 'Have a seat, Commander.' Markkus thanked him and sat in the chair that had been pulled up. He took a deep breath and relaxed. A sparkle caught his eye and he glanced down at the medal pinned to his lapel. He considered it, something akin to guilt rising in him. He hadn't worn his old army jacket in longer than he thought. He unpinned the medal and studied it, rubbing his thumb over it to see it shine. He remembered the day he had earned this medal, the men he had fought with. Some of them were still alive, fewer still were in The Old Boot that night.

He pocketed the medal as a man clapped him on the back.

'Markkus! How are you?'

Markkus nodded.

'I'm fine Sedrick. And you? How are your lovely wife and son?'

'Son's gone into the army.' Sedrick sniffed. 'Leaves this Friday for a tour of Seracombe. We're dead proud, naturally, but the wife is worried. Poor love.'

Markkus wouldn't even pretend to understand how that would feel, for his own son to see and experience everything that he had. He didn't think he would bear it.

'Let's pray we never go to war,' Markkus murmured. Sedrick nodded, then smiled and held his pint glass up.

'To peace!'

They clinked glasses and Sedrick turned to talk to another man. Markkus watched his old friends. They had been through some tough, horrific times and some good times. Not enough good times, not yet, although nights like these helped to balance the tally.

'Markkus! Still working at the castle?'

'Yes. It's good to see you, Arthur. How are you enjoying life as a tailor?'

'Well, if the suit fits.' Arthur roared with laughter. 'Not like working for a king though. That must be interesting.'

'Interesting is a good word. Well paid are two very good words.' Markkus winked at Arthur who roared once more, clasping his oversized gut.

'Excellent! I bet you have some gossip on the king though, ay?'

'Gossip? You've become an old fish wife, Arthur?' Johnny, the youngest of the group, emerged and grinned down at Markkus. 'I bet the commander here is too busy with the castle women to worry about gossip.'

Markkus shrugged playfully, smiling up at Johnny. The age gap between them was significant but that hardly mattered. Johnny had been the one to carry Markkus from the battlefield. He had lost his leg but, because of Johnny, he had kept his life.

'Come on Markkus, tell all. There must be some pretty girls working there.' Johnny pulled up a chair and sat beside his old commander.

'There are. Depending on your taste, of course. How's your work?' Markkus changed the subject, sipping his ale, relishing the bitter tingle on his tongue.

'Johnny! Where are you working these days?' Arthur asked, giving Johnny a hefty slap on the back.

'Mr Brown's accountancy in Old Town, that's where. Every day's filled with the most boring shite.' Johnny grinned. 'Never thought of myself as sitting behind a desk dealing with paperwork.'

'Never thought any of us would leave the army,' said Arthur. 'Life has plans for us all.' Then, seeing someone he knew, Arthur gave warm goodbyes and moved on.

'No.' Markkus frowned. 'No, sitting at a desk doesn't suit you at all. The livery yard suited you more, you should have stayed there. I thought you wanted to work on the docks? Or move to Ushwaithe?'

Johnny shrugged.

'The office job pays better than the docks. Can't afford to travel to Ushwaithe. I'm certainly not going back to the army. Not after everything. Definitely paid those dues.'

'How about the city guard?'

Johnny nearly spat his ale in Markkus's face.

'You're kidding, right?'

'Why? You'd be great. Helping people out, protecting people, standing up for the little person. It's what you were born to do.'

'There's no way I'm working with those bigoted cu-'

'-well, yes, I suppose there is that.' Markkus interrupted. 'But you could work your way up. Army career like yours, you'd be in charge in no time.'

'Really? You don't think someone else would beat me to it?'

'Gods, now that's an unpleasant thought.' Markkus studied Johnny for a moment. 'There must be something else?'

'Well, when I was little…'

'Yes?'

'Nothing. I had these stupid dreams. It's never going to happen, doesn't matter.'

'What? You wanted to be king?'

'No, 'course not. A dragonslayer.'

There was a pause as Markkus and Johnny stared at one another.

'That's perfect!' Markkus beamed. Johnny flinched at the volume of his voice. 'You'd make a great slayer. Why don't you enrol?'

'Do you know how much it costs to enrol at the academy? I can't afford that.'

'You can get sponsored. That's how Del did it.' Markkus instantly regretted uttering that name. He shut his mouth. Johnny sagged a little, watching him.

'I could do. It's an idea. Thanks.' He put a warm hand on Markkus's shoulder. There were no words but the message was clear. Markkus heard it loud in his mind; *she's alive. Somewhere.* 'Anyway, I bet the castle has prettier girls than the academy.' Johnny went back to his ale.

'Probably,' said Markkus, grateful. 'You should get a job there Johnny, I'm sure you'd be kept busy.'

Johnny smiled.

'Oh, I don't know, I wouldn't want any of your rejects, old man.'

Markkus shook his head.

'I haven't touched one. Not one. Hand on heart.' After a pause he placed his hand over his heart. Johnny laughed.

'You still haven't loosened up, Markkus!' They both turned to the voice of Sergeant Don. 'He must be a good employer, our king,' Don said as he pushed through the crowd to his old army buddies. Markkus didn't answer. The walls had ears and at that moment he couldn't think of a kind word that didn't relate to his pay packet. He forced his lips into a smile as he watched Don.

'What's the king done for you lately then, Don? Besides paying for your new role of sitting on your arse and doing nothing all day.'

'Now wash your mouth out, Johnny. I work very hard. But since you asked, my neighbour problem is fixed.'

'Neighbour problem?'

'Yeah. You remember that bad storm a year ago? The fence between our yards blew down and Hodgkin said he'd fix it. He replaced it all right, three inches onto my land. Damn cheek. I told him he'd done wrong but he wouldn't have it. Said last week he'd go to the king about it if I carried on. Last I saw he was headed to the castle, haven't seen him since.'

There was a pause.

'What do you think happened to him?' Markkus

murmured.

'Woah, what do you mean if you carried on? What did you do to him, Don?' Johnny squared himself up to the sergeant. Markkus watched Johnny, the people's hero. He smiled to himself. Johnny should have been a sergeant in a city guard. Don was more suited to a role that was less people orientated.

'I didn't do anything to him. Don't get your knickers in a twist.'

Markkus could feel Johnny tense and he rested a hand on the man's arm. Johnny obediently backed down. Don almost laughed. Markkus looked hard at him.

'So, what happened to him? He should have been back, maybe moved your fence?'

Don shrugged.

'How would I know? Doesn't matter, I moved the fence last night.'

'Didn't he have a family?'

'Yeah, his niece came in this morning and made a missing person's report.'

Markkus risked a glance back at Johnny.

'You're looking for him?'

'Gods no. Good riddance.' Don pulled away, muttering to himself and disappearing into the crowd. Markkus watched him.

'You think something bad has happened to his neighbour?'

Markkus didn't respond. He stared into the tavern at nothing, thinking hard.

*

Tabitha sat cross-legged on her bed, with the thin covers over her knees, staring out of the small window.

It was close to midnight and she had to be at work in four hours but she couldn't sleep. She still heard that scream, now that the lights were out and silence filled the empty spaces. The day had passed with no strange occurrences. There had been no gossip on missing people, no screams, nothing suspicious. It had been a boring day of dusting and polishing, wandering through the servant corridors as if in a dream.

But now that night had drawn in, the shadows lengthened and Tabitha's memories played tricks on her. She stared at the stars and blinked as one twinkled. Her ears buzzed with the silence. She wondered, not for the first time, if her suspicions were all in her head. At first working in the castle had seemed such a glamorous job but cleaning and feeding a gluttonous king had soon become tiresome. Her mother was so proud of her, working in the castle. No other job would measure up. Not that there were many suitable jobs; a seamstress but Tabitha never could thread a needle, a mother but she would need a husband, a serving girl but she had never even stepped foot inside a tavern, a nurse perhaps but Tabitha had watched those women, tired and underpaid. So she accepted her role as a maid. Maybe one day she would be like Doris and manage the other maids. Tabitha pulled a face at the thought. No, there had to be more to life than that. There was, she thought. There was the mystery of Drummbek Castle. There was no explanation for the missing people, and no evidence of a witch at work. Unless, Tabitha realized, catching her breath, the missing people were in the prisons. It didn't make sense, but it was the most logical explanation she had.

That wasn't true. There was another explanation. One that involved the king. One that whispered to Tabitha on nights like these. But she couldn't bear to consider it, didn't dare allow herself to think it. It would be treason. That famous dragonslayer had been exiled for saying such things. Tabitha thought of the pain that would bring her parents. No. That wasn't an option. It had to be something to do with the prison. It just had to be. She lay down and pulled the covers up to her neck. The morning light would bring answers. As soon as she could, she'd make her way into the prisons and find those missing people. Or a witch. Or ghosts. Tabitha twitched as her eyes closed, her mind throwing up shades of men and women taken too early from this world amid howling screams.

Four

Del was awake before the sun and the company rose. Rubbing Shadow down with a rag as he munched on a handful of oats from her lacking supply, she breathed in the silence of pre-dawn and the magical moment of stillness. Red streaks lined the horizon as wisps of cloud hung in the air. Del packed up her few possessions and sat under her tree, leaning back against the trunk to watch the sun rise. As she settled there came the instinctual feeling of being watched. Lowering her gaze, she glanced around the camp until she met Andra's eyes. The sun began to peak over the horizon as Andra pulled herself up and stood next to Del.

'You don't sleep much,' Andra muttered.

'No. I never have.'

There was a pause as Andra turned to study Del. She leaned forward and whispered in her ear, 'Why are you doing this?'

The silence that followed felt longer than it was. Del could almost hear the universe ticking as she faced Andra.

'My reasons are my own, Captain. You can arrest me if it'll make you feel better.'

Andra's brow furrowed. One of the men broke the silence, coughing and spluttering as he woke. Del pulled herself to her feet, ending what conversation there had been.

'When do we leave?'

'When we're ready.'

Del began to fasten her packs onto Shadow's saddle as Andra left to prepare for the day's ride. Del felt the weight of her pistol in one saddlebag. Would Andra keep her secret? If not, the captain would have arrested her by now. Not that being arrested would be such a bad thing, Del mused. In fact, the more she thought about it the better it sounded. It would get her where she wanted to be and she could drop her act, but it would put her out in the open. She'd be vulnerable. No. She'd have to continue with the pretence for now. Until she was back within the walls of Drummbek, until she had worked out her next step. Leaning on Shadow, she felt him lean back against her. She ran her fingers over a patch of his coat as she steadied herself for whatever was to come.

*

The day was quiet with the company riding in companionable silence. As the afternoon grew late, Del rode behind the company. Lawrie was meant to be taking the rear but she had slowed and slipped past him without him noticing. Shadow picked his way through the scrub with experienced sure-footedness. Del had loose reins and allowed him the freedom of his head. She studied the men in front of her, scrutinising their positions in the saddle, the looks in their eyes, the way they spoke to one another. They rode with long reins, giving their horses the freedom to pick their own way across the difficult terrain. Del suspected they were only a day or so ride from the outer villages of Drummbek now. It shocked her a little; she had always assumed she had put a fair bit of distance between herself and the city but in truth she had been creeping back. She could feel her heart pushing at her ribs, urging her forward. It wasn't homesickness. It wasn't a sentimental feeling. It was a warning. Something was going on.

Del's mind quietened.

Something was going on. Something was going to happen.

Del reined Shadow to a halt and allowed the company to move away from her. Sitting deep in the saddle, she lengthened her legs around Shadow's sides. She watched the little horse's ears flick back to her. Perhaps he felt the tension through her hands and seat but it felt to Del that he sensed exactly what she did.

She craned her neck back to stare up at the sky. It was so blue that if she relaxed her eyes and squinted she could see the black of night. To the untrained eye she was just a rider staring upwards to the hidden stars. Del was listening. Listening for that change in the air, for the heaviness, the cry, the thud of wings.

Del swore. She turned in her saddle to look in the direction of the sound as she felt her insides shudder. Another thud vibrated through the air. She was sure that the dragonslayers in front of her had heard it and would be watching the horizon as she was. Searching the landscape, she wondered why she couldn't feel that tingle on the back of her neck that told her someone was at her exposed back. A sharp golden glint in the distance was all she needed. She turned back to the company and stopped with her mouth open. They hadn't noticed, they hadn't heard. They were disappearing from her view at the same steady walk.

'For the love of everything pure,' Del cursed under her breath as she picked up her reins and urged Shadow forward. Shadow had never been a stupid horse and since he had come to be with Del, he had become an educated horse. He knew the signs and although Del urged enough for a slow trot, he broke into a steady canter. As they began to move through the company, Andra and Venkell heard their approach and looked back, pulling their horses to a halt. Andra watched Del for a moment before looking beyond her, her eyes widening. The captain raised her hand, catching Del's eye as she spun her horse around to face her men. The company stopped clumsily, some horses marching into the tails of the ones in front.

'Dragon!' Andra called to them. Del had slowed Shadow by this point and stood beside Andra and Venkell, looking back at the men. Chaos seemed to spread through the company. Some skittered to the left, others to the right, all straining to see the dragon while their horses whined, eyes wide and nostrils flared. Del clenched her jaw.

'Men!'

Everyone stopped at the sound of Andra's voice. Even the horses relaxed a little, ears pricking forward to their leader.

'Peking, prepare the trap. The rest of you make ready your weapons.'

'We don't know that it means to attack,' Del told her.

'What of the horses, sir?' said Peking.

Andra looked around.

'Corporal Lawrence, you and Jude take the horses that aren't required to that area of scrub over there. Where the rocks come out. Hide behind it.'

'It might not mean to attack us.'

Andra looked at Del.

'And what if it does?'

'Dragons do not just attack groups of people.'

Andra raised an eyebrow.

'You've been out of the Order too long,' she said

breathlessly, dismounting and throwing her reins at Del as she stormed away, drawing her sword and barking orders. Venkell followed, shooting Del a warning glance over his shoulder. Del watched them go with narrowed eyes. This just wasn't right.

She looked towards Lawrie who had begun to gather the reins of the horses around him. Del caught reins as they were flung at her. She watched Peking remove the large harpoon from his pack horse and begin running checks. The others dismounted and revealed their pistols and rifles before running into positions. Del realised that Lawrie was waiting for her. She followed him, leading four horses to the scrub. They stopped in a sheltered area once the company was out of sight. Lawrie remained mounted, head cocked as he listened for the action to begin. Del sighed and sat back in her saddle, dropping her own reins. Shadow took full advantage of the opportunity and dipped his head to take a mouthful of grass.

'Is this your usual role?' Del asked Lawrie. The corporal, eyes wide, nodded. 'What about the privates in the company?'

'There aren't any,' said Lawrie, suspiciously. Del ignored the look.

'Have you ever been involved in any of the trials with rogue dragons? Any actual face to face confrontations?'

'I've helped.' Lawrie held his chin up. 'What do you know about it anyway?' His attention was snatched as Andra's voice floated to them on the breeze. Del looked around her.

'I don't see how we're particularly safe here if the dragon does decide to attack.'

Lawrie shrugged.

'We're out of the way. That's all the Captain wants.

They'll protect us if the dragon gets too close.'

'Are you attacked by dragons often?'

'On every job.'

'By dragons you are not sent to try?

Lawrie nodded.

'Every job. How do you know so much?'

Del chewed on her lip, feeling the bile rise in her throat. Andra was right, she had been away too long. Del moved Shadow so she could just see Andra and the company ready in their positions. Andra stood tall with her sword by her side, waiting for the approaching dragon. Peking knelt nearby, hidden behind some bracken, priming his harpoon, and Venkell crouched a little further down, pistol drawn and already taking aim.

Del closed her eyes as the whoosh and thud of a dragon's miraculous wings beat closer. As she opened them, the dragon rose up the path, hovered and roared at Andra. The deep call rumbled through the air and into the ground. Shadow vibrated as it passed up his legs and into Del. Her eyes shone. Andra kept her sword low as the dragon watched her.

It was a medium sized dragon, gold and red in colour depending on how the light shone on the scales. Del noted the angled head, the two small horns and the claws on all four feet, long and yellow. The ridges down the spine, and the long and beautiful wings with skin stretched so tight that Del could see the sky through them. It was a male and he was wondrous. Del marvelled, as she always did, at how such delicate wings could hold up such a large creature.

'I am Captain Andra Ferrer of the Dragonslayer Order of Drummbek, under the command of King Rupert of Drummbek. Stand down,' Andra shouted up to the creature. There was a low rumble as the dragon chuckled. 'Do you mean us harm?'

'Indeed, Captain Dragonslayer. I have come to grind your bones to dust,' the dragon said, flicking out his tongue. He flicked and stretched his wings, sending up a cloud of dirt among the dragonslayers.

There was a sharp bang. Del turned sharply but couldn't see who had fired the pistol. What did they think would happen from such a small shot? Shaking her head, she watched as the dragon roared in anger and faced his attacker.

'Hold your fire!' yelled Venkell, stood on the opposite side. The dragon turned his full attention onto Venkell and opened his jaws. Andra stepped towards the creature, crying out, trying in vain to get the beast's attention. The rest of her company also came out of hiding, shouting, calling, and began firing their small weapons. The dragon twisted one way then the other, taking in each individual. Small bullets grazed his scales and he whined and roared, teeth dripping with thick, pearlescent drool as he flung himself around in the air.

He lunged, mouth open, and scooped up one of his attackers. The man's scream turned to gurgles as the dragon closed his jaws with a snap. He shook his head until the man ripped apart and the gore scattered across the company. The dragon dropped the remains and moved, rumbling, to another man close by pointing a shaking gun at the creature. Del watched with a dry mouth. Now was the time. If it wasn't now, there wouldn't be another chance.

Shadow stepped back as Del shortened her reins and looked to Lawrie. The boy was fighting for control of his mount. The company's horses were skittish. Not yet scared enough to move but the idea had landed in their minds. Lawrie's horse had lifted its head so high that the corporal had no control, the horse's mane twisted through his fingers as he clung to his saddle. Del pushed Shadow up against them, hoping that her little horse would act as a calming influence. Lawrie's mount snorted as its ears flicked toward Shadow.

'Don't you lot use explosives?' Del hissed.

'We have a harpoon gun,' Lawrie protested through gritted teeth, his eyes darting to the riderless horses beside him.

'But no proper explosives?'

'We ran out, during the last job.' The corporal yanked his horse towards the others. Shadow grunted and shook his head as the dragon roared and the vibrating air hit his ears and nose. Del pulled open her saddlebags and found what she needed. Throwing the packs to the ground, she spurred Shadow on and they cantered out of hiding into the chaos. Shadow's ears pricked forward as he lengthened his stride, aiming for the dragon. Del heard her name shouted but she didn't pay any attention. Nor did she see the few dead bodies littering the ground but she couldn't dismiss the stench of blood and fear. There was a boom as the harpoon gun fired. The shouts grew louder as the harpoon missed its target. It went wide of the dragon's heart and the creature dodged before it could puncture a wing. Del pulled Shadow to a halt in front of the dragon. She sat back, looked up and aimed her pistol at his head. The dragon looked down at her and growled. Now it was just the two of them, the shouts and cries of the remaining company becoming muffled background noise.

'Turn back now!' Del shouted to the dragon. The creature lifted his lips in a smile.

'You will all die.'

'You cannot win this,' she told him. 'Turn back now. Let's end this without any more death.'

'Foolish human. This can only end in blood. Not today perhaps, but it is only a matter of time.'

Del heard Shadow snort, she felt him paw the ground. A drop of thick saliva splattered onto her knee as the dragon lowered his body so that his wings encircled her. The creature dipped his elegant head and with a snarl he looked Del in the eye.

'I know who you are, Del Dragonslayer,' the dragon hissed. 'Your name is spoken on the wind. But no more.'

'What is coming?' Del shouted. The dragon only grinned, bearing his teeth, flicking his forked tongue out. They watched each other for a moment and time slowed.

There was nothing in the world but Del and the dragon. She lifted her gun. The dragon opened his jaws wide, showing her each individual sharp tooth. He moved to snatch her from the saddle and Del seized the opportunity. She aimed and pulled the trigger. The bullet went up through the dragon's throat and into his head.

Time stopped.

Shadow backed out, tail swishing, as the dragon crashed to the ground head first. The little horse turned on his hind legs, trotting Del to safety just as the dragon's wings landed sending up a cloud of dirt and dust. The head and neck crashed to the ground and silence filled the air. Del, breathing hard, watched the dragon's body as his wings and a singular hind claw twitched. The creature's chest became motionless, the beautiful, stretched skin of the wings now dirty, torn and lifeless.

A silence fell over the scene as each member of the company turned to look at Del. She kept her gaze on the dragon's body. There was no turning back now.

Five

'Your Grace?'

King Rupert lifted his eyes from the book he was reading. Lord Commander Binkley stood at the door looking absurd in his full uniform. Rupert had often told him not to wear the thing unless the occasion called for it. Binkley had decided that every day called for it.

'There is a woman here to speak with you,' said Binkley. He took a couple of steps into the library. 'She was at the city guard station making something of a scene. It seems that when she realised Inspector Monterey could no longer assist her, she came here. To speak with you. Something about her uncle who has gone missing. He came to the castle, apparently, to speak to you about a troublesome neighbour. We've told her you can't help but...' Binkley drifted off. It took all Rupert's willpower not to roll his eyes, and with that energy spent he saw no reason in holding back any further.

'I will see her.' The king marked his place in the book and placed it on the table beside him.

'Your Grace.' Binkley bowed and turned to leave.

'In my chambers.'

Binkley hesitated and turned back.

'Your Grace?'

'In my chambers, Lord Binkley. Give me a moment to get there, of course. And then I will hear all about her little problem.'

Binkley opened and closed his mouth. Rupert had often thought of Binkley as something akin to a small mammal hiding in holes whenever danger came too close. Now he saw the man as a small fish, hiding in coral and under rocks as the big sharks slunk by. The king smiled.

*

There had been another scream. Whether it continued to echo through the stone passages or only in Tabitha's mind, she couldn't be sure. Was she going mad? It was time to find out. Tabitha followed the echoes. She pressed her back against the cold stone wall as two maids walked past talking in hushed tones. She knew she wasn't the only one in the castle to have suspicions. But no one pressed the matter of the whereabouts of missing servants. When she brought it up, the subject was quickly changed. It wasn't that people were acting as if they'd never existed. She heard people speak of them but silence filled the gaps where their names should have been. People were avoiding the subject. Tabitha shook her head, she was being silly. There was probably no conspiracy. Maybe she just hated her job this much. Tabitha studied at her hands, as if they had all the answers. No, she didn't hate her job. This didn't feel like hatred. It felt a lot like fear and confusion.

She walked up the few steps that served as the servants' access to the king's chambers. Her confidence lasted only seconds. Her heart beat faster as she approached the thickset wooden door at the top of the steps. The sound of her feet clapping against the stone sounded loud in the empty corridor. Realising she was holding her breath, she exhaled in a quiet hiss, stopping as she reached the door. She stood there. Just stood there. Now what? She hadn't thought this far. She turned on her mind. 'Well?' she interrogated it. 'What did you think would happen? That Mr Hipkins or whatever would meet you on the steps and shake your hand? Stupid girl.' She stared hard at the door, anger flaring up in her stomach.

There was a bang from inside the room. Tabitha flinched and caught herself before she yelped. It had sounded like a large piece of furniture toppling over. A scuffling noise followed and then a quiet scream. A scream that was just too terrified to leave the mouth of its owner. Tabitha felt her bowels loosen and her breakfast threaten to reverse back up. She threw out one hand and held the wall beside her to keep her steady. There was a low rumble which vibrated through the stone and up her feet and legs. Her own breathing was now the only sound. She wasn't sure which scared her the most, the screams and rumbles or the utter silence which followed. She managed to lift her hand from the wall and watched as it shook of its own volition. Her eyes shifted to the door handle in front of her while her feet swivelled to leave. No, she thought. She had come this far. She would regret this opportunity if she let it pass. She had to know what was behind the door. Her body screamed for her to turn and run but her mind, her damn inquisitive mind, had forgotten the fear and was ordering her to turn the door handle as quietly as possible. As an automatic reaction, she dropped and crouched on the floor as she pushed the door open by millimetres. The smell of fear hit her in a wave. Her body started trembling again and her teeth began to chatter. The noise was the next to hit her; a squelching, soft rumble. Her face contorted in disgust and her stomach grumbled and twisted, repulsed. All she could see of the king's chambers was the corner of a table. Easing the door open a little more, she put her head through as far as she dared. She crouched lower, her eyes wide. King Rupert had his back to her. Tabitha blinked a few times, not believing what she was seeing. The king sat over a body. A human body. She could see the feet in their shoes. A hand lay flat on the floor. A woman's head with tussled, bloody hair and mouth open in a silent scream staring up at the king. King Rupert's lips were bright red and his huge jaws chewed in delight. His head dipped and his nose disappeared inside the ripped torso of the body.

Tabitha kept calm long enough to ease the door closed before she leapt back, catching her balance in time to stop from toppling down the steps. Breathing heavily, the walls started to close in on her. She grabbed at the flat, cold walls as she stumbled away from the door. Bile rising in her throat, she jogged down the corridor and blindly found her way to a tiny cupboard full of brooms and mops. She shut the door behind her. Falling to the floor, hugging her knees, she allowed the tears and sobs to come.

*

Markkus sat in the courtyard with his fingers steepled. He was staring at the rose bush in front of him, watching the bees move from one flower to the next. Lunchtime was approaching. Markkus tapped his index fingers together. As the city clock struck twelve, rebounding throughout the city, he stood in one easy motion. Ignoring the twinge in his right thigh, he made his way to the grand dining room. He caught the eye of every servant, butler and guardsman as he moved through the room. They all nodded or smiled in their own respectful, quiet ways of acknowledging a friendly presence. He sat in his chair and began tapping his fingers on the polished dining table. A trumpet sounded and Markkus stood as King Rupert entered.

'Ah, Markkus. How are we since this morning?'

'Very well, Your Grace.' Markkus bowed his head as the king swept past him and sat. Markkus lowered himself back into his seat. 'I trust Your Grace has had an interesting morning?'

Each day was the same; the same questions, worded differently, the same responses, the same empty feeling in Markkus's gut. At first he had put this down to the responsibility of keeping the king of Drummbek safe. But he had been in this job long enough for those fears to fade and yet the feeling remained. Markkus felt the king look at him out of the corner of his sharp eye.

'Indeed. Another peasant, another problem solved. And you, Markkus? A productive morning, I hope?'

'Oh yes, Your Grace. Most productive.' But not as productive as the afternoon, he hoped.

Two maids entered and presented the king with a plate of meat and cheese. Markkus scanned their faces but neither were Tabitha. Markkus tasted each type of food laid before him and nodded to the king. With a low rumble, King Rupert began to eat his lunch.

'Your Grace, may I be so bold as to ask you a question?'

'Of course, Markkus,' King Rupert said between mouthfuls.

'I overheard from an old friend of mine that a Mr Hodgkin came to see you regarding a neighbourly dispute. I understand that he hasn't been seen since. Did he come to see you?'

'Hodgkin. Hodgkin,' the king mumbled to himself, crushing a chicken leg between his teeth. 'Indeed, I believe he did. Something about a fence?'

'Yes, Your Grace. Do you know what became of him?'

'I'm sorry to say I haven't seen him since. I told him I would solve his dispute. I do hope his neighbour is pleased with the outcome?'

Markkus blinked at the table.

'Yes, Your Grace. He's very pleased.'

'And you are not, Markkus?'

Markkus realised the king had stopped eating and was now staring down at him. He forced on a smile.

'I am pleased, Your Grace. I'm afraid it has been a trying day. Please excuse my rudeness.' He bowed his head. The king huffed to himself and continued eating.

'You are dismissed then, Markkus. There is only the one course today so I suggest you go have a lie down.'

'As you wish, Your Grace.' Markkus stood and bowed low to the king.

King Rupert watched Markkus leave the grand dining room, his eyes narrowing, chewing slow in thought.

'I believe Charles is waiting for me? Fetch him,' he said to the guards at the doors. One bowed and left. He emerged ten minutes later followed by a tall man dressed all in black with black hair and black eyes. Charlie approached silently as King Rupert placed another polite mouthful between his lips. 'Charles, I'm so glad you could make it to the city in such short notice. I do hope your room is to your liking? We have yet to discuss the work I wish you to undertake. I understand that you are among the best? Then perhaps this first task will be beneath you but it will lead on to brighter things, that I am sure. Things much more deserving of a man of your calibre. For now, I wish you to follow

Markkus Kern, my taster, and report back to me. The payment will be ten gold coins, as originally discussed.'

Charlie bowed low and swept out of the room, the door closing behind him.

*

Tabitha had managed to carry out her duties without vomiting. Thankfully, she hadn't had to serve food to the king. The very thought of it made her double over and gag. Her mother was making a start on the evening meal when Tabitha came home from work. Tabitha sat in her chair at the kitchen table. After a few moments Milly stopped chopping a carrot and glanced at her daughter.

'Tabitha? How was work?'

Tabitha nodded. Her mother looked her daughter over. 'Has something happened?'

Tabitha didn't know how to respond. There was a deep need to tell her mother everything that she had seen but she knew what the response would be.

'Good afternoon, my beautiful women.' Erik swept into the kitchen, wrapping his arms around Milly's waist and kissing her. Milly playfully tapped her husband away.

'Your lunch is on the table,' she told him.

'Ah, a fine meal to break up the day.' Erik grinned, surveying the sandwich and pickle waiting for him. He turned on Tabitha and kissed her cheek. Then he stopped and looked back at his daughter. Tabitha met his eyes and tried to force a smile.

'Tabby?' Erik murmured with a rare seriousness. He pulled a battered chair up and sat opposite her. 'Something's wrong?'

Tabitha shook her head as she thought quickly.

Maybe she could tell them, maybe they would believe her, but then what? They could all leave, maybe move to the outlying villages and live as farmers. Then freeze to death come the winter. Tabitha looked into her father's worried eyes. Maybe she could just tell him, he was more likely to believe her than her mother, but what could one man do? Tabitha looked down at her feet.

What could one girl do?

'I'm fine,' she said. Erik raised an eyebrow. 'It's just...It was a strange day, is all.'

Milly moved back to chopping the vegetables.

'Did you meet someone?'

Tabitha sighed before she could stop herself.

'Has your gentleman found a lady friend?' Erik asked. Tabitha pulled a face at him as her mother spun back round to face her. 'Your young gentleman has another? You must fight for him.'

'No!' Tabitha found her voice again before her mother could start making plans. 'There is no man,' she told her father. 'And I doubt I will ever find a husband at the castle,' she told her mother. 'I saw something today that I didn't like.' She paused to swallow against her dry mouth. 'I think I need a new job,' she murmured.

'Oh no. Do you know how difficult it is to get a job at the castle? You're staying there, my girl.' Milly waved her knife at her daughter. Tabitha stood.

'I'll go and wash,' she said quietly, walking past her father and out towards her bedroom. Erik watched her go.

Tabitha sat on her bed and stared at nothing in particular. She just didn't know what to do. The image of Markkus flickered into her mind. She could tell him. It would be risky, perhaps he was too close to the king. She could be the next victim if Markkus decided not to believe her. Tabitha clenched her eyes shut as her stomach churned with the memory of that broken, open, steaming body.

'Tabitha?' She opened her eyes as her father poked his head into the room. He sat beside her on the bed. 'What happened?'

'Nothing.' The idea of her father worrying so much as to take action scared her more than anything else. Erik nodded and looked around at her walls and the half burnt candle on her bedside table.

'Is there a man?'

Tabitha looked up at her father and smiled the first genuine smile of the day.

'There is someone I admire, if that's the right word. But nothing will come of it.'

Erik nodded.

'I had someone like that at your age. Nineteen is still young, Tabby. There's no hurry, no matter what your mother thinks. Marriage is wonderful but being in love and being happy are better. You need to take your time with love.' He winked at her.

Tabitha leaned forward and wrapped her arms around her father, hugging him. Erik gave her a kiss on the head as he stood before leaving her alone once more.

Tabitha curled up on her bed. She couldn't tell anyone. She couldn't trust that anyone would believe her or, if they did, that they wouldn't do something stupid. But she couldn't accept that there was nothing she could do. She chewed on her lip. After all, she had access.

'Tabby!'

Tabitha jumped up guiltily, relaxing as her father popped his head in again. 'Remember to come eat lunch.'

Tabitha nodded, chewing on her lip as she returned to the kitchen. She could do something, and if she was careful she could do something and not get caught.

Six

'She's a dragonslayer!'
Del said nothing, keeping her back on whoever had spoken. She looked Andra in the eye, her skin prickling as she felt the company circling her.

'When were you going to tell us?'

'She wasn't going to.'

'No. I wonder why not?' Venkell asked, running a thick finger up the blade of his knife. Del knew he had recognised her just as Andra had. He had kept quiet all this time, and Del could guess why.

'We have friends who deserve a decent burial,' Andra shouted above the tension. Some men walked away, mumbling to one another, but others stayed, pressing in. Andra approached Del, her men making room for her.

'What was she doing at that old house?'

'Where's her company?'

'She's turned rogue, that's what!'

'What did you do?'

The questions came thick and fast and all the while Andra and Del silently watched each other.

'I think you're all missing the point,' Del said, giving each member of the company a fleeting glance. 'You have lost some good men today. We are all lucky to be alive.'

Andra nodded as her men grumbled.

'She's right.'

'She's Del Thorburn,' Venkell revealed. 'Exiled by the king and now she's turned rogue. We all saw her kill a dragon.' This caused the men to start talking amongst themselves. 'She's not a dragonslayer now and we all know the law,' Venkell said to Andra. 'We should arrest her and put her on trial before the Order and the king.'

Andra was watching Del thoughtfully and Del saw the regret in her eyes. Regret for what was to come.

'She will be.' Something fluttered in Del's chest. 'Is it true?' Andra asked loudly. 'Are you Del Thorburn?'

Del took a moment to consider her options and came to the conclusion that there were none.

'I am.'

A gasp lifted from the company and the chattering started again. Andra seemed to deflate.

'Del Thorburn, I am arresting you on the charge of being a rogue dragonslayer,' Andra said for the whole company to hear, her eyes glistening. She blinked and looked towards the graves that were being dug. 'We continue with our journey as soon as we have buried our fallen. We will take her to stand before Lord Gerard.'

Del felt her eye twitch and a familiar feeling of rage cloud her insides. The men mumbled to one another as they walked past Del to prepare for the burials. Some pushed her as they went, murmuring threats as they drew close. Others seemed torn, trying not to catch her eye as they studied her, keeping their distance. She forced herself to remain still. Once she was alone with Andra and Venkell, she looked from one to the other.

'Del Thorburn.' Venkell approached Del, long knife easy in his grip. Del held her head high.

'Yes.'

'Del Thorburn, who fought in the Great War? Del Thorburn, who led King Tobyias's royal dragonslayers? Del Thorburn, exiled by King Rupert?'

'That was the first dragon I have killed since my exile,' Del said. 'And you know why I did it.' She held out her arms. 'Will I be bound as I'm dragged back to the city?'

'Will you come willingly?' asked Andra.

'It would be much easier to walk into the city as a free woman but one way or another I think I need to go back,' Del told her.

'You think?'

'I think the time has come, yes.'

Venkell and Andra exchanged a glance.

'I'll prepare the prayers,' Venkell murmured before walking away. Del watched Andra's brief internal struggle.

'They don't train them like they used to, huh?'

Andra met her gaze.

'A lot of things have changed since you were exiled.' She paused, wondering whether to continue. 'I have to say, although I wish the circumstances could have been different, it is an honour to meet you.'

Del smiled.

'Likewise, Captain. It is an honour to meet the daughter of the man who made me my best swords, and to see her as a captain in the Order.'

Andra looked away.

'I didn't want to do this,' she murmured.

'We all have to do things we don't want to.' Del shrugged. 'Is it true yet?'

'What?'

'The rumours of the king eating people?'

Andra's gaze hardened.

'You can't talk like that. King Rupert is an intelligent and good hearted ruler, he has done the city a great deal of good. He's not like some–' She gestured towards the dragon corpse behind Del.

'-Rogue? How can you be sure?' Del smiled sadly. As she approached the dragon's corpse she pulled out her knife and stood by the head of the creature. Andra followed her.

'Why did you become a dragonslayer?' Del asked.

'Because…The Order is based on respect and tradition. I like that. Why did you?'

Del sighed through her nose as she surveyed the corpse's head; the dull and blank eyes, scratched scales, dry tongue hanging loose from the open mouth. Kneeling, she dug the knife into the gums of the dragon and yanked out two long yellowed teeth. Standing, she pocketed one and thrust the other into Andra's hand.

'Give this to someone you love.'

*

Del stared into the flames of the small fire. She sat cross-legged with her hands bound in front of her. Her pistol, sword and knife had been taken but placed reassuringly close to her by Andra. The others sat around the fire, eating the flame roasted meat of five birds. Andra sat beside her, holding two cooked bird legs. Del, stomach growling at the smell of cooked meat, glanced up out of instinct and stared straight into the scowl of Venkell. She shifted her position.

'I don't think Venkell likes me.'

Andra shrugged.

'No one here likes you much. You lied to us,' she said around a mouthful of meat.

'Anyone of you would have done the same.'

Andra took another bite.

'I should hope so.'

'Venkell seems more suspicious than the others.' Del tried not to look at the second bird leg in Andra's hand.

'He's just protective, that's all.' Andra handed Del the meat. She took it and raised her bound hands to her mouth to take a bite. The meat was dry and the skin was oily on her lips but she was ravenous. She took a larger bite.

'Your parents must be proud of you, becoming a dragonslayer.' She swallowed her mouthful.

'Not really. They wanted me to take over the family business.'

'Is a dragonslayer more respectful and traditional than a blacksmith?'

'I had my reasons, as I'm sure you did. Why did you turn on King Rupert?'

'Because.' Del grinned. 'Because of respect and tradition.'

'You accused the king of awful things,' breathed Andra. Del studied her eyes, softening.

'I didn't want to. You'd have done the same, I think.' She frowned. 'Which is why I wanted to return of my own accord. No one else should be involved.' Del looked away.

'I'd get some rest if I were you,' said Andra after a long pause as she waited for Del to continue. 'It's hard going riding with your hands bound, especially if a dragon finds us.'

Del snorted as Andra stood and walked away. She stripped the bone of the last traces of meat, watching each of the men in turn. Dropping the clean bone, she sucked the juices off her fingers and glanced over her shoulder to check on Shadow. Her little horse was tethered with the others, relaxed, his head and eyes drooping. Del scooted herself around, leaned and dropped to the ground. Wriggling to get comfortable, she shut her eyes and willed sleep to come as her wrists and fingers felt for weaknesses in the rope that bound her.

'I don't like this,' said Venkell. Andra sat beside him but he kept his eyes on Del, watching her drop to the ground to sleep.

'It's a strange turn of events,' agreed Andra. She stared into the flames, concentrating on the warmth on her front rather than the cold at her back.

'And what do you think will happen, when we get back?'

Andra daren't think of it.

'This has been a strange time,' she repeated. Venkell looked at her. 'It's been too long to be away from home.'

'Nothing too out of the ordinary. Just a few jobs. It saves time and energy to do them together.'

'Even though we ran out of provisions?' Andra wondered if she should have broken orders and taken her company home. She could feel Venkell's gaze burning her. When she met it she found his softened eyes searching hers. She was held for a moment, heart thumping, acutely aware of how close she had sat to him.

'You did the right thing,' he murmured. Those words brought more comfort than Andra would admit to. She smiled and turned away, still feeling his ever watchful gaze on her.

Rather than meet it she looked up at those still sat around the fire, talking and eating. At the horses behind, grazing and dozing. At their prisoner, shivering as she slept. She ought to put a blanket on her, but Andra stayed where she was.

She no longer felt Venkell's attention on her. Looking out of the corner of her eye, she saw him facing the fire and finishing a piece of meat.

'We're hunters,' he said. 'It doesn't matter if we run

out of food. We will find more.' He held up the last bite before popping it in his mouth. Andra gave a weak smile. Yes, they were hunters, professionally trained and dedicated, not that anyone would have been able to tell from that dragon attack. Andra felt that failure as personal to her. 'It may do your career well, bringing Del Thorburn back to Drummbek as a rogue,' Venkell told her. She looked away from the fire, blinking moisture back into her hot eyes.

'I don't think Lord Gerard or the king will be happy to see her.'

'Perhaps not. But you brought in a rogue slayer, Andra. And not just any rogue. Del Thorburn. The Del Thorburn. You'll go into the history books for this.'

Nausea swelled in Andra and her lips began to tremble.

'Do you think so?'

Venkell was studying her again, his smile dropping as her skin paled.

'The captain who brought Del Thorburn back to Drummbek,' he murmured. 'Maybe they'll give you a pay rise. That will help your family, won't it?'

Andra nodded. He hadn't mentioned what might happen to Del, she thought. She knew, from the rumours and history lessons and her own ears, that Del was a fighter. Maybe she would survive. If Andra brought her home, maybe she would go down in history. Maybe for the right reasons. Her family would certainly welcome a pay rise, if she were that lucky. She smiled at Venkell.

'I would see to it that the whole company were rewarded.'

Venkell's expression didn't change. Still he watched her as she stood and moved away, covering Del with a blanket before checking on the horses in the darkness.

*

The next day, as the sun reached its highest point, the company approached Drummbek. Del watched the city as it came into view. The first thing to greet them, and any historic enemy who had been intent on attacking, was the great castle. Sitting upon its hill, surrounded by the valley and sprawls of streets and buildings, filled with people and dragons of every size, colour and income. At first they could see only the tops of the castle towers, then gradually the castle walls and windows came into view through the cloud. Beyond glittered the grey waters of the bay, the tall masts of the ships in the docks just discernible from the city buildings. The castle appeared ominous as heavy rain clouds gathered behind them, driven over the city by a strong wind. Drummbek shone under rays of sunshine which slowly dwindled as they watched. The clouds grew over the company and it began to rain. Del squinted at the castle, wondering which room King Rupert would be in at that moment. Perhaps relaxing in his bed chamber or sat reading in his library. Maybe he was enjoying the courtyard gardens, the only royal place in the castle that was almost too small for him to fit. He may be in the throne room, dealing with his royal duties. Or perhaps tucking into another rich meal in the grand dining room, the royal taster sat beside him. Was Markkus still the taster? It felt like so long since she had been within the castle, since she had last seen Markkus and the academy. The two years she had spent exiled might as well have been a hundred.

The company had ridden through four neighbouring villages leading up to the city's southern gates. Most of the villagers had been out, on the path or in their gardens or fields. They watched with silent awe as the dragonslayers rode through. One drunkard at the doorway to a tavern had called slurred words to them but none of the slayers replied. Del rode with her hands bound in front of her. Venkell rode beside her, holding Shadow's reins. Del sat deep in her saddle, rocking her body with Shadow's gait and trying to keep her head down. Every now and then she would glance up to peer at their surroundings. Andra rode at the front, bowing her head in a half nod at the well-wishers that met them. One woman came forward and gave a flower to one of the men. He pulled his horse to a stop to accept it and exchange some kind words. Del wondered if he knew the woman, if this was the village he had once called home.

They approached the city gates. There were four guards positioned at the gates and two of them came forward as Andra trotted out to meet them. The gates opened and the company rode through without pausing. Del read the twisted iron inscription that sat above all gates leading into the city, taking comfort from the surge of familiarity that swept through her.

Drummbek Forged Of Flame

She was home.

As they rode into the city she looked up at the old stone buildings. Memories fought for her attention and the comfort of home ebbed away. It felt like a large rock had dropped into her stomach, she was increasingly uneasy and nauseated. Looking to the high towers of the castle rising above the city, her fingers curled into fists, her wrists straining against her bonds.

Andra raised her hand and the company came to a halt. She turned in her saddle to look at them. Del's eyes flicked to her.

'Welcome home,' said Andra. Del took a sharp intake of breath before realising she was speaking to the whole company. She felt the men around her relax. 'We will ride to the academy for debriefing and then you may take leave until further orders.'

There were cheers and whoops. The rain began to fall a little heavier. The company continued to ride through the city, talking amongst themselves. People dodged out of their way with heads bowed and quiet words. Old women with bags of shopping, small children playing, and men and women travelling home from the working day, covering their heads and attempting to dodge the rain. Del watched, remembering the feeling of respect that being a dragonslayer brought. It had been a long time since she had felt that respect and the power that came with it.

Seven

A chill ran through Markkus as he hunched his shoulders against the rain. It was dark as the heavy clouds moved overhead. That didn't stop the street from being busy. The New Town market was just around the corner. The road bustled with those walking to and from the stalls. Some with heavy bags, others with hands jammed in pockets, some holding the hands of small children and one man who was losing a tug of war to a terrier over a scarf.

The city was large enough to accommodate a vast number of humans and dragons. The dragons of Drummbek varied in size, from that of a human toddler upwards. The larger dragons were rare in Drummbek. It was the general consensus that King Rupert was currently the largest. It had been a long time since the Old War, when human and dragon finally learned to live together, but still there were difficulties. Many human employers underpaid their dragon employees and vice versa. It was easier to underpay than to beat them senseless and have to deal with the wrath of the dragonslayers.

The dragonslayers should have had their name changed. Markkus had often discussed the topic with Del, but traditionalists ran the Order. Plus, it was difficult to argue the point since the first dragon king had allowed them to keep the name.

New Town's occupants were no different to Old

Town's, except for their income and maybe their family history. Dragons and humans lived on both sides of the bridges. Perhaps equality could go no further. Dragons were persecuted by humans as humans were by dragons, as women were by men, as the lower classes were by the higher classes, no matter where or how they lived.

The buildings were different in New Town. Markkus had grown up in Old Town where the old cream and grey stone had been worn away by centuries of weather. Here in New Town the bricks were a clean cream and red with shiny brass handles and knockers. There was often the smell of fresh paint and always the smell of flowers. New Town was where the wealthy lived. New Town was where the up and coming lived. He had felt so proud when the king had given him a New Town house. It was clean and crisp and still only a short distance from the castle sat upon its hill. These days he missed the murk and dirt of Old Town. He often felt a fraud, striding along the same roads as the women in their elegant dresses and men in their suits. Even the horses were smarter in New Town, a completely different breed. Not that Old Town didn't have its wealth. It had the long, main road leading up to the castle. At the opposite end of that road was the Dragonslayer Academy, their high spirited, well bred horses mingling with the shaggy carthorses of the poor. Wealth and modernisation couldn't compete with tradition in this city.

Markkus stared up at the houses. One belonged to Sergeant Don and the other to Mr Hodgkin. Markkus had been standing out on the street for three quarters of an hour, huddled in a long coat with a hood pulled over his head and eyes, his hands deep in his pockets. He looked up and down the street one more time and saw neither Don nor Hodgkin. Markkus approached Hodgkin's door and knocked. He waited. No one was home. He wondered if the man had any family. The truth was that Mr Hodgkin could have just run away with a woman to start a new life.

'Chance would be a fine thing,' Markkus muttered to himself. He turned to move on when he spotted Don approaching. Don saw him at the same moment and slowed his pace. His hat sat crooked on his head, channeling the rain down that one side of his body. He shrugged his shoulders as if a cold raindrop had found its way under his clothing. Judging by the position of his hat, it probably had.

'Don,' Markkus acknowledged. Don nodded his head, glancing towards his house. 'Horrible weather, huh?'

'Yeah, and I got a nice warm fire waiting for me. What do you want?'

Markkus smiled his most charming smile.

'I have an enquiry for the city guard.'

'I'm off duty.'

'Oh, well, sorry to bother you. I'll go to the station with my enquiry.'

'No.' Don grabbed onto Markkus's arm as he went to move past. 'What is it?'

Markkus smiled. Don always had been selfishly curious.

'Have you heard anything about Mr Hodgkin? How's the investigation going?'

Don groaned.

'This again? Who cares. He's gone, my problem is over. It's over.'

'Exactly.'

The men stared at one another and Don swallowed hard. They may have different lives now but Markkus had once been his superior and old habits die hard. Don looked down at his polished, rain soaked boots.

'Yes, his niece has been asking. She filed the report. We don't have any leads yet, no news. His house has been empty since the day he went to the king.' Don looked up at the house and sniffed, a raindrop hanging off the end of his nose. 'Creepy really,' he murmured. Markkus patted him damply on the shoulder.

'Go and get dry, Don. Thank you.'

Don nodded and splashed away. Markkus took one last glance at Mr Hodgkin's house before trudging along the street, around puddles, head down.

Charlie emerged from the shadows on the other side of the street. He watched Markkus's back disappear around the corner and into the throng of the market. Turning back, he looked down the road at the houses, narrowing his black eyes. He left for the castle, the crowds parting around him.

*

Tabitha wondered if anyone had noticed that she was shaking as she had made her way through the castle. Her fingers trembled as she lifted the bucket. Soapy water sloshed over the side. She cleaned it up, her fingers losing their grip and the mop threatening to fall to the floor. Straightening, she took a deep breath and lifted her eyes to the service door to the king's chambers. A wave of sickness came over her. She told herself that she had dreamt the visions of blood and death. That she had made up the stench of fear. She wasn't convincing. Being placed on the cleaning rota for these rooms was fortuitous, at least that's what she repeated to herself. There may be clues as to whether it was real.

This was it.

It was now or never.

She stood, a soldier ready to go to war, her gaze dropping to the door knob. She placed down her mop and bucket. A reasonably steady hand reached out and began shaking again as she turned the door knob. The door opened and revealed the largest of the chambers. The living area with the chaise lounge and antique furniture. She fought the urge to look away but her eyes immediately found the part of the floor where she had seen…where she had…the body, the blood, the noise of his crunching jaws. The memory overwhelmed her senses. She focused on the floor and saw that it was clean. Swallowed hard, she picked up the mop and bucket and stepped into the room. She checked that she was alone and then left the door ajar. Just in case.

She picked her way over to the part of the polished wooden floor where the body had been. It was as clean and shiny as the rest of the floor. That was when the doubt began to creep in. Maybe she hadn't seen it, or heard it, or smelt it. Maybe she had imagined it all. Imagined an image so terrifying which had felt so real that it was now etched on her memory. She shook her head. Dropping to her knees, she held her face close to the floor looking for any sign of dirt or discolouration. Her nose bounced off the wood as she scanned the surface. It stank of vinegar and lemon but that was nothing strange. The bucket of water that she had just filled had vinegar in it. Someone had scrubbed the floors, but the floors were scrubbed every day. That was what she was there to do. She gingerly ran a hand over the floor, willing some sort of stain to make itself apparent. Seeing nothing, she stood and hugged herself, holding back tears. She had imagined it all.

The memories were still real. The smell was still in her nose and the sounds roared in her ears, but as every minute passed the more it seemed as a dream. A real and frightening dream, and Tabitha knew she had been awake. Still, there was nothing she could do about it so she did the only thing she could. Tabitha got to work. She dusted each spotless surface. She made the bed in the next room off to the right with fresh silken sheets. She wiped each sparkling window down with a damp cloth. She picked up her broom and began to sweep the floors. There was nothing to sweep up, there never was. Tabitha found it so boring to clean things that were already clean. Where was the dust? Where was the dirt? Where was the satisfaction of a job well done? There had to be areas that the other maids missed. She shoved the broom under the bed and scraped it out, peering down to see what the bristles had brought her.

Nothing.

She looked around the room and saw the wooden cabinet by the disguised servants' door. Running her hand over the red and gold wallpaper on the door, she noticed that she had stopped shaking. Well, she thought, that was what physical work did for you, even if it was pointless work. Propping her broom against the door, she took hold of a corner of the cabinet and wiggled it towards the centre of the room. Once it was far enough in, she trotted round to look behind and gave a small squeal of delight. Dirt! There was dust and dirt and lost buttons and a stray sock. She picked up the dirty buttons and dropped them into her pocket for her mother. It wasn't exactly stealing, not when the buttons must have been lost for so long. As long as the sock, she imagined. King Rupert didn't wear clothing with buttons and he certainly didn't wear socks. In fact, he would look downright silly in socks. Tabitha tilted her head, wondering who it had once belonged to. It was a man's sock. Perhaps it had once belonged to King Tobyias. A royal sock. Maybe it would be worth something. She scooped it out of its resting place and studied it. It carried no embroidered initials, nothing that gave it away as being royal. With a smile, she placed it in a nearby bin which she would empty on her way out. Picking up her broom she began to sweep the dust and dirt out, paying careful attention to the corners.

Her heart began to race as she neared where the edge of the cabinet had sat. Tabitha paused, waiting for her brain to process what her eyes had just seen.

Brown.

Or was that dark red.

Specks of it, on the wooden floor. Tabitha risked a closer look, getting down onto her knees. It was congealed with large grey and black fluffy balls of dust plastered into it. Tabitha swallowed hard. Perhaps it was paint, left behind from when the room was decorated. She looked up at the papered walls. With a shaking hand she poked one of the specks with the tip of her finger, flinching as her skin touched the cold floor. It was completely dry. Sitting back on her heels, she looked at the pile of dust her broom had swept out. Her eyes fixed on a lighter brown dot resting in the pile. She clambered over and brushed the surrounding dirt away. Lifting it up on her finger she stared hard at a small reddish brown speck hanging onto the black dust ball. She sniffed it but it just smelt of finger. She prodded the dust pile some more, desperately trying to think of explanations that didn't contain the word 'blood'.

Footsteps by the main entrance made Tabitha start. She jumped up, pushing the cabinet back into its place. Wiping her red speckled fingers on her apron, she picked up her broom and began sweeping as if nothing were out of the ordinary. The footsteps faded. Tabitha stopped and listened to her own breathing, looking down at the dirt.

Something had to be done.

Her mind threw the memories back at her: the body, the claws slashing to open the flesh, the blood splashing. The maids never moved the furniture, they had no reason to. How long had that blood been there? How long had this been going on? And who had cleaned the floor? Someone in the castle knew because someone was helping to cover it up. King Rupert wouldn't have done it, she doubted the king knew what a mop looked like. She continued sweeping and moved back to the cabinet. Something stuck out from under the front, dislodged from when she had moved it. She bent and yanked at it, lifting the object up.

'Shhhh,' she hissed, another wave of nausea hitting her as she stared at the white and brown of the small piece of flesh in her fingers. She dropped it as if it were hot, turned and vomited into the bin, all over the lone dusty sock. Wiping her mouth on her sleeve, she sat back and stroked her aching stomach.

*

'What do you have to tell me?' King Rupert's voice rumbled.

He sat in his library, a book open, one claw pinning down a page. Charlie emerged from the shadows near the large doors and approached the king. They held each other's gaze for a matter of seconds before Charlie's eyes wandered around the room. The ceiling was far above his head and the bookcases that lined every wall reached right to the top of the room. A large window filled half of one wall. Charlie guessed it overlooked the royal gardens, but now the heavy red and gold curtains were drawn against the dark rain clouds. The light patter of rain hitting the glass was loud in the quiet. It was only his second visit to Drummbek castle. His mother would be proud, were she alive, he thought, to see him working so far up the social ladder. Charlie did not feel particularly proud, but rather pleased with the salary offered. He had done his research into the king's finances before travelling to the city and had started to work on a retirement plan. Not that one took retirement from a career such as Charlie's. He glanced at the nearest bookcase and read the titles of the closest books. He'd always drawn comfort from libraries, such a room as this was a dominant feature in his future plans. He wondered if this may be a hobby that he and the king shared.

'You have an interesting collection, Your Grace.' Charlie's voice was deep, almost as deep as the king's, and rough from years of tobacco and whisky abuse. King Rupert snapped his book shut. 'I understand that many dragons are hoarders. Are books your treasure?'

King Rupert ran his tongue over his sharp teeth.

'The majority of them came with the castle,' he told Charlie. 'Do you have anything to tell me?'

'Yes, Your Grace. I followed Markkus Kern.'

'And?'

'I followed him to some houses, close to New Town market.' Charlie moved over to another bookcase, tilted his head and began reading the titles. King Rupert glared at him. 'He waited outside for a long time.'

'What for?' The king asked. With one slender finger, Charlie pulled out a volume bound in red leather. He gently blew the thick dust from it.

'I used to have a copy of this,' he murmured as he turned the thin pages. King Rupert sighed shortly. 'This is a first edition. Such history that lies within this castle,' Charlie mused. 'I wonder which king added this book to his library.'

'Charles. My patience wears thin.'

'Hmm.' Charlie replaced the leather bound first edition of "*A Beginners Guide to Assassination*" with great care. 'As he was leaving, he met Sergeant Don Alder of the city guard. I believe they fought together during the Great War. They spoke and then Kern left. He headed for his own home. I believe he will be back in the castle for your next meal.' Charlie faced the king, his features giving nothing away. King Rupert glowered.

'Sergeant Don Alder. What did they speak of?'

'You asked me to follow the man, Your Grace. Nothing more.' Charlie moved towards the king, running a finger along the edge of his shiny mahogany desk.

'I am your king,' King Rupert growled. Charlie didn't flinch.

'No. You are Drummbek's king, Your Grace. With all due respect, I am not a man of Drummbek.'

'I don't believe you show any respect, due or otherwise.' The king showed Charlie his teeth as he spoke but Charlie only blinked like a bored cat.

'It will cost you five gold coins to learn what was spoken. Information is expensive, Your Grace.'

King Rupert slowly cocked his head to the side.

'A man who shows no fear in front of those superior to him is an interesting one, although perhaps a little foolish,' he rumbled. Charlie considered this but decided it a waste of energy to point out that no one was his superior. King Rupert reached out to a box on the edge of his desk. He pulled back the lid and showed Charlie a pile of golden coins.

'Take your payment.'

With swift fingers Charlie lifted his original payment of ten gold coins followed by the five.

'They spoke of the sergeant's neighbour.' He examined a coin before pocketing it. 'A Mr Hodgkin, who has recently gone missing.' King Rupert flicked his tongue over his lips in thought. 'Markkus asked the good sergeant if he had seen him, being as they are neighbours. He asked him how the missing persons investigation was going. The sergeant said there was no news. Markkus thanked him and moved on.' Charlie allowed a small pause. 'Will you kill me now, Your Grace?'

King Rupert's far off gaze refocused on Charlie and he looked directly into his black eyes. With a broad smile, the king laughed. The noise boomed around the study. He reopened his book and found his page.

'No, Charles. Why ever would I kill you when you are so invaluable to me?' He looked down to his book, silently dismissing Charlie. Charlie bowed and went to leave, taking note of the door, surrounding walls and that particular first edition as he did so. 'Don't go far, Charles. I will call for you again.'

Charlie let himself out of the study and glanced at his watch. It glittered back at him as the three diamonds embedded in the strap caught the light. It was nearing four o'clock. Charlie glanced out of a nearby window. The rain had eased but the grey clouds still hung heavy over the city. He made his way along the corridor, passing a young maid as he did so. His eyes caught hers for a second.

*

Tabitha turned back to look at the strange man dressed all in black as he disappeared around the corner. She looked back to the library door as there came a low grumble. Shivering, she trotted past the door as the king rang his bell, calling a butler to him. She threw herself down the nearest servant staircase and landed heavily at the bottom. Thankful that no one was around to see her, she leaned against the cold stone. This was no time to panic, or to let fear get the better of her. She had to be strong. Taking another deep breath, she made her way to the kitchens. Through the kitchens she stalked and out into the small courtyard. Along a small alleyway and there was the prison building. A guard who wasn't Richie stood by the stairway leading down to the entrance. Without pausing, Tabitha walked up to the guard. He watched her without expression and moved to block her path down the stairs to the entrance.

'Excuse me.' Tabitha stuck her chin out in an attempt to show authority.

'Sorry, miss. No one gets past.'

Tabitha studied the guard. His eyes were kind, but wouldn't meet hers.

'Why not?'

That made him look down at her.

'Those are my orders,' he said, as if she had asked a stupid question. 'Dangerous men are behind that door, miss. Can't let anyone inside.'

'I work here,' Tabitha told him, in case he hadn't recognised her. 'I'm one of the maids.'

He looked her over.

'You don't have anything.'

'What?'

'In your hands, miss. No cleaning equipment, no food. You don't have anything.'

Tabitha looked down at her empty hands. 'So why do you want to go into the prisons?'

She looked back up at him. He was good.

'Well done!' She grinned. 'You've passed. Erm, the Lord Commander asked me to come out and test you. And you passed. Well done,' she muttered before scuttling back to the kitchens. She made her way through the bustle and smell of warm cooking meats, and down into the servants' quarters where she promptly collapsed into a chair, exhaling in a whistle. She needed to think before she did things, that much was obvious. What she had seen in the king's chambers had rattled her. Yes. That was it. She needed to pull herself together. Tabitha sat up in the chair, oblivious to the two chatting butlers walking in and disappearing into the kitchenette. She couldn't just sit on what she had seen. Something had to be done. Her foot tapped on the floor. She was unable to keep still, so there was no option but to take action.

Then it occurred to her. As if her brain had just passed her the note it had been trying to write since she had witnessed the king…seen the king…

Another person had accused the king of eating people. Another person with authority and some power. A dragonslayer. Del Thorburn. The greatest dragonslayer of recent times and the only female slayer to become a household name. And what had happened to her? She was exiled and likely dead. Tabitha unstuck her tongue from the roof of her dry mouth. If that had happened to a powerful dragonslayer, the slayer who had led the armies of the previous king, what would happen to a simple castle maid? It wouldn't just be Tabitha who suffered. She knew that with a dreaded certainty. It would be her parents too. Not just because their precious only child would be dead, but because of what the king would do to them. The memory of the corpse, torn open and glassy eyed, lying on the chamber floor rose in Tabitha's mind. Only this time the faces of the dead were those of her mum and dad.

'No.' She whispered it, but in that quiet room the word was loud enough for the two butlers to stop their conversation and look at her. Lowering her head, Tabitha walked out and through the servants' corridor towards the laundry room. She was on her own. She couldn't risk endangering anyone else. Her next move needed careful consideration and planning. There was no room to mess up.

Eight

Andra's company rode through the city. Climbing up the hill, they turned down the long, wide road that down to the academy. Del felt the presence of the castle burning into her back. At the end of the road it forked away leading to the docks or the eastern city gate. Here the company approached the large black iron gates that only closed on special occasions. The academy stood beyond. It was a grand building of grey brick gone black in places with age. Moss grew in the cracks and ivy ran up the wall around the large double front doors. There were five storeys, each with large lead lined windows. Over to the right, an arch led through to a stable yard of large grey brick stalls and a well swept floor.

Del had been watching Shadow's ears, flicking to face each direction. He had never been in a city and he was finding the new loud noises and pungent smells alarming. It wasn't helping that he couldn't feel the reassuring pressure of Del against his mouth. He began skipping and shying. Although he wasn't as light and limber as Venkell's horse, he more than made up for spryness in weight. Venkell was nearly pulled from his saddle more than once. He muttered and cussed under his breath, yanking on the little farm horse's reins, much to Del's disgust. Del looked up at the building, her body beginning to shake. Andra led them through the archway to the right where two smart stable boys met them. The company dismounted and began to prepare their horses for the night but Del stayed where she was. She glared pointedly at Andra as one of the boys took Shadow's reins.

'I'm sure you can dismount with your hands bound,' Venkell said.

'You scared I'll run?' Del growled. Shadow threw his head up as the boy attempted to stroke his nose. The horse skittered backwards but Del kept her balance, her eyes never leaving Andra's.

'Fine,' Andra relented, nodding to Venkell. Muttering under his breath, Venkell took a knife from his belt and cut through the rope bonds. He allowed Del to dismount, holding onto her sleeve. Once she was on the ground, he spun her round and retied her hands behind her back. Del looked back to Shadow who was eyeballing her.

'Take it easy with him. He's a country horse. This is all new for him,' she told the boy. He nodded and stroked Shadow's neck until the horse began to calm.

Del twisted free of Venkell's grasp and made her way towards the building. Andra and Venkell followed closely.

'Eager to get before Lord Gerard, huh?' Venkell muttered.

Del didn't respond. Andra opened the doors and the three filed through.

Venkell gripped Del's wrists and pushed her up a large staircase that wound its way up the building. The feel of the carpet beneath her boots was enough to allow the vivid memories of her youth to come rushing back. Of the mistakes she had made, and the victories. She slowed as she passed the oil portrait of Lord Winshaw, grey before his time. Taking a breath, his familiar scent of old leather and cigar smoke filled her mind. There was the door that led to the dining hall, where Del had often feasted and drunk until she collapsed beneath the table. Up another flight and there was the corridor to the dormitories. When she was young, she had lain awake with the others telling ghost stories and making bets and dares. They passed the floor holding the private quarters of the experienced dragonslayers who called the academy home. She caught a fleeting glance of the door that had led to her own bedroom. She could still smell the sheets as she woke in the morning, see the sun light filtering through the curtains and feel the warmth of whoever she had brought back with her that night. They walked almost to the top of the staircase. On the fourth floor, Venkell pushed her hard away from the stairs and Andra led them into a large room. A woman, pretty with blonde hair flowing over her shoulders, sat at a large desk. She looked up as Andra and Venkell approached and smiled. The smile vanished when she caught sight of Del. Del grinned.

'Hello Ami. Long time no see, huh?'

Ami sank back into her chair and looked at Andra.

'We wish to see Lord Gerard.'

Ami glanced at Del as she made her way to the door on the other side of the room. She hesitated as she reached Andra.

'Do you know who she is, Captain? She's exiled,' she hissed.

'Now she's back,' Andra replied. She turned to Del as Ami disappeared behind the door into Lord Gerard's office.

'Nice to see old faces?'

'Some things don't change.' Del shrugged.

Ami reappeared and gave Andra a subtle nod. Venkell pushed Del forward and they followed Andra into the office beyond the door which Ami shut behind them.

Lord Percy Gerard glared at Del. He sat at his mahogany desk, littered with paper, his hands clasped in front of him. His short grey hair was whiter than Del remembered and he had new glasses with smaller frames. He looked over these now, towards Andra. The stress must have gotten to him, Del decided, and carved wrinkles into his face.

'My Lord,' Andra began. Del kept her eyes focused on Lord Gerard. 'We have returned from our jobs in Arisdon and the Wastelands. The Mayor of Arisdon was grateful for the help we could provide and said he would send word to you. We were successful in finding the female rogue dragon in the Wastelands and held her trial. The girl she kidnapped was found in a nearby cave, dead, along with four other corpses. We found the rogue guilty and put her to death.' Andra pulled a purse out of her pocket and gave it to Lord Gerard. 'The villagers offered us reward and payment.'

Lord Gerard emptied the purse and counted the gold coins. Placing them back, he nodded and looked up at Del. She stood her ground and stared back hard.

'Del. I wasn't expecting to see you again so soon. Or ever, for that matter.'

Andra looked from Del to Lord Gerard.

'We came across her on our return, my Lord. She was living in ruins where we spent a night. She's… turned rogue, my Lord.'

Lord Gerard raised an eyebrow, his lips twitching.

'A rogue. You have evidence of this?'

'Her weapons, my Lord. She carries a sword, a knife and a pistol. Her weapons were taken when she was exiled. And we…well…she killed a dragon.'

Lord Gerard leaned forward, his attention focused on Del. Resting his elbows on the desk and his chin in his palms, his lips fought against a smile.

'Did she, indeed?'

Andra shuffled her feet.

'Ms Ferrer.' Del gestured to Andra. 'And her company apprehended me at the ruins. I rode with them. They were attacked. Unfortunately, this academy no longer seems to set high standards for training, my Lord. I was forced to intervene to save lives.'

'Gave yourself away, ay Del?' Lord Gerard smirked. Del searched his features for a hint of warmth, something that might give away his true feelings. There was none. 'She rode with you before the killing?' He turned to Andra.

'No, my Lord. She asked for safe passage to Drummbek. She told me she was a blacksmith.' Andra's voice dropped, regretting the words before she'd finished speaking.

'And you believed her? The daughter of one of Old Town's smithies believed that this woman was a blacksmith?'

'No, my Lord. I knew something was not right.'

'Did you know who she was?'

Andra struggled.

'Have you ever met Ms Thorburn before, Captain?'

'No, my Lord.'

'Then you do not know her. I do. Del, you, have been charged with turning rogue. And we can now add the charge of breaking your exile, which I have no doubt were your intentions when you lied to my captain and joined her company. You will go before the king who will decide your punishment. The punishment for turning rogue, of course, being death. I cannot say what King Rupert will decide on the charge of you breaking your exile.'

'Ah yes, nothing like a fair system.' Del smiled at

Lord Gerard. 'They could have been killed if I hadn't helped.'

'Could, Del. Could.'

'The company saw me talking to the dragon, asking him to back down. He refused and attacked me.'

'And just what were you doing with those weapons before Andra's company turned up?'

'Defending myself. You have no evidence that I have killed before that dragon.'

'That remains to be seen and, of course, will be made available at your trial, I'm sure.'

'If I'm given a trial.'

'We are bound by law, Del. Think before you speak.'

Lord Gerard and Del glared at one another. Andra sank back, cheeks burning.

'Leave us, Sergeant Venkell.' Lord Gerard said.

Venkell gave Del a tug.

'Leave Del here.'

Venkell dropped his grip on Del and left. The door closed with a click.

'Did you lose any men?' Gerard turned to Andra.

'Yes, my Lord. Five.'

'Five. Tell me, were you caught unaware by this dragon?'

'No, my Lord.'

'And if she hadn't come to your rescue? Would I be writing a condolence letter to your family right now?'

Andra hesitated long enough for Gerard to know the truth. Gerard turned to Del. She stood at ease, hands still bound behind her back. She met his gaze.

'So, you wanted to return to the city. Did you forget something?'

Del sighed as if in thought and pulled at her wrists.

'It's hard to think, my Lord. With my hands bound.'

Gerard looked her up and down.

'Does she have weapons?' he asked Andra.

'No, my Lord.'

Gerard looked over his desk. He took a silver envelope knife and a fountain pen, and locked them in a drawer.

'Untie her.'

Andra released Del. Del rubbed her wrists and plonked herself into the soft leather chair opposite Gerard. Andra looked on with horror.

'As a matter of fact, I do have unfinished business in the city.'

'Such as? Unpaid debts? I never took you for a gambling type.'

'Then perhaps you don't know me as well as you think.'

Lord Gerard gave an uncertain smile and glanced up at Andra, gazing down at Del.

'Do your men need extra training, Captain Ferrer?'

'My Lord?'

'You were nearly butchered by a dragon who didn't even catch you unawares. Do your men need extra training?'

'No, my Lord.'

'Then explain to me, please, how so many of your men died.'

There was a silence. Del glanced at Andra before turning back to Gerard. She leaned forward in her seat. Gerard flinched back and then relaxed with a huff. Del smiled at her short triumph.

'My Lord, Captain Ferrer was not at fault. Her leadership was impeccable. Her men may have let her down but I'm sure it was a one off occurrence that can probably be blamed on the new distraction in the company.'

'You consider yourself to be a distraction?' Gerard raised an eyebrow.

'You do,' Del said playfully, her eyes finding a stray metal paperclip on his desk. Gerard followed her gaze and she watched him swallow. He leaned forward and removed the thin piece of metal, keeping it clasped in his fist.

After a moment of quiet contemplation, he murmured, 'So. Why are you here?'

When Del didn't answer, he looked up at Andra. 'She was one of our best, you know. Managed to get herself into the castle, didn't you, Del. Under King Tobyias. His own personal mercenary. You led the dragonslayers in his army. You brought him nine victories during the Great War. Nine victories out of nine battles. You could have thrown Andra. You could have lost her. Hell, you could have killed her. So why are you here?'

Del avoided looking at Andra who was staring hard at her.

'Maybe I was homesick.'

Gerard gave a small laugh.

'King Rupert won't be pleased to see you.' He sat back, studying Del as if she were a puzzle he could solve. 'You shouldn't have come back.'

'There are a lot of things I should not have done, Gerard.' Del noticed Andra flinch. 'Lots of things,' she murmured. After an uncomfortable pause, Gerard cleared his throat and looked down at his desk.

'Captain, take our rogue here to the cells. She will be taken before the king as the king sees fit. Your men will report for training tomorrow morning. Eight, sharp. Your whole company.' Andra bowed her head. Del stood and the captain gripped her arm.

'My Lord. Her bonds,' Andra said quietly.

'What? Oh, she'll be fine. Just lock her away.'

Gerard swept them out of his office with a wave. Before the door closed, Del saw him place the paperclip back onto his desk with a shaking hand.

On the ground floor Del was led down some steps and towards the row of three small dark cells in the basement of the large academy. These were the cells reserved for the dragonslayers, those who came home drunk or broke the law. The cells for the dragons that broke the law were on the other side of the academy. Built with thick walls and wide doorways to accommodate a small dragon's strength.

In the human cells, the scent of sweat and urine in the darkness behind the heavy set door was overpowering. Andra led her to a cell, opened the door wide and allowed Del through before locking it. The cell, with walls of bars, was bare save for a blanket in one corner and a pot in another. The floor was black with grime. Shadows moved across the cell, created by the light from a tiny square window chiseled into the top of the stone wall that made up the foundations of the academy. Andra watched her through the bars. Del rubbed her wrists where her bonds had chaffed on the long journey.

'You shouldn't be afraid of Gerard, you know,' Del told her.

'*Lord* Gerard.'

Del shrugged.

'How can you be so relaxed?' Andra asked. 'You're going to be put to death.'

Del didn't respond. She was trying not to think about it which was hard when people kept bringing it up.

'You were a household name.'

'Am I not anymore?'

'No female dragonslayer has ever been as successful as you. You made history.'

Del looked up at Andra.

'Is that why you joined? I would have thought Ferrer's firstborn would take over the family business. He's the best smith in the city, even though he isn't recognised for it. How did you afford a dragonslayer education?'

'Same way you did.'

Del smiled.

'Not exactly the same, I hope. Your father is well?'

'He's still alive, if that's what you mean.'

'I should hope so, I was only gone for two years. He's a good man. Made me my finest sword.'

'He doesn't make the dragonslayer weapons.'

'No, but he should. I do hope you get yours from him.' Del turned and looked around the tiny cell again. She looked between the floor and the blanket, wondering where would be safer to sit. 'Is this all I get?'

'I'll see what I can do.' Andra left, a dizziness coming over her.

*

As night fell over the city, Andra walked up the road from the academy towards the castle. She stopped outside the blacksmiths on the right and looked up. The windows above the shop were lit by candles and she could see the shapes of figures moving inside. Andra moved to the front door to the side of the shop, unlocked it with the key in her pocket and pushed it open.

'Andra!'

The tension in Andra released. She hadn't realised

that she was hunched over until her shoulders dropped. Grinning, she crouched and opened her arms wide as a small boy with scruffy blonde hair ran into her. She held him tightly. 'You're back.'

'Told you I'd come back,' Andra said, her nose and mouth in the boy's hair. She pushed the boy back and looked him over. 'And I thought I was only gone a matter of months but here you are, almost a man. You don't fit your clothes anymore.'

The boy giggled. Andra stood as her mother walked around the corner.

'Welcome home.' Her mother rushed towards her and they held each other. 'Come in. You must be starving.'

Andra couldn't deny that she had been thinking about her mother's cooking for most of the time she had been away. Andra's stomach rumbled as she caught the scent of roasting vegetables and boiling potatoes drifting through the house. She followed her mother through the house and into the kitchen.

'Andra.' Ferrer the blacksmith sat at the kitchen table with a glass of ale. He raised this as she walked in. He looked tired and older than when she had left, and a twinge of worry marred the comfort she felt from seeing him. 'Welcome home.'

Andra smiled at her father, her fingers running through the boy's hair as he grasped her leg.

'Cayden. Come and sit down. Give your sister some space.' Andra's mother turned to her stove. Cayden looked up at Andra and grinned. He was missing two of his teeth. Andra placed her bag on the floor and sat in a chair opposite her father. Her little brother curled up on the floor beside Andra's feet. Ferrer watched as she pulled out her sword and pistol, and set them on the table.

'No,' snapped her mother. 'Not on the table.' She gave Andra a meaningful glance and a minute gesture towards Cayden.

'Did you bring me anything?' Cayden asked, oblivious to the weapons.

'She's been working, Cay. She can't bring you something every time she goes out working. Did you see any action?' her father asked. He picked up her sword and looked down the blade with a keen eye. 'This certainly hasn't seen any.'

'Arisdon was nice, as always. The men found it quite boring. We found the dragons we were sent to investigate out on the Wastelands, on the outskirts of Arisdon.'

'And?' her mother asked, stirring the gravy.

'Did you kill them?' Cayden asked.

'We did our job,' Andra told him, ruffling his hair.

'That means yes,' Cayden told his parents.

'I did get you something.'

Cayden sprang to his feet and jumped up and down on the spot. Andra pulled out a small wrap of cloth from her pocket and handed it to her little brother. 'Careful now.'

Slowly, Cayden unwrapped the cloth. The tooth gleamed up at him. He stared, wide-eyed and open mouthed, up at Andra. 'It's a dragon tooth,' she told him. Their father leaned over to look at it.

'I can make you a chain for that, Cay. It'll look good around your neck.'

Cayden ran on the spot as he looked down at the tooth.

'Thank you thank you thank you,' he breathed, throwing his arms around Andra's neck and holding her so tightly that she might have choked had he been a little older. Laughing, Andra untangled herself from him. He sat down on the floor and stared hard at the tooth. Andra watched him, wondering how to say the next words.

'When we were coming home we stayed in the ruins of this big house,' she said. 'Del was there.'

'Del? Thorburn, Del?'

Andra nodded.

'She's alive? One of my best customers, she was.' Andra's father placed down the sword.

'Isn't she the one you used to go on about?' her mother asked.

'She's back in the city.'

'But she was exiled?'

'She's turned rogue…I had to arrest her.'

Andra's parents both turned and stared at her.

'You arrested her?' her father asked.

'The woman who is the reason you became a dragonslayer?'

Andra stared hard at the floor.

'I was trying to do my duty.'

'But she'll be hanged,' murmured Ferrer. His wife smacked him on the shoulder and he looked down into his son's wide brown eyes. 'I mean...there's no other way of putting it. Not if she's turned rogue.'

'What does rogue mean?'

'It means that she's killed. She killed a dragon,' Andra told her brother.

'Like you do.'

'Well, yes, but not with the authority. It's not her job to kill dragons anymore.'

'Did she kill good dragons?'

'Well...it's complicated.'

Cayden wasn't satisfied with this but his father spoke before he could.

'You did what you had to do to,' he said with a loud

voice.

'Where is she now?'

'At the academy. In the cells.'

'Poor thing,' her mother murmured. Ferrer stood.

'Come on. I'll help you take your things to your room.' He picked up Andra's bag. Andra collected her weapons from the table, Cayden close by her side.

'No, no, Cayden. You go wash up. Dinner'll be ready soon.'

Cayden pouted, placing his prized dragon tooth on the table before running to the sink. Andra followed her father out of the kitchen and towards her bedroom.

'You did the right thing,' he told her as he set her bag down on her bed.

'Did I? I thought I had but now I'm not so sure.'

'You didn't know Del. You only saw her on parade and in the shop sometimes. I often wondered why you looked up to her so much when you never met her.'

'I knew of her.'

'Everyone did.' Ferrer gave his daughter a smile. 'You did the right thing, Andra. People say that Del spread rumours about the king, but she didn't. Del wasn't the type for rumours. She was onto something. I just know it. And now she's back. She won't be easily hanged.'

Andra sat on her bed.

'I hope you're right. I don't know what I was thinking, bringing her back here to die.'

'Your duty, pet. You were doing your duty. And she knows that. Hell, I'd bet she was relying on that.'

'You think so?' Andra looked up at her father.

'If there's one thing I learned about Del, after all those years? It's that she never does anything by accident. It'll work out, I'm sure. Now, put that sword and pistol where Cay can't get them and go wash up.'

Ferrer left Andra sitting on her bed.

*

Andra had an early night. She climbed into bed and clenched her eyes shut, willing the numbness of sleep to come over her. Her eyes opened rebelliously and she stared up at the ceiling. She was thinking about Del. About how she had listened to the woman's voice when she was no older than Cayden, helping her father in the shop. How she had watched Del on parade, wearing her every day clothes, surrounded by uniformed dragonslayers. A well-used sword and pistol, made by Andra's father, at her hips. Andra remembered the moment she had decided that she wanted to be like Del. She wanted to be a dragonslayer. She wanted to walk on parade with used weapons, her name on everyone's lips, surrounded by history and tradition.

Andra looked over at her dragonslayer uniform hung up on the door. Swinging her legs over the side of the bed, she sat with her face cupped in her hands. She couldn't see how Del would escape death this time. Andra dropped her hands and clenched her eyes shut tight before opening them wide. Del had come so easily. That wasn't the Del whose name was whispered in taverns throughout Drummbek. Her father was right, she had wanted to return. What was she planning? Andra fell back onto the bed with a loud sigh. She wouldn't sleep tonight.

Del had made herself a bed as best she could. Now was not the time to plot and plan. She had spent two years doing that. Now was the time to sleep. She was right where she should be. She hoped. Del was used to sleeping rough now and the clean, dry straw she had been given as per Andra's orders was almost a luxury. The blanket gave some warmth and Del slept well. She didn't dream. She allowed the blank nothingness to overwhelm her.

Tabitha lay in bed and stared at the ceiling. Her eyelids would droop periodically and she would start to drift chaotically into sleep. The darkness consumed her, throwing her from side to side as visions of dragons with blood dripping from their teeth loomed into view. The dragon spotted her and roared, charging towards her. She woke with a jolt, eyes wide, and spent the next hour going over and over the situation, until her eyelids began to droop again. Over and over.

Markkus didn't sleep. He made it home in the dark early hours of the morning with the tang of ale still on his tongue. Lying on his bed in deep contemplation, the hours passed as he drifted through complex thoughts. The first rays of light fought their way over the cityscape and into the bedroom. Markkus stood to look through the window at the sky, eyes narrowed against the bright morning light. Palms on the windowsill, he lent out and took a deep breath, listening to the city awakening.

Nine

The sun had barely risen over the hills on the horizon as Tabitha crept through the castle kitchens. A skeleton staff were already in, cleaning and making preparations for the day's meals. Breakfast wasn't for another few hours, but already one chef was butchering a side of pork for the king's dinner. Tabitha tried not to look, holding her breath against the sharp smell of fresh meat. The chef didn't notice her. Why would he? She was just a maid. There were perks to be so low in the hierarchy. She trotted out of the kitchen and into the courtyard, ran through the dark alleyway between buildings and stopped in the shadows, watching the entrance to the prison. There was the guard. It looked like Richie, leaning against the wall, head tilted down to his chest. In the soft silence of the morning Tabitha fancied she could hear him snore. But he was stood next to the entrance. She couldn't sneak past, no matter how quiet she was.

The jangle of cups on a tray tore at Tabitha's attention. Daisy, a maid roughly Tabitha's age, walked down the alleyway behind her. She held a tray of bread and cups full of water which splashed as she manoeuvred the cobbles. Tabitha rushed towards her.

'Daisy!'

'Tab? What're-'

'Erm. Agnes asked me to take over.'

'She did? But, why? You don't start for another hour, don't you?' Daisy had a tight grip on that tray.

Tabitha took a breath and glanced over her shoulder at the prison and sleeping guard.

'It's just handing the tray to the guard. It's fine. I can do it. Save you some time.'

Daisy twisted her lips.

'But Richie's on guard, isn't he?' She went on tiptoe, nearly tipping over the cups, to peer over Tabitha. Tabitha deflated. This was going to be more difficult that she thought.

'You like Richie?'

Daisy shrugged.

'He's cute.'

Tabitha tried to keep disgust from her face.

'Does he know how you feel?'

'I try to talk to him when I pull this shift,' Daisy whispered with a sly smile. Tabitha returned the smile, seeing the solution to her problem.

'And he still hasn't done anything about it? Sounds like he needs a prod in the right direction.'

Daisy nodded.

'That's what my mum says.'

'I can help,' offered Tabitha. 'Why don't you go to the pantry. It'll be empty and quiet this time of the morning. I'll tell Richie to meet you there.'

'What if he doesn't come?'

'Of course he will. I'll make sure of it. Then you can have a proper talk.'

Tabitha waited, holding her breath, as Daisy thought about it.

'Okay,' said Daisy.

'Here. Give me the tray. I'll make sure it's sorted. Hurry now. And I'll send Richie along to you.'

'Thanks Tab.' Daisy thrust the tray into Tabitha's arms and gave her a kiss on the cheek. 'I owe you one. If it works,' she added, before turning and running back towards the kitchens.

Tabitha stood frozen, waiting for something to go wrong. When Daisy didn't return after a few seconds, she turned back to the prison and Richie. Standing tall, head back, Tabitha approached the guard.

'Morning Richie.'

With a snort, Richie woke up and stood straight. He blinked at Tabitha as he got his bearings.

'Where's Daisy?' He wiped his mouth and nose on his sleeve. Tabitha pulled a face.

'Funny you should ask that. She wanted a quiet word with you. If you know what I mean.' Tabitha wasn't entirely sure what she meant, she had never been good at this, but apparently Richie did. His eyes lit up.

'Oh yeah?' He slicked his greasy hair back.

'Yeah. She's in the pantry. You know where that is?'

He nodded and then looked down at the tray in Tabitha's hands. 'Oh, don't you worry about this,' she told him. 'You get to Daisy, while she's got a minute. I'll take this down and cover for you both. Go on.'

'Okay.' Richie handed her the keys, which she folded in her grasp under the tray. 'Wait. You sure? It ain't right, a girl going down there.'

'They're locked up right?'

'Right.'

'And I just hand out the bread and water, right?'

'Ain't right,' Richie murmured, his expression showing the silent battle waging in his head.

'Well, I don't know what to say. Daisy's waiting for you. She won't have long.' Tabitha turned to glance up at the clock just visible on the side of one of the castle towers. Richie followed her gaze.

'Okay. Just don't get too close to them. Heck, Tabby, just leave the tray here and I'll do it afterwards, err, when I get back.' Richie ran off towards the kitchens before Tabitha could answer.

'And let the poor prisoners go hungry and thirsty?' she murmured. 'I don't think so.'

She walked down the steep steps, leaving the sunrise and flickering lamps behind. The darkness came over her with each step. At the bottom, she shifted the tray onto one arm and tried each key in the lock, a chill sweeping over her. Don't think, just get on with it. Tabitha gritted her teeth. The lock gave way under the third key and the door opened. She pushed it and let it swing wide so she could see what she was walking into.

The prison was silent. The door gave way to a wide corridor with cells on either side made up of walls of metal bars. There was no privacy, there was no glass in the tiny, high windows and there were no torches to give light. Then there was the smell. Sharp, thick and so strong that Tabitha could taste it on the air she breathed. Out of the gloom, gleaming eyes watched her. She considered holding her breath, but then she wouldn't be able to talk. Which was the whole purpose of her coming into these cells. To talk to the men inside.

The door bumped against her as it tried to close, shutting out the light that had managed to creep in from up the stairs. Tabitha, again balancing the tray on one arm, studied the door and found a latch on the outside. By fitting the latch to the outside wall, the door remained open and the slither of orange light trickled into the prison. Tabitha began a slow walk down that corridor.

The silence of the prison gave way to murmurings.

'That's not the guard.'

'Shhh.'

'It's a girl.'

'Something's going on.'

'Is the king dead?'

'Shhh!'

Tabitha stopped between the first cells.

'Here, child.'

She looked to her left. An old man sat close to the bars, his remaining hair white and long, his face full of whiskers and bristles. His eyes, from what she could see, were watery and light. 'Here.' With a long, trembling finger, he pointed to a hatch at the bottom of the cell door.

Tabitha bent and placed a cup of water at the hatch, pushing it through with a finger. He took it and gulped it down.

'What's going on, child?' he asked, wiping his mouth on his arm and licking at the watery remains. Tabitha swallowed hard.

'That's what I came to ask you.' She looked up at the other men. Now that her eyes had adjusted she could see how wretched they were. Seven of them, with one cell at the back that appeared empty. There were seven hunks of bread on the tray, and she offered one to the old man through the bars. He eyed it but wouldn't take it. 'Why are you here?' she asked him. 'What did you do?'

He looked up at her and snatched the bread.

'Killed my good for nothing brother,' he growled, ripping off a bite. Tabitha stepped back, fighting to remain calm.

'And you?' She turned to the prisoner opposite. Placing the cup of water and hunk of bread in the hatch and quickly stepping away. The man in the cell, younger than the first with meat still on his bones and muscles still showing through his shirt, gave her a wry smile.

'Why do you want to know, girl?' He took the cup but left the bread, moving to the back of the cell and into the shadows.

'Why do you ask?' came a voice from further inside the prison.

'I...' Tabitha found she couldn't speak. She was scared to say it out loud.

'What have you seen?' asked the voice. Tabitha moved towards the sound, deeper into the prison, dropping off water cups and bread hunks at each hatch. In the back cell there squatted a man with dark hair. He was young, not much older than Tabitha, but his clothes were hanging from him. His pale face was gaunt and his bones were visible pushing through his skin.

'What have you seen?' Tabitha asked him. 'Why are you here?'

'Treason,' he said, watching her place the last cup and bread at his hatch. He took the cup but pushed the bread back to her. 'I'm not eating.'

'You have to eat.' Tabitha frowned. 'Or you'll die.'

The man barked a laugh which turned into hacking coughs. He took a sip of the water, splashing some as his body shook.

'I'll die anyway. We all die. But me? I'll die sooner than most. At the hands of a demon.'

'What do you mean?'

The man cocked his head at Tabitha.

'Do you know what happens to the men kept here?'

'It depends.'

He nodded.

'Yes. Yes, it depends. Some are freed. Some live out their sentences and then are freed. But that's rare now. King Tobyias. That's what happened when Tobyias was king. Not now. Not anymore. What's the point in eating? It only fattens us up.'

Tabitha looked down at the small hunk of bread.

'I don't think anyone could get fat on what they feed

you.'

The man smiled, showing gaps where his yellow teeth had fallen.

'This is just breakfast. They offer us food throughout the day. Whatever the king don't eat. How old are you?'

Tabitha could feel the eyes of the other prisoners on her and was suddenly aware of just how far away the door to freedom was.

'It don't matter.' The man waved his question away. 'You prob'bly don't remember.'

'You don't remember,' muttered the man in the cell next door.

'That as may be. But I know where I'm headed.' The man watched Tabitha with a keen eye. 'Into the mouth of the king,' he whispered. With a short giggle, he coughed again, his body heaving. When he looked back up at Tabitha, there was spittle on his lips.

'You think the king will eat you?' Tabitha asked, breathless.

The man stood, pushing himself against the bars, getting as close to Tabitha as he could.

'That's where we go,' he whispered. 'We're fed and broken and we're dragged from this place of darkness.'

'How do you know?' Tabitha asked. 'If everyone here is eaten and no one returns, how do you know?'

The man's eye twitched and again, Tabitha stepped away.

'I'll not give it to him,' he said. 'He'll crunch on my bones but nothing else!'

Tabitha wanted to run. The stench was in her nose now, on her tongue and stuck in her mind. Richie would be back soon. She had to go.

'What was your treason?' she asked.

The man stopped smiling. His face crumpled and

with a burst of noise, flinging his arms out, he began to wail. Tabitha backed up until she hit the wall of the empty cell behind.

'His wife!' called out the man's neighbour, over the crying. 'He says the king ate his wife. She came to the castle to visit her sister, who worked 'ere. She was with child. Both her and her sister ain't been seen since.'

Tabitha rushed to the neighbour's cell.

'Who was the sister?'

He shrugged.

'Angelinaaaaaa,' cried the man. 'Angelina Carter.'

'Carter?' Tabitha blinked at the men. 'Carter.' She rushed out of the prison, not looking back. She slammed the door closed, fumbling with the key. Breathing hard, she ran up the steps and stopped, taking in gulps of fresh, clean air.

Carter. There had been a Sophie Carter. She had worked in the laundry room, supervising the staff to keep the king's sheets, tablecloths and curtains clean. She had stopped coming to work the year before. Tabitha counted on her fingers. Six months. Sophie Carter had stopped working six months ago. No reason had been given, just as no reason had been given for many of the staff departures. She had just been replaced.

Only an hour after Tabitha had crept into the prison, the kitchens were heaving with people all hard at work, sweating and shouting. All in their own little worlds of baking powder, onions, chicken breasts, gravy, roulade and raspberry sauce. Tabitha wiped the sweat from her brow with her sleeve. Still in a daze, she had volunteered to cover a shift in the kitchen after someone had gone off sick. Agnes had berated her for being too slow at chopping the vegetables. When she tried to speed up,

Tabitha had caught the side of her finger with the knife. Now bandaged, she stoked the fires and set to work with a wooden spoon, stirring a cauldron of soup. She watched large chunks of carrot and parsnip bob up and down as she stirred, chewing on her lower lip, mentally studying each of the prisoners' words.

Richie and Daisy had appeared shortly after Tabitha had made her escape. Both with a stupid smirk on their faces. At least some good had come from it, Tabitha thought.

'Sophie Carter,' she had asked Daisy. 'Did you know her?'

'No. But my cousin did. She works in the laundry room. I remember her being angry that Sophie just didn't turn up one day. It was the day after her sister came to visit. They all got to feel her baby kicking.'

'What does your cousin think happened?'

Daisy had shrugged.

'Her sister disappeared too. My cousin reckons the husband was beating her, so the sisters left town.'

Tabitha remembered the wailing man, his despair and grief.

'Did they see the king the day before they went missing?' Tabitha regretted her choice of words immediately but there was no taking them back.

Daisy had looked sideways at her.

'I think the king wanted to congratulate her sister, or something. I dunno. Why?'

'It doesn't matter. Did Richie find you?'

Daisy had beamed and spent the next ten minutes telling Tabitha details that she didn't need to know.

It felt as though the weight on Tabitha's shoulder had grown heavier. There were too many voices in her mind, all screaming at once. She needed to do something about the king, she knew that. She considered the people she could, or should, go to for help. Would the Dragonslayer Academy help her? This was what they did, wasn't it? She had seen them on parade, marching, saluting the public and the king. Some wearing the traditional garb of ironed black cloth with a small red dragon emblazoned on the jacket. A leather belt around the waist where an ornamental sword hung on one side, a knife on the other and antique pistols sat in holsters. When she was a small child she had watched those men and women with awe. They were so disciplined and polished. As she had grown older it had dawned on her that those that walked in torn and dirty clothes with dull but sharp swords and worn pistols, were more deadly. There weren't many like that. The only one that stood out had been…Tabitha shook her head. They wouldn't believe her. They hadn't believed Del Thorburn. She was probably dead now. All because she had spoken aloud what Tabitha now knew. An experienced and trusted dragonslayer had failed to bring the king to justice. What hope did a young castle maid have? But what choice did she have? Who could say who would be next? Tabitha held up the wooden spoon, wondering briefly how it would fare as a weapon.

'Tabitha?'

'Hmm?' Tabitha turned to Agnes. 'I mean, yes ma'am?'

'Water and mop, Tabitha. One of the lads has had an accident.' Agnes stormed off across the kitchen bellowing orders before Tabitha could open her mouth to respond. Placing down the wooden spoon, Tabitha headed into a small room just off the kitchen. She opened the large cupboard doors, pulled out the bucket and stopped as she reached for the mop. It was dark with grime and dirt. Tutting and muttering under her breath about feeling like the only maid who tidied up after herself, she changed the dirty mop head for a clean one. As she lifted the clean white mop head a flash of red caught her eye. Tabitha dropped the mop head to the floor and swallowed the squeal that threatened to burst from her.

It was a box of rat poison. Only a box. Tabitha looked around guiltily but she was alone. Everyone nearby in the kitchens was too wrapped up in their own responsibilities to notice the maid in the cleaning cupboard. Before she could think it through Tabitha picked up the box of rat poison. She found a small cap used for measuring soap and almost filled it with the white powder from the box. She stuffed the box back into the cupboard and placed the cap of poison into an empty corner of the cupboard. Then she filled the bucket with soap and water, and carried it, careful not to spill, to the obvious mess of the kitchen. The boy who had spilled the tomato sauce on the floor looked down his nose at Tabitha. She thrust the mop at him.

'Here you go.'

'I don't clean.'

Tabitha glared at him. He didn't look a day older than her and the idea of cleaning up after him made her sick. It was the principle of the thing.

'My soup will burn,' she told him, offering him the mop again. He shook his head, almost turning away.

'Saunders, you will take that mop and you will clean up your own mess. If you don't like it, I suggest you don't make a mess in the future!' Agnes's voice boomed at them. Snatching the mop from Tabitha, the boy dipped it in the bucket, grumbling under his breath.

Tabitha left before he could change his mind. Returning to the cupboard, she retrieved the cap full of poison and attempted to walk through the kitchen as if nothing were awry. Picking up the wooden spoon, she dipped it into the soup and stirred. She looked around her and in one swift motion tipped the rat poison into the soup.

It flashed across her mind that the king might not be the only one to eat the soup. Leftovers were given to the staff and, now she knew, the prisoners. No matter, she would have to dispose of the rest. Tabitha nearly dropped the spoon.

Markkus.

She bit hard on her lip. Her hand began to tremble. Was Markkus immune to rat poison? The back of Tabitha's eyes began to burn. The image of the mangled corpse in the king's chambers and the warm feeling that Markkus's eyes inspired in her fought violently in her head. She clenched her eyes shut as they filled with tears and she prayed to whichever gods might be listening. Stirring the soup, she wondered how much would be enough to kill a dragon. How much would be enough to kill a man. Two tears fell down her cheek. She couldn't bring herself to add any more. Wiping her cheeks on her sleeve, she took a deep, shaking breath.

'Everything ok, girl?' Agnes asked as she approached. Tabitha nodded. 'It's time to plate up.'

Agnes stepped to the side to reveal two junior cooks carrying the royal soup bowl between them. There was nothing else to do. Tabitha moved aside and watched Agnes pour half of the soup from the cauldron into the bowl. Tabitha swallowed hard, forcing the tears to stay behind her eyes. The cooks left, the soup sloshing as they walked with grunts and quiet moans. Agnes turned to Tabitha.

'Tidy yourself up, girl. We're short staffed and you're serving.' Tabitha looked down at her soup flecked apron and shoes. She gave the cauldron a long lasting glance, desperately trying to think of how to dispose of the poisoned food. 'Tabitha. Now.' Tabitha jumped and made her way out of the kitchen and down to the servants' quarters to change. She swallowed against the lump in her throat as she entered the small rooms, scanning the chairs by the fire and the small kitchenette for Markkus. He wasn't there. The room began to spin, her head feeling light, her heart thumping in her ears. She took deep breaths as she grabbed the serving uniform hung by the door and moved into one of the small bedrooms, closing the door behind her. As she stripped, she thought about the cauldron of soup but there was nothing she could now. Fully dressed, she straightened her hair in the mirror on the wall and stopped as she met her own eyes. Wisps of brown hair curled around her face, the rest tied back in a bun. Her large, sorrowful eyes looked back at her. She hadn't realised how much she had been holding back the tears, now her eyes were rimmed red and swollen. They filled, glistening as they began to drown. The tears welled and fell. She sniffed and wiped her eyes with the back of her hand. After another deep breath she opened the door and trotted back to the kitchen to resume her duties.

Tabitha and Daisy heaved the large bowl of soup between them, being careful not to spill any. Tabitha found her eyes drifting down to the soup before she would tear them away to stare ahead. Two large guards opened the great doors for them. She composed herself as the king and Markkus came into view. The king ignored them. Tabitha was glad, she could hardly bring herself to look at him. When she did glance up, the light from the large windows along one wall bounced from the jewel encrusted rings around his claws, dazzling her. The girls lifted the bowl of soup onto the table in front of the king. Markkus caught Tabitha's eye and gave her a brief smile. He stood and lifted his shining spoon.

Tabitha held her breath as he dipped the spoon into the soup. He held the soup in his mouth and as he swallowed his eyes flittered back to Tabitha. She let out a shuddering breath, her mouth dry and her head throbbing. He hesitated, his gaze fixed on her. Tabitha pleaded with him. Be okay. Don't say anything. Be okay. She felt at one moment that he might run to her, his eyes seemed filled with concern rather than anger. Finally, he lifted his face to the king and smiled.

'It is delicious, Your Grace.'

Tabitha drooped a little. Markkus may not have been harmed and he may not have said anything but he knew what she had done. She cursed her red eyes, following Daisy out of the dining hall. As she turned her back on the king, she waited for a noise, a crash, any telltale sign that the poison had taken effect. There was none, just the sound of the king slurping up the soup and crunching on the vegetables. The door closed behind her and silence filled her ears as she padded back to the kitchens, hoping that the remains of the soup would still be there.

The soup was still there, growing cold in the cauldron. Tabitha felt a surge of relief at the sight of it. She absent-mindedly took a mop handed to her.

'Tabitha.'

Tabitha looked up at Agnes. 'Mop, dear girl. Start in this corner and move on as we plate the main meal. Daisy will help you.' Agnes walked away, shouting orders. Tabitha looked back to the soup and groaned, watching Daisy mop close to the cauldron. She soaked her mop in the bucket of soapy water and wrung it. As she began to clean the tiled floors, she tried to think of a way to get to the leftover soup. Each plan that came to mind was quickly dismissed, it wouldn't work or it was too complicated. Stopping to soak her mop, she stared hard at the cauldron, willing it to disappear. She needed to be quick. Soon they'd pour it into a suitable container to be divided up between the kitchen staff and prisoners.

A junior chef walked into the kitchen and smiled at Daisy, saying something to her as he passed. Tabitha couldn't make out the words but she watched him turn to flash another grin and as he did his foot slipped on the wet tile. His forceful walking pace carried him forward and he landed heavily on his rear end with a crack as the bottom of his spine hit the floor. Tabitha watched his feet as he slid forwards and one toe met the cauldron. The rest of his foot smashed into it a second later, followed by his other foot. He curled up, hands above his head as the cauldron tipped and rocked and worked its way off its hook, spilling its contents over the wet floor and ending with a climatic crash and boom as the cauldron hit the ground.

Silence followed.

Tabitha let her breath out slowly. The silence lasted mere seconds. The amount of time it took for Agnes to figure out what had happened and to come flying across the kitchen towards the junior chef.

'What in the king's breath do you think you're doing?' she yelled. Daisy was pulling the junior chef to his feet, her cheeks flushed red, eyes down. Tabitha walked towards them, mop in hand.

'It was my fault. An accident,' the junior chef said, standing with a wobble and looking down at his shoes stained with soup. The thick liquid and leftover vegetables seeped over the tiles, one carrot rolling under a cupboard. Tabitha looked over the carnage, not daring to think she had gotten away with it yet.

'From now on I suggest you spend more time

looking where you're going and less time looking at the virtues of my serving girls,' Agnes told him.

'Yes ma'am, it won't happen again.' He rubbed his head, turning to hurry away.

'Well I don't see why the girls should have the clean up this mess if it was your fault.' Agnes stopped him. He pouted, opening his mouth to protest.

'I'll clean it, ma'am,' Tabitha piped. Agnes turned her fierce gaze on her. 'I mean, I don't mind,' Tabitha finished with a stutter.

'You're needed to serve the main course, Tabitha.' Agnes's eyes narrowed.

'I'll do it. Now. Before the next meal is served.'

Agnes nodded and turned back to the junior chef.

'Remember to thank her.'

'Thank you,' he mumbled. Tabitha gave him a hurried, small smile as he left, Daisy scurrying along with her mop behind him. Tabitha turned to Agnes, urging her to leave. The dragon surveyed the scene.

'Such a mess.' She tutted. 'Very good of you to offer, Tabitha. I've always said you'd go far.' She glided away before Tabitha could tell whether she was being sarcastic. Exhaling, Tabitha glanced around. The kitchen had returned to normal as the king's main meal was prepared and no one paid her any mind. She tipped the cauldron upside down and emptied the remaining drops onto the floor. After picking up the scattered vegetables, she added more soap to the water and scrubbed the floor until it gleamed, ignoring her throat tightening and eyes burning as she held back the tears.

*

As the sun dipped beneath the horizon, King Rupert sat in his library and tapped his claws one by one on his desk. There was a soft noise as he sucked on his teeth. His forked tongue protruded and licked at his lips as he stared at the far wall in thought. Then his eyes flicked to the shadows and he narrowed them to reptilian slits before relaxing back.

'Charles,' he purred.

Charlie emerged from the shadows and tilted his head in what constituted a bow from him. King Rupert sneered at it.

'Something was amiss tonight.' Rupert looked down at his claws tapping on the table. 'Markkus hesitated. It was slight but there it was,' King Rupert mused to himself. The king had tasted the poison. Why would he leave his life in the hands of one man? No, he had built his immunity to poisons from a young age, just as Markkus had. But it wouldn't pay to let the staff know this. No, by keeping this secret, Rupert had exposed that someone in his castle wanted to kill him. He just needed to figure out who, and why Markkus was covering for them. He obviously wasn't helping them. Even a man like Markkus knew that it would take much more rat poison than that to bring down a dragon Rupert's size. 'He has been acting strangely of late, hasn't he. Looking for missing people that are not his concern, asking prying questions. Something's going on and Markkus is involved.'

There was a pause.

'Your Grace?'

The king lifted his noble head.

'It appears he can no longer be trusted.' The king turned to Charlie and smiled, his lips lifting gently over his teeth. 'Kill him.'

Ten

Del was rudely woken by a cockerel crowing in the yard. With a groan she pulled herself up, stood on the unused upturned bucket and squinted out of the tiny window. The bird sat on the stable block roof, its feathers vibrant in the morning sunshine. It crowed again and flapped its wings. The yard was empty but she could just make out the scent of horse and somewhere someone was brushing the floor. Del lowered herself back into the straw. She wondered what time it was and when breakfast might be, stroking her empty stomach. Her eyes instinctively moved to the hinges on her cell door, at the joins on the bars, at the pointing in the nearest brick work. She noted at least three choices of escape should she decide to take the opportunity. Sitting back against the corner of the cell, she stared at the door just because it was something to do.

It was an hour before the door at the top of the steps opened and Del heard footsteps approaching. Tilting her head for a better view, she waited. A worried young man wearing a private's uniform and carrying a tray appeared. A smile danced across her face. She was always amused to see the dragonslayer uniforms. She had rarely worn her own and only in her days as a private and corporal. In any case, she'd lost it the day she was exiled. The boy's uniform was clean and crisp. There were no signs of blood stains or mud or indefinable patches that couldn't be washed out. Del doubted the boy had ever seen any action, let alone killed an actual dragon.

'Who are you?' she asked as he looked into her cell. He appeared startled.

'Private Noah Strangles,' he said without much conviction.

'Unfortunate,' Del muttered. 'And you drew prison guard duty, huh?' The private didn't respond. 'It's nothing to be ashamed of. We all start somewhere. I started in the kitchens.' Again, Noah remained silent. 'How's my horse?' Noah stared at her. 'Black cob. Shadow. Can't miss him round here. How is he?'

The boy blinked.

'I don't know.'

'Well, find out for me, will you? Would hate to think he isn't being looked after. It's not his fault he's mine.' Del flashed him a smile. 'Brought me breakfast, have you?'

Strangles pulled himself together.

'Yes.' He opened a small hatch in the bottom of the cell door and shoved the tray through.

'Lovely,' Del muttered, looking at the soggy bread and dirty glass of water. She looked back up at the private. He was still staring at her. Realising she'd caught him, he snapped to attention. He avoided her gaze for a while, staring up at the ceiling then down at the floor, off to the left, heaving a nervous sigh.

'You'll bring me word on my horse?' Del prompted, before he became any more uncomfortable. The private nodded.

'Yes.' He turned to leave and stopped. 'You're erm…' His fingers played with the hem of his jacket. 'You're Del Thorburn.'

'I am.' Del dragged the tray of breakfast over to her corner.

'Who led King Tobyias's dragonslayer army. The first dragonslayer army for centuries?'

'Yep.' Del poked a slice of soggy bread.

'Who led them to victory?'

'Yes.' Del examined the water.

'Who was exiled by King Rupert?'

'Hmm.' Having made her decision, Del pushed the tray away and turned her attention back to the private. He was looking at her with keen eyes.

'Why?' he asked.

Del considered this question. She took a deep breath and looked up at the ceiling.

'Why what?'

'Why were you exiled?'

'Oh.' Del smiled. She shrugged. 'The usual reason a dragonslayer gets exiled.'

'Everyone says something different,' Strangles murmured. He lent against the bars, forgetting himself and staring through her. 'I was wondering which one was true?'

'What are the stories?'

'Well, the less fanciful ones I've heard are that you threatened King Rupert somehow.'

'A big, strong, formidable dragon king like Rupert, threatened by little me?' Del smiled dryly. The private shuffled his feet.

'You were the mistress of King Tobyias and had his son and rightful heir?'

'I've never been pregnant.'

'Then you refused to obey orders?'

'That's closer to the truth, I guess.'

'What is the truth?'

There was a pause as Del considered her response.

'There wasn't a story that suggested the king had a secret?'

'Some say that was why you threatened him.' Strangles nodded.

'Interesting, how stories can become twisted,' Del murmured. She looked up at the boy. 'Maybe I just couldn't bear to serve under a dragon.'

Strangles seemed disheartened.

'Oh.'

Del, an eyebrow raised at the idea of him believing that, watched the private turn away and disappear up the stairs.

'Strangles!'

He stepped back into view.

'My horse?'

'I'll look now,' he mumbled.

Del sat back and waited, listening to the marching feet and shouting coming from the yard as companies, privates and officers began to come and go. Her stomach rumbled its protest. She closed her eyes and drifted into a state of sub consciousness. The sounds of life echoed in her ears, her mind distorting them into dreams.

She opened her eyes with a start.

Andra was looking down at her. Private Strangles stood behind her. Pulling herself out of her slouch and stretching her tired back, Del watched them.

'How's my horse?'

'He's fine,' Andra answered as Strangles opened his mouth. 'You're dismissed,' Andra called over her shoulder.

'But, Captain. I have orders to-'

'You are dismissed.'

Andra's teeth were close to gritted. Del watched her as the private left.

'Lord Gerard wishes to speak with you.'

Her teeth were definitely gritted.

Del sat up, crossed her legs and cocked her head, looking at Andra from different angles.

'You have every reason to be angry,' she said, carefully. 'You believe your leadership has been questioned. Your company is being forced to undergo further training. I notice, however, that you are not.'

She didn't get a response. She hadn't expected one. 'Perhaps that indicates that your leadership has not, in effect, been questioned. Perhaps the best captain in the world could not have led that company with the skills they possessed. The academy is at fault, not you. Perhaps.'

'Lord Gerard wishes to speak with you,' Andra repeated.

'Oh he may well do, but I do not yet wish to speak with him.' Del studied Andra's posture. 'I thought that maybe we needed to talk before I'm dragged back before his Lordship.'

'About what?'

'About what's happened. If you don't want to then that's fine. From the look on your face yesterday I thought you may have some questions. Am I wrong?'

Andra sagged her shoulders. She leaned against the bars and looked past Del, collecting her thoughts.

'I never thought I would get the chance to meet you, not after your exile.'

'Did you think I was dead?'

'Of course. We all did. Not once did it ever cross my mind that I would find you living in a ruin riding a farmer's horse.'

Del snorted.

'I'll have you know that Shadow is not only braver than the academy's high and mighty horses but he's a damn sight more comfortable.'

'You're the reason I'm here,' Andra blurted.

'Well, if you wish to visit me you must come here, me being locked up and all but I don't think that's what you meant?'

'The reason I'm a dragonslayer.'

'Oh.' Del waited for more, getting a rush of pride at being the inspiration for someone. She frowned at a sudden pang of guilt. 'I made you want to join?'

'I first saw you when I was little. When you would come to my father's shop. I saw you on parade. I wanted to be like you.'

Del looked down at the floor.

'Then I wish I had spoken to you when you were little. No one should ever want to be like me.'

'You were the best. King Tobyias's protector. You were victorious in every battle. You've killed more dragons than anyone else.'

'You believe all that? That last one is certainly not true. And I was victorious in battle and, arguably, in court, because I killed people, not dragons. People died because of me. That's nothing to be proud of. There's no pride in being good at war.'

'But you were…' Andra drifted off. She wanted to say a saviour, she wanted to say hope, but looking down into Del's face she couldn't bring herself to say the words out loud.

'I haven't killed that many dragons,' Del said. 'That isn't what being a dragonslayer is about. Not anymore. It's about protecting the king. It's about protecting the city, the villages that belong to the city and its inhabitants. Do you ever talk to the dragons you kill?'

'I don't think so.'

'I noticed you talked to that dragon who attacked us.'

'I asked him to back down. That was all.'

'Did you consider asking why he was attacking?'

'No.'

'Why not?'

'Because we're not there to talk. We're there to do a job.'

'Is that what they teach you now? No wonder you all need retraining. Your job is not to kill. Your job is to keep the peace. Don't you think that it's better to try talking first?'

Andra looked down, her face and neck flushing.

'Hey, I'm not criticising you,' Del murmured, shuffling closer to the bars. 'I just want to give you another option.'

'I wanted to be like you but I'm nothing like you. I'm not the person I thought I would become,' Andra said.

'You don't want to be like me. Look where I ended up. In a rotting cell under the academy, most likely going to my death,' Del told her. Andra flinched. 'Be like you. Forge your own path. You're a great leader, you just need to trust your own instincts.'

'Be braver?'

'Trust yourself,' Del corrected. Andra thought about this, looking up and out of Del's tiny window at the bright light of midday.

'Why are you back?' she asked in a soft voice.

'Because you brought me here.'

'You could have stopped us. You had more than enough opportunity.'

'I have unfinished business. I believe the time has come to finish it.'

'And what's that?'

Del untangled her legs and stood.

'I think I'm ready to see Lord Gerard now.'

*

Lord Gerard was moving the nib of his pen over a piece of paper. His eyes glazed, the text on the paper a blur. The king hadn't been happy at the news. King Rupert's booming voice still rebounded through Gerard's mind, drying his mouth. His heart beat in a way that made his chest ache as he conjured all sorts of images of what might happen to him. All because of Del Thorburn. The door opened and he startled, the pen nib drawing a cragged line across the page. He gave it a fleeting look of disgust.

'My Lord, Captain Ferrer and D...the prisoner are here to see you.'

'Yes, yes, show them in.' Lord Gerard waved Ami away.

Once she was gone he took a deep breath and turned his chair around to face the window behind him. He straightened his clothing and adopted a thoughtful pose as he looked out over the city. The door opened and he heard Andra and Del enter. There was a puff noise. Old memories stirred and he knew that Del had sat in the chair off to the right. She always did. She would sit there, examining her dirty fingernails as lords, captains and the king's advisers talked and discussed urgent and important issues. Lord Gerard had watched her do this, always with the utmost faith that she would succeed in everything she did.

Now she was back.

Andra was just as predictable. She would be standing to attention.

'Sleep well, Del?'

'Very well, thank you,' came her voice. Lord Gerard forced a smile onto his lips and swiveled his chair around to face them. Andra was stood to attention to his left, Del slouched in the leather chair to his right. Ah yes, both of them so predictable. His forced smile became easy.

'Good. I imagine our cells are more comfortable than the ruins you've been frequenting.'

Del shrugged.

'I never was one for luxury.'

'No.' Lord Gerard glanced at Andra. The captain was staring straight ahead. 'I think I know why you're here, Del.'

'Oh, I'm sure you do.'

Lord Gerard looked at her to find that she was staring straight at him. It gave him a small jolt. She never used to do that. Del had always been a woman of sly smiles and glances. She always looked down at her hands or with disinterest at the wall. Only when she was leading the army into battle did she ever look you in the eye. It had fooled many men who had later paid the price. Lord Gerard had never been fooled. But never before had she looked at him with such menace. Was she just that angry, or had she changed? Lord Gerard leaned forward and clasped his hands in front of him on his desk.

'You will soon stand before King Rupert and face his wrath,' he told her.

Del smiled.

'I'm sure I will.'

'I imagine he will have you put to death.'

'I imagine he'll kill me where I stand.'

There was silence. A heavy, static silence.

'The king always follows the law,' Lord Gerard said through gritted teeth. Del laughed. The sudden loud noise made Andra jump. 'Del, are you suggesting that King Rupert is anything other than honourable and gracious?'

'Indeed, my Lord. I am suggesting that King Rupert is utterly dishonourable and most ungracious.'

They glared at one another.

'The king knows you're back.'

'Oh, good. How did he take the news?'

Lord Gerard gritted his teeth.

'He wishes to see you. Until then you will remain here in your cell.'

'I'm surprised he's keeping me waiting.'

Lord Gerard grinned. Yes, Del could be tricky but King Rupert could be cunning.

'Oh, he has much better things to be doing than dealing with you.'

'And there was me thinking I was the thorn in his claw.' There was another silence as they watched one another, Gerard searching Del's eyes for a clue to her plan. 'Fine.' Del continued. 'I will wait in my cell but I demand time outside in the yard and I demand to see my horse.'

'Sentimentality? I never thought I'd see the day. Fine. You may have your fresh air and horse. Captain Ferrer, take her to the yard.' Lord Gerard picked up a stack of papers and shuffled them to signify the meeting was over. Andra opened the door. Del stood and left the office. Andra paused before leaving, turning back to Gerard.

'My Lord, is my presence required at the meeting with the king?'

'Yes, Captain. You will be among the first to know when.' Lord Gerard looked up at her. 'I assume you won't be leaving the city before then?'

Rather than looking horrified at the notion, Andra looked thoughtful.

'No, sir.' She left and closed the door behind her.

Lord Gerard watched the now empty space she had occupied. Captain Ferrer was not as talented as Del and it appeared that this stretched to hiding her changes in thought and character. Gerard would have to watch her. Del was a bad influence. The sooner the king dealt with her, the better.

*

Del filled her lungs with city air and exhaled as she stepped into the yard. The chill of the breeze hit her skin and made her smile. Without thinking she made her way to the stable block, Andra following. The stable block was two centuries old, give or take a decade. Large, airy stables lined either side. There was a deep shine to the swept cobbled ground and down the opposite end would be a room of gleaming harness, buckles and bits. The only dust that existed in this place were the small clouds glistening in the sunlight that filtered through the windows and doors as horses pulled hay from the racks on the walls. Del breathed in the scent of fresh hay, straw and dung.

'Old Mister Smith is still here, isn't he,' she murmured. Andra made a quiet noise in response. A small black head with hairy triangles for ears and a pulled, trimmed and plaited mane looked over a stable door and whinnied.

'Shadow.' Del advanced upon her horse, ignoring the gallant, muscled horses that she had to pass to get to him. Shadow greeted her with a head nod and pushed his nose deep into her open hands. She rubbed it and her brow creased as she stared at his mane. 'What in the king's name have they done to you?'

'Looks like they tidied him up.' Andra was smiling, troubles forgotten for a moment as she reached out and patted the cob.

'Ridiculous.' Del looked down Shadow's body. He shone. His tail was straight and gleaming, and his coat was brushed and preened. She pulled a face at his plaited mane again, at the small tight bundles of bound hair dotted down his neck. She took hold of the top one and began to gently undo it.

'When…when you said that the king will kill you on the spot, you meant he wouldn't give you a trial. Right?' Andra asked as Del worked her way onto the second plait. Andra stroked Shadow's nose as the horse snuffled at her. 'I know what you accused him of. But it can't be right. The king has been a gracious ruler. He may not be popular with the poorer people in the city, but he only raises the taxes because he has to. King Tobyias made a mockery of the exchequer.'

Del smiled to herself, running her fingers through Shadow's freed hair.

'Murderers can be good with money. King Rupert is not as he appears. I thought he would be a good king too. He let me keep my position as the king's protector. I naively thought he would be like Tobyias.' Del sighed, moving down Shadow's neck as she worked on. 'I became suspicious of the king after a couple of years. It was something and nothing. A servant had disappeared. I didn't know him but I had overheard the castle staff talking about him. He was never found.'

'Maybe he just left town. It happens,' Andra offered.

'Yes. That's what I thought. Don't get me wrong, Andra. I'm not against dragons being part of our society. Not at all. I've had many pleasurable conversations with dragons. The king's advisor in Ushwaithe, he's a dragon. He's wonderful,' Del mused, tackling the last plait. 'Anyway, I sent a note to my contacts outside of the city, asking after this man. No one had seen or heard of him. Again, not that surprising. It wasn't until the second servant went missing, and the third...' Del smoothed Shadow's mane down. 'I asked the king about it. He said he hadn't seen any of them and he didn't seem to particularly care. I visited the second man's family and they were distraught. He had no reason to leave.' Del met Andra's eyes.

'You think the king had something to do with it?'

Del nodded.

'I couldn't be sure, of course. I had no evidence. So I waited and watched.'

'And?' prompted Andra after a moment of silence.

'And I got the evidence. It was late one night. The majority of staff had finished for the day. Only the night staff were around. I had stayed late at the castle to eat. I sat in the kitchen and ate alone. The kitchen staff had gone home. And I heard a scream. A gut wrenching, terrified scream. I ran towards it and ended up at the king's chambers. I didn't have my pistol on me, or any kind of weapon for that matter, which was a shame. I peeked around the door and saw him and what he was doing to that poor woman. Her husband was stood close by. Somehow he escaped, for a while at least. I admit I didn't act immediately after that. Who would? For all I knew, I'd be killed on the spot or I'd put even more lives in danger. But I couldn't sit back and do nothing. So I went to Lord Gerard who didn't believe me. He marched me back to the king who exiled me.'

Andra allowed this to sink in.

'And what you saw...happening to the woman. The king was..?'

'The king was eating her. Alive.' Del gave Shadow a smart pat.

'He wouldn't.'

'He did.'

'Then it would only have been the once.'

'I wonder how many missing persons reports have

been filed in the last two years?'

Andra blinked and shook her head.

'You can't go around damning the king's name just because he's a dragon,' Andra murmured.

Del looked up, her eyes soft.

'Like I said, I'm not against a dragon being king. Far from it.' There was another pause. 'Have you noticed the number of rogue dragons lately?' Andra looked at Del with renewed focus. 'I've seen a few but you would know more about it than me. Do many companies go out at once these days?'

'That was our third job in a month. We haven't been home for two months. Every time we finished a job, a messenger would arrive with another.' Andra told her. 'It's always been like that though. I guess the rate of jobs has been increasing. But slowly. It's hardly noticeable. But I don't know, that might just be my company.'

'I very much doubt it.' Del rubbed Shadow's nose and turned to leave, heading back to the yard. 'But maybe it's something you should investigate.'

She walked alone, stopping just outside the stable block. Turning her face towards the sun, she closed her eyes and enjoyed the warmth. Andra came up beside her.

'What will you do when you see the king?' Andra asked. Del lowered her face and opened her eyes.

'Nothing that concerns you.'

'And what if it does?'

'I don't want to ruin your career, Andra. Mine is already ruined, I don't matter. I can't prove what I know, so I must do what I must.'

Andra swallowed hard and nodded. Del began to walk away.

'Are you coming?' she called back to Andra. 'It

looks strange if I escort myself back to prison.'

Eleven

'I wish to see Lord Gerard,' Markkus said to the top of Ami's head as the secretary bowed low over her work. Ami glanced up at Markkus. 'Is he available?'

Ami scraped back her chair and moved to the door of Lord Gerard's office, sticking her head through. There was the sound of muffled voices. Ami's head re-emerged and she walked back to her desk and sat down.

'Lord Gerard of the Fourth Corner of Drummbek will see you now,' she told him stiffly.

There were five Lords of the Corners of Drummbek, born from ancient families dating back to the first prehistoric construction on the land. No one knew why there were five corners, and now it didn't matter. The Lord of the Fifth Corner had disappeared without a trace a century ago.

Markkus rolled his eyes and entered Lord Gerard's office. Gerard sat at his desk, writing in an open file.

'Lord Gerard-' Markkus began as he closed the door behind him.

'Ah,' Gerard looked up and examined Markkus. 'Commander Kern, it's been a long time. How are you?'

'I'm fine, I-'

'Good. Please, take a seat.'

'Thank you.'

'And how may I help you?'

'I wish to speak with you about…dragons,' Markkus attempted, realising now how stupid he sounded. He had tried to rehearse this conversation but there was just no good way of approaching the subject.

'Well, after all, sir, I am the Head of the Dragonslayer Order. I know all about dragons. Although I'm sure one of my captains or administrators could help you just as well. I'll just-'

'-No! No, I'm afraid it has to be you.' Markkus took a breath as Gerard sat back in his seat. 'Tell me, my Lord, if it was thought a dragon was breaking the law, what would the procedure be?'

'Breaking the law, sir? The Order would investigate the claims, sir. Those who do break the law are often classified as rogue. The majority live in the wilderness, away from society and civilisation, but near to villages. That's where they steal their food and thus break the law. We deal with them accordingly. I assure you the city is full of law abiding dragons. Much more so than humans, it sometimes seems.'

'What do you mean by 'deal with them accordingly'?'

'Once we receive a claim, we investigate and hold a trial if there is reason to. If the dragon is found guilty they may be given a warning or, if the situation is dire, slain. It depends on which law they have broken.'

'So if a dragon steals?'

'The law with dragons is the same as humans, Commander. If anyone, human or dragon, steals they receive a warning, should it be their first offence. A prison sentence if not.'

'So if a dragon kills, they are punished by death. As with humans?'

'Of course.'

'Because if a human kills a dragon, then they are

executed.'

'If they kill outside of the law, then yes. My dragonslayers are the only ones authorised to take life. It requires stout training.'

'And what if the dragon suspected is part of a civilisation, in the city?'

'Ah. In a rare event of that happening, the case is discreetly investigated and dealt with according to the results of the investigation.'

'And if the results show that the dragon was breaking the law?'

Lord Gerard sighed with exasperation.

'What is it that you are getting at, Commander?'

Markkus glanced at his hands curled in his lap.

'As I ask, my Lord. I am curious what would happen to a city dwelling dragon should it break the law. If it committed murder.'

'And do you have a dragon in mind when you ask me these questions?'

Markkus hesitated. This was the man that had turned against Del. Markkus also couldn't escape the truth that he had no evidence against the king. Just Del's word and Tabitha's actions. Somehow, though, that seemed enough. He looked Gerard in the eye, searching for the possibility of change.

'I have no dragon in mind, my Lord. I just want to know what happens to a dragon living in the city that breaks the law,' he repeated.

'The same thing that happens to a human when they break any law.' Lord Gerard's tone had changed. Frustration, boredom, it was hard to tell. 'It depends on the crime. If a human kills a dragon or human, then they are put on trial and, if found guilty, executed. If a dragon kills a human or a dragon, then they receive the same treatment. It is the same for all crimes.'

'Any human or dragon?'

Gerard paused before answering.

'Any human or dragon. The Dragonslayer Order keeps this peace, being the only ones who may take the life of a dragon legally. But they are still bound by the law. As the city guards are the only ones who can legally take the life of a human, but are still bound by the law.'

'Yes, a great weight upon their shoulders I imagine.'

'As I'm sure you would know,' Gerard agreed. 'Our dragonslayers are well trained and managed, don't you worry about that. They get everything they need. Of course, every now and then one will turn rogue and break the law, but we deal with them according to that same law. As I just described,' he added.

'It seems like a fair system, I've always said so. I heard there was talk, when King Rupert came to the throne, of the Order allowing dragons to join.'

Lord Gerard gave a small smile.

'There was. Nothing much has come of it. It would require a name change. Whoever heard of a dragon being a dragonslayer? There is a lot of bureaucracy surrounding a name change, however.'

'Of course. I imagine that's why other cities disbanded their Orders.'

Lord Gerard gave Markkus a cold look.

'Was there anything else?

'Yes. So a suspected dragon would be given a trial, as with humans. You would need evidence, I assume?'

'We would require evidence to begin the investigation and, indeed, to come to a decision. Who are you thinking of? One of those small fellows who work at the docks?'

'No. No, I'm just curious as to the law.'

'The law that has remained unchanged since the end

of the Old War? You must have a purpose?'

'Laws do change, my Lord.'

'Yes but I'm sure you would be aware of any changes. You do work in the castle. I seem to remember you were close to Del Thorburn.'

'My Lord.'

'These questions don't have anything to do with her, do they?'

'No, my Lord. Del is in exile. In truth it's a long time since I even heard her name.'

Lord Gerard gave Markkus a twisted smile.

'Yes, well. Be careful, Commander. Asking inappropriate questions can lead to suspicion. That is what led the crown to charging Miss Thorburn with treason and exile. Exile being the lenient punishment for that particular crime, of course. Miss Thorburn was perhaps saved only because of her notability.'

'I am not suggesting that I know of anyone who has broken a law, my Lord. I only wish to confirm that the law remains unchanged. Having done so, I will take my leave.'

Markkus stood and left before Lord Gerard could say another word, slamming the door behind him. He walked out into the corridor. Not a lot had changed since Del's time and now Markkus would have to be careful where he trod. Lord Gerard had most certainly just threatened him.

Lord Gerard stared at the closed door. Troubled, he turned back to look out of the window over the city. He would have to report the conversation back to the king of course and he made a mental note to do so when he took Del to the castle. What was happening? He had thought these troubles were over after Del was exiled. It was enough that she had returned but to have others asking such questions. The king's own taster. The person who was supposed to protect Rupert. Gerard shook his head. He was being paranoid, that was all. Markkus's questions had nothing to do with the king. These were two separate incidents. Did Markkus even know that Del had returned? He couldn't, and he wouldn't. Not while Del was in the cells. At least, not until Del stood before the king. By then it would be too late.

Gerard took a deep breath to steady himself. Soon this would be all over. Although he doubted he would ever sleep soundly again.

Markkus walked down the stairs, muttering. He swung round the corner and straight into a woman. Correcting himself, he apologised as his eyes focused on her. Her blonde hair was short, accented by her high cheekbones. She wore muddied clothes and appeared tired, with red eyes above dark circles. Behind her was a woman with black hair pulled high into a ponytail. Wisps were escaping and falling down her face. Her hands were bound in front of her. Her eyes were hard and stared right into him. Markkus felt a pain in his chest.

'I'm sorry,' Markkus said, not taking his eyes from Del.

'No problem,' Andra murmured, looking to push past.

'Are you,' Markkus started, stopping Andra as she headed towards a door behind him. His eyes still fixed on Del. 'Are you a dragonslayer?' He tore his gaze back to Andra.

'Yes. Captain Andra Ferrer. Can I help you?'

'Hello, Markkus.' Del smiled sweetly.

'Del.' Markkus bowed his head a little. He wanted

to pick her up, to hold her. He wanted to swing her around whooping with the joy of her being alive. Instead he swallowed it back down. 'I didn't think I'd ever have the pleasure again. Been doing things you shouldn't have?'

As Del opened her mouth to speak, Andra repeated, 'How can I help you?'

Markkus hesitated.

'I came to speak with Lord Gerard.'

'He's upstairs. His secretary will help you.'

'I know. I've seen him and no, she won't. I wonder if you would be able to help?'

'With what?'

Markkus looked into Del's eyes. There was a hardness there that was new. He wondered what she had seen, what she had done. She looked well enough.

'Dragon law.'

'Concerning?'

'Well, that is, murder.'

'Captain Ferrer?' Ami came down the stairs. She stopped when she saw Del and Markkus. 'Lord Gerard wishes to speak with you, Captain.'

Del was searching Markkus's eyes. He hoped she couldn't read his thoughts. He knew she was trying, she always had. Just as he had always tried to read hers, in the castle and on the battlefield. He was one of the few people who often knew where her mind was going.

Andra nodded up to Ami and turned back to Markkus, looking between the taster and the rogue.

'I have to take you back to your cell,' she said uncertainly, reaching for Del's bound hands.

'I am allowed visitors, I believe. Just the one won't do any harm.' Del's eyes remained concentrated on Markkus.

Andra hesitated.

'I'll have someone sent up for you,' she told Markkus. He watched them both leave through a side door and down the steps to the cellar and cells.

Andra reappeared a few moments later. She began to climb the stairs to Lord Gerard's office, catching Markkus's eye as she passed. Another man, in a crisp uniform, followed behind Andra and stopped before Markkus. He saluted.

'Sir. If you'd like to follow me.' The private led the way down the stairs. Del stood inside a small cell, the barred door closed and locked, and the bonds removed from her wrists. The private stood in a nearby corner, trying his hardest to disappear into the shadows. Markkus stepped up to Del and cleared his throat.

'What have I missed?' she asked conversationally, sitting down cross-legged in front of him. She looked up through the thick, black and red rusted bars. The private stiffened as Markkus moved towards him and took a chair from the opposite wall, seating himself in front of Del.

'Nothing.'

'Nothing? All this time and nothing?'

'Where have you been?'

'Around.' Del shrugged. 'Captain Ferrer found me in a ruin, not far from here.'

'Doing what?' Markkus had always known that Del would not be easily exiled. She was never the type to slink away quietly.

'Polishing a sword that I wasn't supposed to have. They arrested me on the charge of being a rogue after I killed a dragon that was going to kill me and them. Fact is,' Del lowered her voice to a whisper. 'I may have killed another dragon or two. And a man. You don't want to know what he was doing. The dragons were attacking villages. I watched them kill people.' Del frowned, immersed in her own thoughts. Markkus waited for her to return. 'There were more than two, you know, over the two years. More than I thought there would be.'

'Dragons killing people?'

Del looked up at Markkus.

'Yes. Maybe the academy has always kept secrets about the true figures.' She didn't sound convinced.

'Perhaps,' Markkus murmured.

'Are you still at the castle?'

Markkus nodded.

'Still the king's taster.'

'Lucky you.' Del smiled. 'Anyway, enough of this catching up. Why are you here?'

'The king.' Markkus glanced at the private. He leaned close to the bars as he turned back to Del. 'There's something...well, what you accused him of before he exiled you.'

Del nodded.

'Have you seen something?'

'No. That's the trouble. I have no evidence, just a gut feeling.'

'Well, your gut feeling has saved my gut enough times.' Del leaned back and glanced at the private, stood awkwardly in the shadows.

'Did you ever have evidence?' Markkus asked after a pause.

'Yes. A witness.'

'Where are they now?'

'Unlike me, he didn't survive.'

'He was...I mean, the king…'

'Ate him? Yes. I believe so. Or maybe he just had him killed. But he ate his wife. That was my evidence. Right in front of the poor man. He even had his clothes, stained with her blood. Blood that had dropped off His Right

Royal Highness's right royal teeth,' Del sneered with a shudder. Markkus closed his eyes tightly before releasing them. He was getting a headache.

'How did you survive?' he asked.

'Who says I did?' There was a short silence. 'I mean, of course I did. But I wasn't meant to. A few days after I was kicked out of the city, a dragon found me.'

'That doesn't mean the king sent it.'

Del raised an eyebrow.

'You know, I was exiled without a single thing. No sword, no pistol, no rifle, no horse. Nothing. He should have sent that dragon the same day. And the king sent him. I know because I asked him.'

'You had time to have a chat before he tried to kill you?' Markkus didn't know why he'd asked that. Of course Del had struck up a conversation with the dragon. That was what she did. It didn't make killing any easier, he knew that, but he suspected that was why she did it. Killing wasn't meant to be easy. It was a job, a duty and above all else it should never be easy to take a life.

Del smiled knowingly. It was an expression that only those close to her ever saw and that was why Markkus treasured it. It gave reassurance and hope. Hope that you would survive the next battle, hope that she would defend you, hope that she had a cunning plan that would get you out of any sticky situation. He shuffled closer to her, keen to be let into any secret she might possess.

'You know what that dragon said to me? It was the strangest thing. He said that it was just a matter of time. That it was inevitable, I guess.'

'What was?'

'I don't know. That's what bothered me. But the annoying little lizard said it right after I'd put a blade through his heart so I never found out what he meant. It bothered me though. And the dragon that attacked Andra's company said something similar. I don't suppose you've heard anything like it?'

Markkus shook his head.

'Where did you get a sword?'

'I told you. He found me about three days after I left the city. I'd already got myself a sword, rifle and horse within four hours of leaving. He should have come for me right away but I imagine Rupert wanted me as far away as possible so as not to raise suspicion.'

Markkus sat back in his chair.

'Just a matter of time,' he repeated. 'How are you going to get out of here?'

'Hmm?' Del turned back to Markkus from staring at the wall. 'I don't have to. Gerry's taking me to see Mr Rupert any day now.'

'What are you going to do?' Markkus expected that wonderful Del smile again but instead she became serious. Her face darkened and she leaned close to Markkus, her nose poking through the cell bars.

'You leave this to me, Markkus. This is my business, not yours. I don't want you involved.'

'But I already am,' Markkus told her. 'I allowed the king to eat poison. And he knows I did.'

'What? Who poisoned him?' Del hissed, glancing at the private who was inspecting his fingernails and very close to whistling inconspicuously.

'One of the castle maids, I think.'

'Do you know who?'

'Yes. Her name is Tabitha Dunn.'

'Do you know why she tried to poison him?'

'No. But I can find out for you?'

Del nodded.

'Only if no one else sees or hears you. You are not to get yourself into any more trouble with this, Markkus.

Just get her out of harm's way if you can. If Rupert knows you allowed the poison to get to him, he might know who put it there. Get her and yourself safe. Don't try anything stupid.'

'I fought in the war you know,' Markkus blustered.

'Yeah and how many dragons have you killed?'

Marrkus didn't answer. It was true that he'd killed plenty of men. But no dragons. He was not a dragonslayer, nor had he ever had any inclination to be one. He was a soldier and a damn good one.

'I know you're a good fighter.' Del softened. 'You're the best I've ever known. How's the pain, by the way?'

Markkus shrugged.

'Usual. Always there.'

There was a pause as they looked at one another.

'The captain you saw me with up there?' Del pointed to the ceiling. 'She's the blacksmith Ferrer's daughter. She's a friend. And while I don't want her involved in this either, you can trust her. Just be careful what you tell her. We're not going to compromise her career. Equally, she can be trusted not to turn on us. That I believe.'

'You said she's the one who brought you back.'

'She did. Very kind of her, don't you think?'

'Del-'

'It's time to end this, Markkus. I'm tired. I'm getting old. And I'm sick of having to keep looking over my shoulder. It's time.' Del leaned back. 'Keep yourself safe.'

'I'm not going to let you do this alone.' Markkus told her.

Del smiled.

'I know.'

Andra was at the bottom of the staircase as Markkus

appeared up the steps from the cells. She knew him although she couldn't place him.

'I'll escort you out,' she told him. They walked in a palpable silence at first through the front door of the academy and up to the gates.

'Del says you're a friend,' said Markkus, his voice low.

'Yes.' Although Andra wasn't quite sure what that meant.

'She says you can be trusted.'

'I can.'

'Good.' Markkus stopped and faced her as they reached the gates. 'Take care of her, Captain. Be her second pair of eyes. Help her where you can. She wants to do this alone. Something in her head tells her she can do these things alone and she can't. No one can. She's a dear friend of mine, Captain. And if you help her, she'll be a dear friend to you too.'

Andra studied Markkus, unsure of whether she could trust him, unsure of whether she agreed with him. So instead of replying, she only nodded.

'I'll do what I can,' she said after Markkus didn't move. She would do what she had to.

She watched Markkus leave. The taster didn't look back. He pulled his coat up around his neck, shoved his hands into his pockets and walked briskly up the street into Old Town. Andra strode back into the academy and down the steps to the cells. Del was sat cross-legged, leaning against the wall. She glanced up at Andra.

'What did his Lordship want?'

'We're taking you to the king tomorrow morning.'

'You don't sound too happy, Andra. Something wrong?'

Andra took another step towards Del.

'Who was that man? He seemed familiar.'

'You didn't recognise him? Probably for the best. He's an old friend. That's all.'

'What are you planning?'

'Me? Plan? Oh, I never plan.' Del turned away from her, closing her eyes.

Andra watched, wondering what to say, what to do.

'You don't want to be involved in this, Andra,' Del said, still not looking at her. 'You're a good slayer. Take me to the king with Lord Gerard and follow your orders.'

Andra opened her mouth to speak. The words were there, ready, but nothing came out. She couldn't ignore the idea that Del would just dismiss her. She stepped back and walked up the stairs. At the top, she closed the door and leaned back against it.

Twelve

It was dark by the time Tabitha could close her bedroom door on the world. She sat cross-legged on her bed listening to the sound of her parents busy in the kitchen. Happy that they were otherwise engaged, she took a package from her aprons and placed it on the bed in front of her. Carefully peeling back the layers of thick cloth, Tabitha revealed a butcher knife.

King Rupert had lived. It had been a stupid thing to do, putting Markkus and herself at risk like that. She wouldn't make that mistake again. This was too big. It was beyond her. This had occurred to her towards the end of her shift, as Tabitha mopped the kitchen floors. She was being selfish. What made her think that a simple maid could destroy the king of Drummbek without anyone getting hurt in the process? It was over. The thought made fresh tears spring to her eyes, but it was the right thing. It was over.

That was when she'd seen it. Above her head, the array of knives shining down on her. Larger, sharper and sturdier than any knife her mother owned. Without thinking she reached up and took one, weighing it, finding a good grip on the handle. No one around her took any notice of the mousey maid seemingly tidying away kitchen utensils. So why not? She couldn't fight what the king was doing and she was too scared to tell anyone what she had seen. That didn't mean she couldn't protect herself. She should protect herself.

Any second could come the message, calling her to the king. He knew, she was sure. He must have noticed Markkus's reaction to the taste of the food. He had probably tasted it himself. Tabitha imagined the poison was bitter. He would find out it was her, one way or another. That would likely involve Markkus and that didn't bear thinking about. Then it would be too late.

She had taken the knife. She had stolen the knife. It wasn't a good feeling, but at the same time she felt stronger for it, in a way she couldn't explain. She hung up her aprons and wrapped up the knife again, placing it back in the large apron pocket.

There was a knock at the door.

'Tabby?'

'Coming.'

'Is it safe?'

'Yes, dad. I'm coming.'

Erik opened the door and peered inside.

'Food's not ready yet. I just wanted to check that you're okay?'

Tabitha sat on her bed.

'I'm fine.'

Erik gave her a knowing look and walked into the bedroom, sitting next to her.

'I don't believe you. You forget, Tabby, I've known you since you were a baby. Before then, even. I know when something's not right. Is it your mother?' Erik asked in a hiss.

'What?'

'All this talk of finding a husband, all the time. It's only because she worries for you.'

'I know. It's not that.'

'Oh. Is it work?'

Tabitha didn't answer. 'Ah, it is work. Tabby, if you don't like working at the castle, we'll find you something else. Maybe down at the tavern.'

'Mum would never allow that.'

'Well, no, but I can talk to her.' Erik studied his daughter. 'Is that what you'd like?'

Tabitha shrugged. To escape the castle? It wouldn't solve the bigger problem but it would take Tabitha out of it. She could forget it all, leave it all behind. The screams, the rumours, the gossiping. Markkus.

'Tell me what happened at work.'

'Nothing happened. Just a bad day, is all.'

'So I'll talk to your mother.'

Tabitha straightened out some wrinkles in her dress. Sitting with her father in her small room, in the gloom of evening, they were apart from the world and its evils.

'Do you think King Rupert is a good king?'

'Oh, Tabby.'

'What if he was worse than you thought?'

'You don't know what I think. Why? Has something happened?'

'Nothing. No. Not really. Just, a feeling I get.'

'Always trust your instincts,' her father told her. 'And to prove it, I will trust mine. I'll speak to your mother in the morning.'

'It won't do any good,' said Tabitha.

'Perhaps not.' Erik put an arm around his daughter and drew her close. She snuggled into his chest and breathed him in. 'But it's always worth a go. She only wants what's best for you. As do I. Your happiness, Tabby, is our happiness. Don't ever forget that.'

Tabitha forced away the tears that were building. She couldn't tell him, or her mother. She had to keep them safe. She had made one mistake already and placed Markkus in danger. That was bad enough. If something were to happen to Markkus, she would never forgive herself. But if something were to happen to her parents…Tabitha couldn't bear to even finish that thought.

*

Venkell slammed his glass down and wiped his lips on his sleeve, staring ahead.

'Everything okay, Ven?'

'No, Bobby.' Venkell brought the glass to his lips again. Bobby leaned his forearms on the bar and watched him.

'Not happy to be home?'

'I should never have joined. Give me another.'

Bobby straightened. He was used to this. This was Venkell's routine. The night he returned to the city he would sit at the same stool, at the bar of The Old Boot tavern and drink ale. Bobby poured another for Venkell and turned to the customer who had approached the bar beside the dragonslayer.

''Ello Johnny. What can I getcha?'

'All right, Bob? Ale, please.' Johnny placed the coins on the bar before turning to survey the people that filled the tavern. He landed on Venkell beside him.

'Hey. You're a dragonslayer, aren't you?'

Venkell glanced at Johnny out of the corner of his eye.

'Might be.'

'What's that like then?'

Venkell turned to face him.

'Why?'

'Hey, I was just asking.' Johnny held up his hands. 'Looks like interesting work is all.'

Venkell turned back to his ale.

'S'all right. If you like ironing uniforms and polishing metal. I'd rather be in the army.'

'Oh, being in the army isn't all that. You still have to like ironing and polishing.'

Venkell turned and looked Johnny up and down.

'How would you know, boy?'

'I served in the Great War.'

A smile touched Venkell's lips.

'So you're not a boy.'

'It ain't true what they say. War doesn't age you.' Johnny winked and turned back to the patrons of the tavern. 'It just leaves you with not a lot afterwards. Unless you're Bobby here.' He gestured back to landlord. 'Unless you're lucky enough to buy a tavern.'

'Hmm. Lucky,' Bobby grumbled and moved away from the two men to another customer.

'Bet there are some pretty girls at the Dragonslayer Academy, huh?'

Venkell smiled to himself.

'There are some.'

'Yeah. Don't get me wrong. There are some pretty girls in the army now. 'Course there weren't many allowed in when I fought. They certainly weren't allowed to fight.' Johnny paused, studying Venkell swaying on his stool. 'So, you want to join the army?'

'I did. I joined the academy instead.'

'How come?'

Venkell swallowed a mouthful of ale. He had never admitted the truth to friends or family, he'd be damned if he would admit it to a stranger.

'It's an honourable and traditional role, to become a dragonslayer.'

'I need a new job. I always thought I'd join the academy if I could afford the fees. What's the pay like?'

'Good.' Venkell had to admit. 'Benefits are good too.' It just wasn't what he wanted to be doing.

'Good benefits, pay and women? It's starting to look very attractive.' Johnny supped at his ale. 'Not sure I could be bossed around by a woman, though.'

'It's not that bad. My captain's a woman.'

'Yeah? What's that like?'

'She's a good captain.' Venkell hesitated, thinking about Andra. Beautiful, sweet Andra. Twice he had turned down the opportunity for promotion. Just one more job, he thought. The next job, that's when he would tell her. He stared down into his glass miserably. Here he was, home again and another opportunity lost.

'You don't get to fight in wars if you're a dragonslayer. Not these days,' he told Johnny.

'Eh. I've done that. Wouldn't want to do it again.' Johnny looked around to see where Bobby was before leaning close to Venkell. 'Seeing your friends die every day. Watching them being blown to pieces and burnt to ash...it's not glamorous. You probably already know that, though.' Johnny straightened and smiled. 'All right, Cassie.' He raised his glass to the barmaid as she walked past. Then Johnny spotted Markkus stood at the door. 'Markkus!' He turned back to Venkell. 'Here's someone who could tell you the horrors of serving in the army. Our commander. Had his leg blown clean off. We found him unconscious one time, lying in a fire. Another time I watched him get sliced shoulder to navel. It's a wonder to see a man's intestines and then he survives. And what does he do now? He tastes the king's food for poison. It's disgusting. The man's a hero. Good talking to you.' Johnny raised his glass to Venkell and moved away from the bar and into the crowd of the tavern. Venkell watched him and saw him approach an older, bald man who must have been Markkus. Markkus smacked Johnny on the back, a huge grin on his face. He didn't look unhappy, he didn't look too bad at all. Venkell turned his back on the tavern and lost himself in the drink.

Markkus put a pint of beer down in front of Johnny and sat opposite him, slurping at the head of his own drink.

'What brings you in here at this time of night?' Johnny asked him, bringing his glass to his lips. Markkus shrugged.

'A bad day at work. I couldn't sleep.'

'Ah, well the beer will help with that.'

Markkus nodded and took another gulp.

'What made it bad?'

Markkus looked away, perhaps a little too quickly and Johnny immediately leaned forward.

'Was it something the king did? Oh, come on. You can tell me. I won't tell a soul, you know me.'

Markkus looked at his friend, searching those old eyes in a young face. He shook his head.

'I can't, Johnny. Let me say only this. I have compromised my situation. I don't want anyone else involved. No more than they already are,' he said, thinking of Tabitha.

Johnny leaned back, scrutinising Markkus.

'Okay. Fine. But if I can help-'

'I know. You'll be the first to know.' Markkus smiled and felt a welcome piece of comfort. He sat back and took a deep breath. The tavern wasn't too busy, but busy enough that no one was paying them any mind. The volume of voices and laughter was at a bearable level and the whole place stank of ale, men and cooked food. It was warm and dry and, Markkus felt, safe. He turned back to Johnny.

'Anything new with you?'

Johnny shrugged and shook his head. 'No girls in

your life? No girlfriend? King's teeth, Johnny, what's happened to you?'

A smile picked at the corner of Johnny's mouth.

'Oh, don't you worry old man. I've still got the charm. But there's a lack of women to use it on.'

'What? You've got the whole city at your fingertips.' Markkus spread his arms to emphasise.

'I dunno. I'm just not much in the mood lately.'

'That's the job,' Markkus told him. 'If you're unhappy at work, you'll be unhappy elsewhere in life. You need a new job. Go back to doing something fun, and life will become fun again.'

'So why not take your own advice?'

Markkus smiled down at the table.

'I don't know why you stay at the castle. Especially if it's bringing you trouble,' continued Johnny. 'You get to keep the house, you keep all the benefits. So why stay?'

'I don't know,' murmured Markkus, and he meant it. For that moment it was as if he hovered over himself, looking at his life from a distance. 'Have you ever been in love, Johnny?' He meant to try and move the subject back to something easy, focused on his friend, but as the words left his mouth he heard how it sounded.

'Who is she?' Johnny asked, his eyes sparkling as he sipped his drink.

'Oh no, no. I didn't mean that.'

''Course not.' Johnny smirked.

'So, have you?' Markkus asked, knowing he hadn't done well at dodging his error.

'Once, when I was five or seven but I don't think that counts. Have you?'

'Once.' Markkus paused to think. 'At least, I thought I was.'

'How can you get to your age and not have been in

love?' Johnny asked, his voice low with sudden seriousness. Markkus swallowed another mouthful.

'I was married to the army. My life was one of death, you know that. Can't bring a wife into that, let alone children.'

'My dad always told me that you don't choose love. Love chooses you,' Johnny told him.

'Well, maybe love didn't like the look of me.'

'So even now, there isn't anyone?'

Markkus didn't reply. He took a swig and held it in his mouth until he could no longer take the sour taste.

'No,' he said, knowing it to be a lie the moment his mouth formed it. Johnny looked at him with something akin to pity.

'That's a shame. We should fix that.' He began looking around the tavern. Markkus laughed.

'No. Please, no. If love wants to choose me, then it can come find me.'

'There's no harm in helping it along the way. What's your type? How old?'

Markkus nearly choked on his beer.

'What?'

'Well, there's a young woman over there. Very pretty. Or how about over there? I know for a fact she's a widow. Or how about Cassie?'

The barmaid turned at the sound of her name and smiled at them.

'No,' Markkus whispered through a smile, so that Cassie wouldn't hear. 'I don't know. Why don't you try your luck with them. Leave me out of this.'

'No, you're right. I need a new job first. It's weighing on me.' Johnny stared down to the bottom of his pint.

'Yeah, well, maybe I do too.'

They sat in glum silence for a moment. Would it be

hard, Markkus thought, to leave the castle now? The king knew about the poison, it would look suspicious if he left now. No, Markkus had unwittingly signed his own contract for the next few months. Maybe even a year. He downed the last of his drink, feeling it trickling down his chin. He wiped at it with his arm.

'Another?'

Johnny nodded. Markkus fetched another two pints and attempted to lighten the mood.

'What happened with the last girl you were with?' he asked. 'I liked her. She seemed the sort you should settle down with.'

'She was. But I'm not the sort to settle down.'

Markkus snorted.

'I can see you as a husband and father. Be a good one too. Any woman would be lucky to have you.'

Johnny laughed.

'Maybe when I'm older. Not yet. Still plenty of fun to be had.'

'So what about that young woman over there? She's about your age.'

Johnny watched her over the rim of his glass before turning back to Markkus.

'She's pretty. You don't like the look of her?'

'She's too young for me.' The words sounded hollow to Markkus.

'Age hasn't got anything to do with it. Like I said, love chooses you.'

Markkus tried not to look at Johnny.

'Do you really think that?'

Johnny shrugged.

'It's whatever you and her are comfortable with, isn't it.'

Markkus supped at his drink to stop himself from saying any more. By the end of the pint, conversation had turned to reminiscing. They guffawed, and then became quiet as they remembered their fallen friends. Most nights in the tavern ended like this. Markkus didn't like it but it seemed inevitable. It was the drink, unlocking those boxes of horrid visions. Just like the night did, replaying those sights and sounds and feelings. Except this time, Markkus found he wasn't quite as upset as normal. Instead, Tabitha played on his mind. Johnny was right, you don't choose love, love chooses you. Not that he loved Tabitha. He didn't know her. And anyway, he told himself, she was too young and he was too old. He would be foolish to think she would want anything to do with him. Him and his battle scars and one leg.

He looked at the suds at the bottom of his pint glass. His seventh pint glass. He frowned, wondering how he had drunk that much. Cassie interrupted as she collected all fourteen glasses from the table.

'Closing time, boys.' She smiled and sauntered off. Johnny turned and watched her go. Markkus stood and wavered.

'Time to try that sleep thing again,' he said, although it didn't quite sound right out loud.

They left the tavern together, parting out on the road. Johnny hugged his old commander and Markkus gripped him for a moment.

'Sleep well, friend.' Johnny grinned. 'Whoops.' He slipped on the wet cobbles, regained his balance and turned to wave at Markkus before shoving his hands in his pockets and walking away. Markkus watched him go until he was out of sight.

Wrapping his coat around him, Markkus became aware of how alone he was. Out in the dark and cold, the air still damp from the rain and a sharp wind rushing at his face. He picked up the pace, extending his stride every time a shadow seemed to lengthen towards him. A few times he grunted, his heart jolting, as a raised voice or a fox knocking over a bin startled him. Every shadow was someone sent by the king lying in wait to kill him, every noise was someone on their way to stab him. And why not, he thought. He was old, his best days were behind him. Perhaps he should welcome death. What did he have to look forward to? Again, he thought of Tabitha but pushed the idea away. No, she was too young, but that didn't mean love wouldn't find him elsewhere. If he could just leave the castle unscathed, find new employment, stay alive. He didn't even have to find love. He'd done pretty well without it so far. Just a new life, that was what he needed, he decided as he walked over the bridge into New Town. A new life, away from Drummbek.

Markkus strode down the street that led to home. The chill night air was sobering and as his thoughts became clearer, so did his future. If only he could avoid whatever punishment the king would send, Del would solve everything. On the battlefield, faced with human generals, Markkus had ruled. But against a dragon foe, there was no one greater than Del. That was why King Tobyias had employed her into his royal staff. She was loyal and bright and deadly. If only she had been born with a silver spoon in her mouth, she would be the Head of the Dragonslayer Order. She was also akin to Markkus's little sister, his confidant and friend. They met in court, he as a young commander and her as a young dragonslayer captain. She had been new and fresh but already her reputation had begun to build.

She rose through the dragonslayer ranks to general. King Tobyias always wanted her close, trusting her more than any bodyguard. There had been rumours of an affair. Tobyias's wife was a beauty but she was quiet and unassuming. Natalia never took part in courtly duties and was rarely seen by the public. She had given Tobyias a son who had died young in battle during the Great War. She had never forgiven her husband, or Del, for that. The prince had been a dragonslayer and under Del's command. The night of the king's death had been the beginning of Del's fall. Somehow King Rupert had descended on the city and calmed the three nights of rioting. He reorganised the city guard and returned order. Perhaps Rupert had been fearful of changing things too quickly, because he kept Del as an advisor and protector. Markkus could remember the night when he knew he would lose her.

Only a couple of years into the reign of King Rupert, Del grew quiet. One night they walked back to Markkus's town house after a few drinks at The Old Boot tavern. Her steps were wobbly and her speech slurred. She collapsed onto a comfortable chair before Markkus's fireplace.

'D'know what I know?'

'Wassat, Del?' Markkus had asked through a drunken grin.

'Shhhh.' Del held a finger to her lips. 'People are dying,' she hissed in what she thought was a whisper.

'What?'

'Because the king's eating them.'

They had stared at one another but spoken no more of it. Del had fallen asleep and Markkus had gone to bed. The following morning Markkus had made her breakfast.

'You said some crazy things last night,' he told her. 'I'm glad you said them here where no one could hear you.'

'It was the truth.'

'You need to watch your mouth. That's treason,

Del.'

'The king is eating people. He's a murderer. I shouldn't have said anything and I'm sorry but it's true. Watch yourself, Markkus.'

The king exiled her from the city a week later.

Something lifted Markkus from his memories. He began to hum as he concentrated on the sensation that he was being followed. He barely had a chance to work out his pursuer's location when Charlie was on him. The assassin leapt onto Markkus's back and pulled him into a dark, wide alleyway. Markkus, alcohol still working its way through him, lost his footing and fell. Pain shot up his leg and into his gut, his metal leg grinding against the stump of his right thigh. He lay winded, struggling to meet his attacker.

Charlie slid a knife from a hidden sheath and moved it towards Markkus without hesitation. Markkus brought up a fist and clumsily smacked it into Charlie's cheek. It stunned the assassin for a moment, long enough for Markkus to roll away and get to his feet.

Markkus, breathing hard, focused on the assassin. Charlie stood with knife poised.

'The king sent you?'

Charlie made no response. He advanced on Markkus, raising the knife. Markkus sidestepped and swung out an arm to catch the assassin. Charlie anticipated this move and grabbed Markkus's arm, twisting it behind his back. Markkus let out a loud grunt of pain and dug his elbows into Charlie's ribcage. The assassin struggled backwards and then lunged forward again. Markkus didn't have time to catch his breath. He turned to flee but Charlie was on him again. Markkus grabbed the assassin's wrist and squeezed hard. With a small yelp Charlie released the knife. Markkus picked it up before Charlie could move and they faced one another. Markkus panting, Charlie silent.

'I think it's reasonable for a man to know who wants him dead,' Markkus breathed. 'Who sent you?'

Charlie didn't respond.

'Okay, well, what's your name?'

Again, Charlie remained silent.

'Oh come on, man. Who's going to know once you've killed me? Where's the harm in telling me?'

Charlie looked down at his knife in Markkus's hand.

'Oh, you doubt yourself.'

Charlie glared.

'No, no, I understand. You don't know who you're up against,' Markkus sneered.

This man knew exactly what he was up against. He had obviously done his research and knew what Markkus was capable of. Markkus contemplated the assassin in his black clothes and black scarf that covered his nose and mouth. He was waiting for Charlie to reveal another weapon. No assassin only carried one measly knife and Markkus knew King Rupert only employed the best.

'Did the king send you?'

Charlie stepped forward but Markkus was ready. He'd spent the precious few moments gathering himself. Catching his breath, coiling his energy up like a spring. He charged at Charlie, smashing him into a wall to the side and pinning him there, pushing his body weight against the assassin.

Charlie struggled, air rasping in his throat.

'Stop struggling and it'll hurt less,' Markkus growled between gritted teeth. Charlie became still and his breathing eased. 'Good. Now tell me, did the king send you?' Charlie's black eyes hardened and he gave a small nod. 'Excellent. Do you know why?'

'He knows of the poison.'

Markkus wasn't sure whether the assassin's laid back attitude was insulting or not.

'That I poisoned him?'

Charlie looked back at him calmly.

Markkus ripped the scarf away from Charlie's mouth and took a good look at the man's face. He was older than Markkus had initially assumed. Lines touched his eyes and lips, and his skin was beginning to sag under the weight of years and exposure to the sun. His eyes remained youthful and hard, and his body lithe like that of a young man.

'I don't want to kill you.'

'Could have fooled me,' Markkus snorted, his body beginning to complain with aches and pains.

Markkus needed to think this through. What was he going to do here? He had taken many lives, his dreams resonated with the screams and blood. On one hand he didn't want to add to the pain, on the other what was one more soul?

'I know who you are, Markkus Kern,' Charlie said. 'You were one of the best commanders during the Great War. Why would I want to kill you?'

'Because you're getting paid to?'

'I am able to pick and choose my jobs. Tell me, Markkus, why did you try to poison the king?'

Markkus threw Charlie's knife to the ground so that it slid away to a safe distance. He released the man and studied him. An assassin could prove helpful. Even though Markkus didn't know Del's plan, he was sure she would be happy to have paid, professional help.

'Have you heard of Del Thorburn? The dragonslayer who fought for King Tobiyas in the Great War?'

'Del Thorburn, exiled years ago for treason. Yes.'

'She's back.'

'So I understand.'

'She accused the king of a specific crime.'

'I remember the rumours well.'

'The rumours are true. She needs help to finish this.' Charlie didn't respond. 'What is the king paying you? I can double it.'

'I will not kill the king.'

'Fine. I imagine Del would not hear of it.' Markkus wobbled a little as his legs began to tremble. He tensed his body, fighting to stand upright and stay strong, drawing breath through his teeth.

'Then what would you have me do?'

'Whatever Del asks.'

*

'Tabitha!' Tabitha woke with a start and sat bolt upright. 'Tabby, are you awake?'

It was her father.

'Yes. Are you okay?' she croaked, clearing her throat and making sure she was decent, pulling her covers up to her chin.

'I'm fine, Tabby. Can I come in?'

'Yes.'

Erik poked his head round Tabitha's bedroom door, his smile lighting up the room. He came in and sat on the edge of her bed.

'I've been down the tavern.' Tabitha could smell the ale on his breath. 'I heard something. I had to tell you.'

'What, dad?'

'She's back.' He sat back with a smug grin.

'Who's back?' Tabitha found herself smiling.

'Del! Del Thorburn.'

Tabitha climbed up onto her knees.

'What?'

'Del Thorburn the dragonslayer. She what led King Tobyias's dragonslayer army during the Great War, is back in Drummbek.'

'But. No. She's. How do you know?'

'A couple of dragonslayers were in the tavern. They brought her back to the city.'

'Why? Why is she back?'

'I dunno, but probably not for anythin' good. It'll be the talk of the city soon.'

'Yes.' Tabitha sat back.

'You're tired, sweetheart.' Erik yawned. 'I'll let you go back to sleep.' He kissed his daughter on the forehead and left her alone once more in darkness. Tabitha lay back, sinking into her pillow. Del the dragonslayer was back. Tabitha had a vague memory of seeing Del mounted on a large strider, riding past her during a parade. Although she had been young, she still remembered that sense of loyalty and pride in watching the famous slayer. How could she be back?

Maybe it didn't matter. She knew the truth about the king. Everything would be okay now. Tabitha closed her eyes and drifted back into a sleep filled with dragonslayers, swords and horses.

Thirteen

Del stood on the upturned bucket, peaking through the bars of the tiny window to the blue sky overhead. She breathed in the breeze, fresh against her face, and calmed herself. Wishing she couldn't hear the three sets of footsteps falling on the stone staircase behind her. Her cell door swung open with a creak as she closed her eyes against the ray of sunshine that found its way to her as the wisps of clouds parted.

'Are you ready?'

Del climbed down and faced Lord Gerard as a private approached to tie her wrists together in front of her.

'Why did you become a dragonslayer, my Lord?' she asked.

Gerard clasped his hands behind his back and exhaled through his smug lips.

'To serve my king and country, of course. You once had a great gift, Del. Not every street urchin can become a dragonslayer. Not every woman is lucky enough to have a man as rich and drunk as your husband choose them. How lucky you were that he led you to our doors.' Chased me, thought Del. He chased me to the academy doors. Gerard knew that, so she didn't correct him. 'Come, the king requests your company.'

'Are you sure you don't want to help me?' Del asked, not moving. 'He's killed, my Lord. I just need time to get the evidence.'

Gerard's face became thunderous.

'Del, come with me now or we will use force.'

To make his point, the private tugged on the rope binding her. Del walked out of the cell, and allowed the private to guide her up the steps.

*

Andra smoothed a crease out of her crisp, black trousers. She was thirsty, her dry mouth ached and cried out for water. She stood to attention next to her horse, the mare's red coat gleaming in the sunshine. People bustled around her, making preparations. Beside Andra and her horse was Lord Gerard's carriage and behind that, the prison coach. Andra blinked back hot tears before they could form. Today might be the day. She daren't think it but it insisted on creeping into her thoughts. Today might be the day Del died.

*

Del sat alone in the small windowless prison coach pulled by one horse towards the castle. The wooden bench running along the length of the coach was hard and Del bounced as the wheels hit the cobbles, staring in thought at her hands. There was a maid in the castle who knew about the king, someone who was trying to take matters into her own young hands. She couldn't think of that. Markkus would take care of the maid, Del had no doubt. She had other things to concentrate on. She wondered if the king would do the sensible thing and rid himself of her today. If she did not do the deed today she would have to ensure she lived until the next opportunity.

Not for the first time she wondered what would

have happened to her had she kept her mouth shut or had Rupert not become king. Where would she be now. Settled down with a lover? The Head of the Dragonslayer Order? The corners of her lips twitched in a sad smile. It wasn't the king's fault that she didn't have those things, it was her own bloody mindedness.

The coach bumped to a halt and Del lifted her head, waiting for the doors to open. She squinted against the bright light as a guard pulled her out into the castle forecourt. Gerard and Andra, smart in full uniform, stood by the main entrance to the castle. Gerard spoke with a manservant who then rushed inside. Shortly after, an older man dressed in full army uniform, medals lined up on his breast and glinting in the sun, appeared and spoke with Gerard. He glanced at Del as she approached. The guards pulled her to a stop before them and the uniformed veteran looked down at her. Lord Commander Binkley of the royal army. She should have known he would take her job, it was a good fit for the king to take the old royalist out of retirement. She wondered what he knew, what he had seen.

'The king will see you now,' the lord commander told them.

Gerard and Binkley swept in front of her and led her into the castle. Andra moved to the back and followed as Del began to walk into the castle, giving the illusion of escorting her. Two royal guards took the rear. Del kept her head held high, making eye contact with every servant and dignitary that they passed. She especially noticed the maids, wondering each time if she might be the one who knew the king's secret. Their footsteps echoed down the wide, luxurious corridors. Red and gold tiles decorated the floor and thick red velvet curtains hung at the large windows to the side. Del had often walked this corridor as a dragonslayer with her colleagues, as one of the king's men. Only once before had she walked it as a condemned woman.

Tabitha stepped away from her work, considering the window glass. Noting her own reflection, she tucked a stray strand of hair behind her ear. The clipping of footsteps echoed down the corridor. Tabitha turned to see Lord Gerard in full regalia and Lord Commander Binkley stride around the corner. Following them was a woman with dirty skin and filthy clothes. Her black, greasy hair pulled back and her head held up. Behind her was a young uniformed female dragonslayer. She stared hard at the back of the woman in front, her expression both sad and serious. Following her were two armed royal guards. Tabitha made eye contact with the woman with dirt smeared across her neck and, while she felt she had to look away immediately, the woman held her gaze.

Was this her? Tabitha wondered. Del Thorburn, exiled by the king? Tabitha swallowed hard, her stomach fluttering. It was her. She held herself with such confidence and power, it could only be the infamous dragonslayer. This woman knew what Tabitha knew. This woman was here to kill the king. Or be exiled. Or worse. Tabitha began chewing on her lower lip.

Del caught the eye of a castle maid. She was young but her eyes were hard, they made Del falter in her step. The maid had turned from polishing the windows when she heard them coming. She was curious, Del liked that. She held the girl's gaze. Was this the one who knew the king's secret? Del didn't have a chance to find out. She was whisked past the maid and toward the large double doors leading to the king's throne room.

The first King of Drummbek was a man, not dragon, and, actually quite small in stature. His castle was a house surrounded by a stone wall atop the hill. His farmers and labourers building their homes along the slope down to the coast, which then became the docks. The doors had been average height and the corridors of average width for a human. Dragons had been the main predator of humans then. Animals known for their intelligence and rumours of magic. But both dragons and men are stubborn and so neither would talk to the other. They had been killing one another since the first written record. The first King of Drummbek created the Dragonslayer Order. A league of well trained, disciplined men who would defend the city from dragons, who would hunt the beasts down and slaughter them. Any opportunity to talk of peace between dragons and men broke down. After a spate of deaths in the outer lying villages, the people became desperate. This marked the beginning of the Old War. Dragons and men fought and tens of thousands lost their lives. The first King of Drummbek died and was replaced by his son, killed years later by a war protestor. The Old War was ended by a dragon, Hermann the Wise, and a man named Wallace, the General Commander of Drummbek's army. The throne was empty as Hermann, Wallace and their witnesses signed the First Law between dragons and men.

Wallace was crowned and Hermann the Wise became his key advisor and most trusted friend. They extended the castle and rebuilt in places to allow passage for the great dragon. King Wallace kept the Dragonslayer Order but decreed that they were now defenders of the city. It became their duty to uphold the First Law; a man may not kill a dragon and a dragon may not kill a man, the punishment for breaking the law being death. Men and dragons were now equals and the dragonslayers stood as a constant reminder of the Old War should anyone forget.

King Wallace lived well into old age and died peacefully. A bronze statue of him astride his large steed stood in the park near the castle hill. All of Drummbek knew it well, it was the only statue that remained clean and unmarked. Hermann the Wise lived to be over a thousand years of age and served Wallace's son, grandson and great grandson as they inherited the throne.

It was only when the fourth king came to power that the city began to question the system. King Wallace's great grandson had no sons or daughters. When he passed there was a quarrel throughout the city's noblemen over who should be his successor.

Hermann the Wise suggested a voting system and, confident that each would win, the arrogant noblemen agreed. The city and its inhabitants voted for their new king and Hermann the Wise was given the crown. He became Drummbek's first dragon king. The great house and its outbuildings were extended once more and the bed chambers rebuilt for the stature of such a large monarch. So the castle still stood, atop its hill, as the small town grew around it into a city. Old Town, weaving its way down the slope of the hill, spread into New Town on the opposite side of the valley. Bridges were built to connect the two and still the city grew.

King Rupert was not a descendant of King Hermann the Wise. King Hermann's lineage had died out long ago. Del would have liked to have met King Hermann, it was common knowledge that he had been a just and fair king. She wondered what he would have done with Rupert.

The doors swung open and the group stepped forward. Del stared straight ahead towards the large red dragon sat on his throne. He wore a thick crown of gold upon his head and was trickling jewels through his claw as he watched Del approach.

Lord Gerard and Lord Commander Binkley stopped before the king and bowed low. Andra stopped behind Del and bowed. King Rupert ignored them, keeping his eyes on Del. Del stood tall, staring back. Her stomach twisted with nerves at the sight of him but she was determined not to let it show. She forced herself to remember what Rupert had done. The crimes he had committed, the blood dripping from his teeth and the twisted ball of nerves within her began to turn to rage.

'Your Grace-' Lord Gerard began as Lord Commander Binkley stepped aside.

'Delilah Dragonslayer,' King Rupert interrupted, rolling the words around on his tongue as if enjoying the taste. Del's eyes narrowed. 'You're alive.'

'Well observed, Your Grace,' she said.

'Yes. What a survivor you are,' Rupert rumbled. He focused on the jewels in his claw and dropped them, one by one, into the bag at his feet. Rupert wasn't the largest of dragons, Del had seen bigger, but he was a particularly fat dragon. All the rich food that adorned his plates for three meals a day, along with whatever else he was eating day and night, had taken their toll. Del could use this to her advantage. It meant that he wasn't fast but he was still strong. His claws were capable of snapping her into pieces and the beating of his wings would shake the castle in its foundations.

'Well well, this should be easy enough, don't you agree Lord Gerard?' King Rupert grumbled.

'I do believe she was arrested on the charge of killing dragons, Your Grace. It would appear she has turned rogue.' Lord Binkley croaked.

The king's smile was slick with saliva dripping from his sharp teeth.

'Yes. Tut tut, Delilah Dragonslayer. Now, the law states that rogue dragonslayers are punished by, oh remind me, Lord Gerard. How are rogue dragonslayers punished?'

'By execution, Your Grace,' Lord Gerard murmured. Del wondered if he was changing his mind about supporting her.

'Yes.' King Rupert turned back to Del. 'Punishable by execution.'

'Will it be a public execution or private, Your Grace?' Lord Binkley asked without even a hint of compassion.

'A public execution may rally the peasants to your cause,' Del mused.

'You wish for a public execution, Delilah Dragonslayer?'

'Or are you afraid of my last words, Your Grace?'

The king made a tight fist of his claw and pounded the arm of his throne. The room shook, pieces of plaster falling from the ceiling around the heads of those who stood before him. He smiled again at Del.

'Yes, a public execution for the dragonslayer guilty of treason and murder.'

Del closed her eyes and took a deep breath. When she opened them she saw Andra out of the corner of her eye, stood just within her vision, looking between Gerard and the king. She opened her mouth and closed it. She daren't speak in front of the king.

'Delilah Dragonslayer will be executed tomorrow morning,' King Rupert decided.

'Your Grace. With all due respect, less than a day is not enough time to do the public execution of such a prominent figure justice. Indeed, I regret to inform you that the public are not content at this moment what with another rise in taxes. A public execution, done in the right way, could re-inspire their love and loyalty.' Lord Binkley clasped his hands before him and bowed to the king.

King Rupert thought about this, lifting a claw and running it down his chin.

'Very well. The morning after tomorrow then. Delilah Dragonslayer will be executed the day after tomorrow. Do you hear that Delilah?'

'Yes, Your Grace, I heard. Your people are just waiting for a chance to riot against you.'

King Rupert looked down at her sharply.

'Your death will make them love me,' he growled.

'They will know the truth, Your Grace. One way or another,' Del said.

'You are a trouble maker, Delilah Dragonslayer,' King Rupert rumbled. 'Make sure you say your goodbyes. Tomorrow night will be your last.'

The guards standing behind Del lunged forward, grabbing her arms and pulling her backwards.

'Easy boys,' she murmured.

Lord Gerard's palms were slick with sweat. He inadvertently tried to wipe them on his trousers, which wasn't particularly difficult given the king's attention was on Del. He had almost spoken up. The list of Del's achievements on the tip of his tongue, the arguments for her to be exiled once more rather than face death. It came seconds too late, the words unable to form. He grasped his hands before him to stop them shaking. With the matter of Del settled, he had to push all thoughts of what could have been from his mind. He had other issues to deal with, other matters to bring to the king's attention.

'Lord Gerard, a moment to plan a time for the spectacle.' King Rupert didn't take his eyes from Del. Gerard bowed low and watched as the guards pulled Del out of the throne room. Andra followed and the doors closed.

Lord Gerard looked to Lord Binkley and the king.

'The morning after tomorrow,' Lord Binkley said. 'Shall we say at eleven thirty? Not too early and in time for the lunch trade. It will be a great spectacle. We can arrange market stalls selling food and drink to make a day of it. The public will not be able to complain.'

King Rupert nodded.

'Yes, yes. Fine. Organise it. As long as the woman dies.'

'Your Grace.' Lord Binkley bowed low.

'Your Grace, if the business of Del is complete here, I do have something I think you should know.' Lord Gerard stepped forward.

'And what is that?'

'The royal taster visited me recently.'

'Markkus came to see you?'

'Yes, Your Grace.'

'Regarding?'

'He asked me some curious questions, Your Grace. About what the law was regarding dragons that kill humans.'

There was a pause as King Rupert inhaled.

'Did he mention the names of any dragons?'

'No, Your Grace.'

'And he knows that Delilah has returned?'

'Your Grace, most of the city is now aware of Del's return,' Lord Binkley said. 'I'm afraid rumours spread quickly.'

'The sooner she is dead, the better,' Rupert

muttered. Gerard glanced down at the floor, the sudden desire to be safe at home overwhelming him.

'As I understand it, this is a delicate time, Your Grace. The rumours are spreading fast and it may be that the public do not wish to see Del hang,' he attempted.

'I don't care!' King Rupert boomed. He snarled and spat. 'Let them riot. She will die.'

'There will be no riots, Your Grace. We will organise everything.' Lord Binkley stepped backwards, away from the force of Rupert's anger. Lord Gerard tried not let his expression give him away and hid it by bowing low.

*

Andra and a private took Del back to her cell. The private locked the door, saluted to Andra and then left. Andra watched him go. She looked troubled. Del couldn't blame her, she was feeling a little troubled herself.

'I'm sorry,' said Andra.

'I didn't expect anything less.' Del shrugged. She could feel her eyes burning with tears but refused to let them fall. She kicked at the straw on the floor, hoping that Andra would leave soon.

'I want to help.'

'You'll damage your career. At the very least. At worse, you'll join me on those gallows.' Del shook her head. 'I can't allow that. Everything will be fine.'

'But-'

'Please.' Del looked up at Andra and sniffed. Andra looked shocked for a moment and Del realised how her face must look. Straining to hold back the tears, two years of tiredness now mixing with the fear of what was to come. She looked away, embarrassed that Andra should see the woman she looked up to like this. 'Please, just leave me be. Just for a little while. Everything will be okay. I'll figure this out. Just go. Please.'

Andra left. Del could hear her whispers at the top of the stairs followed by the private on guard duty acknowledging whatever order he had received. Del didn't have the energy to worry about what Andra was doing. She turned her back on the door, the stairs and the academy, curled up on her straw bed and allowed the tears to come.

Andra hesitated at the bottom of the giant staircase. She watched some dragonslayers filing into the dining room. Climbing the stairs, she stopped by the door and peaked inside. Lord Gerard was still at the castle but his place had been set, his bread and a glass of red wine waiting for him. No one paid Andra any attention as she strode up to the fourth floor. Ami was not at her desk and Andra wondered how long she would be gone. She moved to the door of Gerard's office and eased it open. The office was empty. Andra made her way to the desk and glanced over the immaculately piled papers, scanning the words that she could see. Moving between piles she found a few reports of completed jobs signed by captains. Flicking through them, Andra dismissed her own report and pulled out the others.

They were all familiar. All investigating rumours of dragons attacking villages in the Wastelands. The reports told of the investigations, what had been said, the trials and the outcomes.

A few words stood out to Andra. Stunned, she found the words repeated on each page as she leafed through each report. Shuffling the papers back into order, she counted the reports. Eight. She glanced at the dates on each. Eight over the last week. That did seem rather excessive. Placing the reports down, she looked around for archived files. Spotting the cabinet across the room, Andra approached it but found the drawers locked. She needed a key. Who would have a key?

She walked out of the office and stood by Ami's desk. The secretary had not returned and silence filled the two rooms. Glancing around, Andra moved behind the desk and searched the drawers. There were two keys pushed to the back of the top drawer behind a tub of biscuits. Andra grabbed them and returned to the cabinet in Lord Gerard's office. She needed to be quick and hoped that one of the keys would work.

The second key opened the cabinet. Diving straight in, Andra tried to understand the filing system. She found the reports from the last month with ease and counted them. Hearing footsteps outside the office, Andra closed the cabinet as quietly as possible and locked it. She hurried out of the office and halted when she saw Ami sat at her desk. Ami looked up in shock.

'Captain Ferrer?'

'Hello Ami. I, erm. I was just putting my report on Lord Gerard's desk.'

'You could leave it on mine.'

'Yes, but you weren't here and I...wanted to make sure it was safe.' Andra cleared her throat, the key burning in her hand, biting into her fist. She smiled at Ami and turned, attempting to surreptitiously drop the key. She released the key into the soil of a pot containing a large, leafy plant and felt Ami's eyes on her back as she trotted down the stairs.

*

A tapping noise broke into Del's dreams and woke her. She stared, listening, into the shafts of afternoon light coming through the window. Deciding that the noise had been in her dream, she relaxed and her eyes closed. They opened wide as the tapping sounded again. With a rustle of straw, Del sat up. She looked up at another tap. Clambering to her feet, she reached up on tip toes, looked out of the small window and into the quiet yard. Although empty, there had to be some people around. It had been someone cleaning, or a horse seeking attention.

'Hello?' she whispered, just to be sure.

'Del Dragonslayer?'

Del tensed.

'Yes?

'Markkus Kern has sent me.'

'Oh? And who are you?'

'Someone who can help.'

'Is that right? And how can you help?'

'My name is Charlie. The king sent me on an errand.'

Del held her breath. She only knew of one person named Charlie, but that didn't mean much. There had to be a lot of Charlies in the city. If this was the right Charlie, he could prove useful.

'What sort of errand?'

'To put an end to someone.'

Markkus. Or the maid.

'But you didn't?'

'I was made a better offer. I am at your service.'

Del smiled. Good old Markkus. It was true that an assassin could prove useful but she was uncomfortable about including any more people in her plans. Far too many were already involved.

'You could do one thing for me.'

'Yes?'

'Send a message. To Seracombe. To the High Council.'

'Seracombe is many miles away. It will take me time.'

'Yes, but I need the message to get there tomorrow. I'm being executed the following morning and it would help if the message is received long before I'm hanged. Is that possible?'

'Not for everyone.'

'But for you?'

'Perhaps.'

'How much did Markkus offer you? I can double it. I will double it. If you succeed.'

'You mean if *you* succeed.' There was a pause. 'Very well. What is the message?'

Fourteen

People clung to the walls as King Rupert passed. Diverting their eyes to the floor and waiting until the *swoosh* of his tail told them he was gone. Tabitha, wiping the skirting boards, felt her blood rush as he passed her. The dragon king smelt of sweat and iron, light bouncing from his scales as he strode along. Tabitha waited a few seconds before following on nimble, silent toes. She had no plan, no reasoning behind such a stupid act. Only a compulsion.

The doors to the king's chambers were closed when she reached them but there came noise from inside. Feeling exposed in the wide corridor, Tabitha turned back and sped through the door to the servants' access. Back to those steps leading up to the door to the king's chambers. Out of breath, she climbed the steps and steadied herself against the door for a moment. Once her breathing steadied, she pressed an ear up against the door.

'Your Grace is troubled by Del Thorburn's return?' The voice was old and male but too soft for Tabitha to distinguish. There was a loud smash and Tabitha jumped away. The king's voice boomed.

'Blast that creature. She has been nothing but trouble and now she's not alone.'

'Your Grace?'

'You say she has been in the academy cells since she returned?'

'Yes, Your Grace. Lord Gerard had her sent straight there.'

'There was poison in my food, Lord Binkley.'

Tabitha clapped a hand over her mouth to stop her panic escaping.

'Poison? But surely the royal taster-'

'Markkus knew. I saw it in his eyes. I tasted the poison. It wasn't enough to kill me, it merely tickled at my tongue.' There came the sound of King Rupert smacking his lips together. 'But Markkus allowed me to eat it.'

'Then he can no longer be trusted,' the other voice mused.

'Indeed. You notice he is not in work today? Sick, apparently. But he is of no concern.'

'Your Grace?'

'We are dealing with him. Guard!' the king bellowed.

'Inform me at once when Charles returns.'

Tabitha imagined the guard bowing and leaving the room.

'Charles? Charlie? *The* Charlie? You have sent an assassin after Markkus, Your Grace?'

'Indeed I have, Lord Binkley. Charles is deft, I'm sure that the job is already complete as we speak.'

Tabitha's chest hurt. As if the king had ripped it open, exposing her heart which beat so hard and fast it left her nauseated. Her throat seized. Her knees gave way and she sank onto the cold floor, resting her head against the door. She wanted to storm in and plunge her butcher knife deep into Rupert's head. She wanted to tear away and run after Markkus, to warn him or save him. So she remained collapsed on the floor, her breathing shallow, unable to get the image of Markkus's bloodied corpse from her mind. Tears spilled from her eyes and she sniffed, wiping away any wetness with her fingers.

'Charlie is an excellent assassin, Your Grace. One of the best.'

'You sound uncertain, Lord Binkley.'

'It's just that this is no ordinary foe, Your Grace. This is Commander Markkus Kern. He led King Tobyias's army to victory on no less than ten occasions and lived to tell the tale.'

'He is crippled.'

'But he lives. And I have seen worse, Your Grace.'

'Do you think that Charles might not be capable of bringing down an old man like Markkus?'

'I think it would be an interesting fight, Your Grace.' There was a stiffness to Binkley's voice that Tabitha recognised as respect. She wasn't the only one unhappy about this news. 'Do you have any idea who may have tried to poison you, Your Grace?'

'No. It couldn't have been Delilah Dragonslayer, she is far too direct for poison. Although she was close to Markkus, was she not?'

'They fought together in the Great War, Your Grace.'

'Hmm, Markkus didn't orchestrate this. Whoever it was doesn't know what they're doing or I would be dead.'

'The gods forfend, Your Grace.'

'No, this person is not a threat. They may try again and that is when I will have them. Where is the maid? I grow hungry.'

A ball of fear dropped into Tabitha's stomach. She pulled herself to her feet and stepped away from the door.

'I shall enquire for you, Your Grace.' Tabitha heard Lord Binkley moving.

'Don't be in such a hurry, my Lord,' King Rupert

smiled. 'It would never be you.'

Lord Binkley attempted a laugh but it came out small and false.

'Thank you, Your Grace, but nevertheless, I shall enquire.'

*

Andra entered the stable block to find Del running a brush over Shadow's back.

'They let you out?'

Del smiled, working a shine into her horse's coat.

'That was part of the agreement.'

There was a pause as Andra watched Del bend to brush Shadow's legs.

'The king didn't eat you.'

Del straightened and stared at Andra.

'Didn't he?' she feigned shock. 'Are you sure?' She made a show of patting herself down before shaking her head and throwing the brush into a box full of assorted combs, brushes and picks. She untied Shadow and began to lead him outside.

'Where are you going?'

'We are going to enjoy the sunshine and eat some grass. You're welcome to join us.'

Andra followed Del and Shadow out, opening a gate for them and walking towards a large oak tree in the corner of the paddock. Shadow immediately lowered his head and began ripping at the lush grass.

Del patted his neck and unclipped his lead, giving him his freedom. Del and Andra sat side by side in the shade of the tree and watched the horse glittering in the sunshine.

'Isn't there a guard watching you so you don't escape?' Andra asked.

'He's over there.' Del pointed to the private by the stable block, leaning on the fence, watching them. 'You think I want to escape?'

'You said you were going to do something.'

'And I will. I didn't say when.'

Andra looked at Del.

'You only have a day left.'

Del shrugged.

'When the time is right.'

'What will you do?'

'The less you know the better off you are. I don't want to incriminate you. You're a good dragonslayer and a good captain. You have a bright future. I'm already condemned. I'm going to be put to death, I have nothing to lose. Are you married? Any children?'

'What? No.'

'Right, well, I would hate to take the opportunity away from you. Look, I started this, this is my fight. I will finish it. Why are you so concerned about it? If I'm successful then there will be someone new on the throne and you will still be a dragonslayer captain. If I fail then you will still be a dragonslayer captain. It's win-win for you. So just let it be.' Andra picked at a small wild flower nestled in the grass. Del turned and looked at her. 'You think I'm right? You believe me? Is that it?'

Andra spun the flower between two fingers.

'A lot of people have been going missing. The castle is always recruiting,' she told Del.

'Don't let it question what you do, Andra.'

'You questioned it.'

'No, I took it to Gerard and he ignored me, or didn't believe me. No. He knows. He ignored me.'

Shadow gave a small whinny and sprang forward. Head held high he trotted around the tree and stopped abruptly at a new patch of grass. Del and Andra watched him, bemused.

'This only needs one of us, Andra. You don't need to be involved.'

'What if I am? What if the whole academy stormed the castle?'

'You can't just overthrow a king. It's a lot more complicated than that.'

'But you can just kill a king?'

'Sure, assassinating a king is different to overthrowing one.'

'You'll be sentenced to death.'

'I already am.'

Andra watched Del as she looked toward the stable block on the horizon, squinting her eyes against the bright sunshine.

'What about the High Circle? We should go to them.'

Del laughed.

'Don't you think I've done that? After they kicked me from the city I found my weapons, bought Shadow and went straight to Seracombe. I gained an audience and explained. They didn't want to know. Not without evidence and back then I had nothing. I still have nothing.'

'There has to be another way. Let me help you,' Andra urged.

'No.'

There was a pause.

'You're right. About the number of rogue dragons, about the number of jobs.'

'Oh yes? You looked into it, did you?'

'Yes. There have been eight jobs in the last week. Over fifty this month. It's so many. I didn't have time to count them again. Maybe I'm wrong but...even eight in a week seems a bit much.'

Del stared forward at nothing.

'I hope you don't get into trouble for doing that,' she murmured. Andra shrugged.

'That isn't all,' she continued. 'You remember what that dragon said to you? When it attacked us?'

Del looked at her.

'That it's a matter of time?'

Andra nodded.

'That was in the reports. Every single one. Every dragon that was put to death after being found guilty of murder, each one declared that it was "just a matter of time". What does that mean?'

Del didn't respond. She looked up to the sky and rubbed her eyes and face with both hands.

'Let me help you,' Andra repeated. 'Del, I want to be a part of this. I need to be. You're…I mean, I… I need to be a part of this.'

Del searched Andra's eyes and finally softened.

'Okay, if you're going to be a pain about it, I guess there are a couple of things you could do.'

'What?'

'I'm hoping you've visited Mackay's shop in Old Town before?'

'Only the once, when I was a private.'

'Really? I used to be a regular. You can get me some supplies from there.'

'Supplies?'

'I'll make you a list.'

Andra nodded, looking down at the grass.

'I wonder if Markkus got to the girl,' Del mused.

'The girl?'

'There's a maid in the castle. She tried to poison the king. I told Markkus to get her out.'

'She what? How? Why?'

'I imagine she knows what I know. Maybe she's

even seen it. She might be the evidence I need.'

'Markkus?'

Del nodded.

'The royal taster. He's in trouble too but he can take care of himself.'

'So it's not just you, is it? Others are involved.'

'Others are involved but not by my hand.'

There was another pause.

'I'll get your supplies now.' But Andra didn't move.

'And that will be the end of your involvement.' Del gave her a small smile. Andra lowered her eyes to the grass. Del was right, she was putting her job at risk. She glanced up at the reason she wore the uniform. The reason she wasn't a blacksmith, or a housewife, or seamstress, or anything else expected of her for that matter. Andra owed her this much, she owed Del her life.

'After your exile, stories spread about you, you know,' she said.

'Oh?'

'Stories of how a dragon raised you.'

Del grinned.

'Of how you're an immortal witch, over a thousand years old and the king discovered your secret.'

Del laughed.

'My personal favourite was that you're actually a dragon. King George's daughter and the true heir to the throne, cursed to live in human form. The king found out and exiled you to save his crown.'

Del stopped laughing.

'How did you know?' she asked, seriously. Andra hesitated. Del burst into peals of laughter again and slapped Andra on the back. 'I think that's my favourite too.'

'What's the truth?' Andra asked once the laughter

had quietened.

'The truth? It's boring compared to those tales, I'm afraid. I was born in a little village on the outskirts and told I wouldn't ever amount to anything. Showed them, didn't I.'

'My father says you were married?'

'Widowed. I escaped the village thinking the city would be a better place for me. More opportunities. I was so naive, but I was only fifteen. Or was I sixteen? Anyway, I found work in a tavern. Not the nicest of places, but still, it paid for food and a roof. I met my husband there. A word of advice, Andra. Never marry someone you meet in a tavern. He was a lot older than me and had money and seemed kind enough. I didn't love him. That was my mistake. I should never have said yes when he proposed. Marriage to a drunk was a much darker place than staying at that tavern would have been, I'm sure. He would get angry and...well, one night I had enough. I ran away. He followed but was so drunk that I lost him. I ended up at the academy where they took me in. Me and my broken arm and bruised face.' Andra stared wide-eyed at Del. 'The Head of the Order at that time, Lord Winshaw, spoke to my husband when he was sober. Next thing I knew I'm enrolled in the academy. My husband paid for everything. He died five years later.'

'I can't imagine any man being able to do that to you.'

'No, well. Back then I wasn't who I am now.'

'Del Dragonslayer.'

'Soon to be Del Kingslayer.' Del smiled to herself. Shadow moved around the tree, snuffling at Del's hair and she reached up to stroke his cheek.

*

Tabitha walked home, her belly aching from the kitchen scraps she'd forced down for lunch. She normally enjoyed the freedom of early shifts but the sickness in her stomach made it difficult to think. She had to find Markkus somehow. All she knew about him was that he was a war veteran still working for the king and so likely lived in New Town. She had no idea where exactly, or where he spent his time between home and work. She had no idea where to start. The image of him lying in an alley somewhere dying made her stomach churn.

'Tabitha?'

Tabitha turned, stunned.

Markkus. She stared at him dumbfounded, relief washing over her in cold waves. Markkus put an arm around her shoulders so that she was partly covered by his long coat. Looking around him, he guided her along the road.

'Where are we going?' Despite the immediate fear, there was a thrill of being so close to him. He smelt warm, of skin and faint cologne. She tried hard not to breathe it in, for fear of giving herself away.

'Somewhere safe. I must speak with you.' He turned her towards The Old Boot tavern and pushed her gently through the door.

'I'm not-' Tabitha stopped as the darkness and stench of stale men hit her. She had never been inside a tavern before. Her mother told her that real ladies did not venture into taverns. Especially ladies who worked at the castle and would one day marry a nobleman. Tabitha didn't believe her mother but had still never had a reason to go to a tavern.

The room was large and full of people, mostly men, sat at tables scattered around the room. There was a large fire burning to her left, filling the place with a stuffy heat. The bar was to her right, behind which stood a bald man with tattoos across his scalp, cheek and neck. He was polishing a glass and nodded to them as Markkus closed the door. Everyone in the place stopped in their conversations and looked at the newcomers. They must have recognised Markkus as they soon returned to their own conversations and lives.

'Bobby, we're going into the back. Not to be disturbed.' Markkus herded Tabitha past the bar and through a door at the back of the room.

'Sure thing.' Bobby placed down his glass and leaned on the bar, giving Tabitha a smile that was probably meant to be comforting.

Even during her interview for the role of castle maid, Tabitha had never felt so small. She hugged herself as Markkus locked the door behind them. They were in a cramped room with no windows, two doors and one large table in the middle surrounded by chairs.

'Take a seat,' Markkus offered, moving to peak through the second door and then lock it. Tabitha sat on the edge of the nearest chair.

'What do you want?' she asked in a small voice, furious with herself for ever having the slightest of feelings for this man. Markkus took a seat about three chairs away from her.

'To keep you safe.' He looked shocked. 'I'm sorry. This must all seem a bit much. I never meant to scare you. Look.' He leaned closer to her. 'Did you put poison in the king's food? It's okay, you can tell me. You won't get into trouble. I'm not going to take you to the king. I want to take you home but I need to know the truth. I must know what you know so that I can protect you.'

All the feelings Tabitha had ever felt, denied and bottled up for Markkus came flooding back. Blood rushed through her body and her cheeks blushed. Her hands, stuffed between her thighs as she rocked to herself, were now freed. Her fingers played with a knot in the table.

'I used rat poison from the kitchen.'

'You didn't put enough in. Was it a spur of the moment idea?'

Tabitha nodded, deflated and ashamed. She bowed her head and the wisps from her bun fell around her face. Markkus smiled.

'It's okay.' He reached out a hand and placed it on the table close to her. 'I need you to tell me why you did it.'

'I saw something.' Tabitha lifted her head, tucking the escaped hair behind her ears.

'What did you see? It's important that you tell me everything.'

'Why? What are you going to do?'

'Do you know who I am, Tabitha?' Markkus asked gently. Tabitha nodded.

'You were a commander in King Tobyias's army but you were injured in battle.'

'That's right. I was in the army and I worked with a dragonslayer. Her name was Del Thorburn, do you know about her?'

'She was exiled but she's back. I saw her going to see the king.'

'The king is hanging her tomorrow morning. We don't have much time. Do you know why they exiled her?'

'She committed treason. She spread rumours about the king.'

'Right. She believes the king has been eating people.'

There. The words were out, spoken aloud. Tabitha

looked at Markkus.

'Why didn't the king kill her when he exiled her?'

Markkus paused long enough that the silence should have been uncomfortable, although Tabitha didn't feel it was. He sat back in his chair.

'He tried to. But public opinion is important to him. He wants to keep his crown and couldn't risk an uprising. The rumours died down when Del disappeared. Now that she's back he needs to dispose of her fast and properly, this time. He's hardly everyone's favourite at the moment, not after the latest tax rise.'

'That's why he's making her death public.'

'Yes. And he'll make sure the job is done this time. She's my friend and I want to help her so I have to know what you know.'

Tabitha nodded and took a deep breath to steady herself. Already feeling giddy with the loss of that heavy weight on her shoulders.

'I saw him, I heard him, eating a person. He didn't see me. People at the castle go missing all the time, there's a high turnover. Usually it's because families move away or someone gets ill and dies. I never questioned it before.'

'And why should you.'

'I overheard the king speaking. About you,' Tabitha blurted.

'Oh?'

'He sent an assassin named Charles after you.'

'Yes, he found me.'

'You're not hurt?'

'No.'

Tabitha scanned Markkus's body doubtfully. Markkus watched her and smiled.

'But he was sent to kill you. They said he's one of the best.'

'I can't explain it now.'

After a pause, Tabitha said, 'I'm so sorry.'

'For what?

'Getting you into this. I should never have poisoned him. I don't know what I was thinking. I was just scared.'

'I know. It's all right. Really. Do you think that you're the first person to try and poison him?'

'You've let him eat poison before?'

'Well, no. That doesn't matter. What matters is that the king is after me and he'll soon be after you. I need to get you somewhere safe.'

Markkus stood.

'Until when?' Tabitha looked up at him. 'Is my family safe?'

'Your family is fine, I'll make sure of it. But there is something you should consider. When the time comes, would you be willing to testify?'

'To who?'

'A jury, the High Circle. That is, a group of noble dragons and humans. Think about it.'

*

Binkley fretted. Charlie hadn't returned. He should have finished the job by now but the assassin had vanished. That didn't surprise Binkley, Charlie was a master of shadows. But he should have returned, at least to collect his payment. Binkley stood outside the king's library, deliberating. Eventually he knocked.

'Enter.'

Binkley made his way inside. He felt tiny in the vast room, standing before the dragon king immersed in a book.

'A journal of Hermann the Wise,' King Rupert

mused. Binkley smiled, comforted at the thought of his king studying those particular books. 'A fool.' King Rupert snapped the book shut as Binkley's face fell. 'Lord Binkley, has there been no word on Charles? What should I make of this, do you think?'

'Perhaps, Your Grace, he is not yet finished?' Binkley croaked.

'Hmm. That man does not respect authority. I want an update on the situation. Have the city guard sent out to find Markkus. I want him brought to me. If Charles cannot do the job quickly then he will not do the job at all.'

Binkley didn't know what to say.

'Very good, Your Grace,' he managed, bowing and leaving the library. His chest tightened as he strode through the castle. Markkus was a good man. They had fought together, they had worked together and now the commander might die at his hands. He looked down at his wrinkled, trembling fingers. Binkley tried to swallow but his mouth was too dry. He was too old to save anyone now.

Binkley found the inspector of the city guard in the main station, on the road between the castle and Dragonslayer Academy. The constables and sergeants inside stood to rigid attention as Binkley entered.

'Well? Don't just stand there! I wish to speak with Inspector Monterey. Now.'

'Yessa!' Sergeant Don gave a hasty salute and tripped over himself running to the inspector's office. Binkley followed him and pushed past Don as he opened the door.

'Inspector? I wish to speak with you.'

Monty looked up from the piles of paper and reports on his desk and sighed through his nose. Tapping the top of his pen against the desk, he watched the lord commander. 'I come on urgent business, Inspector. From the king.'

Monty placed down his pen and folded his hands on top of the reports.

'Please, Lord Commander, do take a seat.'

Binkley gave a gracious nod and sat opposite the inspector, catching Del's name written on the report at the top of Monty's pile.

'I come to you with business of a sensitive nature.'

'We have experience with such business, Lord Commander.'

'Hmm. Indeed. A well-known gentleman was recently employed by King Rupert. Unfortunately, he has failed in carrying out the work asked of him.'

'But he took payment?'

'Well, no.'

'Not a lot we can do about that, I'm afraid.'

'No. I understand. What I would like you to do is the work that this gentleman failed to undertake, in a manner of speaking.'

'And I suppose we might get the payment instead?'

'Certainly not. The king has already raised the taxes, what more do you want?'

Monty twisted his lips but said nothing. Binkley knew what he was thinking, but it was hardly his place to suggest to the king that the city guard needed to see some of those taxes. 'You will arrest the king's royal taster and bring him to the castle.'

'Arrest? On what charge?'

'That is none of your concern,' Binkley told him.

Monty sat back.

'Actually, Lord Commander, I'm afraid it is. We need to have a reason to arrest the man.'

'Then the charge is treason.'

Monty pursed his lips.

'And the man who was originally assigned this job?'

'Again, none of your concern.' Binkley squirmed in his seat, sure he could feel something crawling up his spine. 'You will undertake the task?'

'I will send some of my men to find him,' Monty told him, returning back to his paperwork. Binkley didn't question the dismissal, choosing instead to leave as quickly as he could.

*

The afternoon was beginning to turn as Andra pulled her hood up so that it partially covered her eyes. She gathered herself and walked down the steps, leaving the street behind. Darkness overwhelmed her and she had to stand still a moment until her eyes adjusted. Using one hand on the wall to her right as guidance, she continued down into the darkness.

The bridges that connected the Old Town to New Town had houses and shops underneath, between the struts and supporting walls. In-between these walls and storage rooms were caverns, linked by cold, damp tunnels. There were rumours that these tunnels were haunted. That may or may not be true, but they were certainly frequented by people of a less than friendly nature.

The chamber opened up before her. Trying hard to ignore the faint sound of voices and a scream, Andra moved into the right corner. She looked up at the sign above the doorway. Carved in elegant but scuffed and eroded letters read the words *Our Lord Is Our Refuge And Helper*. On the edge of Old Town, it had once been home to the priest of the local temple. When the bridges over to New Town had buried and covered the building the priest had moved out and a lone man had moved in. He created a shop which he passed onto his son who passed it onto his son, and he onto his. It was now owned by a small, hairy man named Mackay. Andra pushed open the door and stepped inside.

A small bell rang and the door closed behind her. She took a moment to look around, lifting her head to see beneath the rim of her hood.

'Ah, welcome, welcome. Perhaps I can help in some way?'

Andra looked over at Mackay and inadvertently screwed up her nose. His chin was bristling with dark stubble but his skin looked clean enough. Still, he had an aura about him that made her shiver. Maybe it was his eyes, small but keen. She looked up at the shelves full of jars. At the barrels lining the shop floor piled high with stock and at the cards stuck to each one proclaiming the discounted bargain that was on offer.

'I need these.' She passed Mackay the list Del had written for her. He took it, the dirty grin never leaving his face, and unfolded it. His lips moved as he read the items.

'Of course, of course. I have these in stock I believe. I can bring them out to you. You know, it's funny,' the little man paused, glancing up at Andra. 'I recognise this handwriting.'

He bent, trying to see beneath Andra's hood.

'I 'eard a rumour,' he murmured, taking a step closer. 'I 'eard that Del Thorburn was back. She what led good old Tobyias's army into war. She what won us the war. I know her handwriting, see.'

With a sigh, Andra pulled down her hood.

'Oh,' Mackay said, disappointed.

'Can you get me the items?'

'Yeah. I mean yes, yes of course.' Mackay

disappeared into the back of the shop.

Andra cleared her throat softly. She wasn't sure what to do with her hands so she clasped them behind her back. In the silence of Mackay's departure she could hear a ticking. Looking round she finally discovered an old clock, behind the till, nailed to the wall surrounded by ornaments, swords, pistols and...

'What is that?' Andra pointed as Mackay reappeared carrying a box. Mackay looked where she was pointing and beamed up at her.

'Oh that, miss? That's a device which breathes fire. My own invention. I designed it after Del were exiled. I wish I'd done it sooner but if wishes were gold coins.' Mackay looked Andra up and down. 'May I ask, if I be so bold, what you mean to do with these items?'

'No, you may not.'

'Ah yes. Del used to come into this shop and enquire about these very things. Funny that.'

'Hilarious. Is everything there?'

'Oh yes.' Mackay placed the last item in the box on the worktop and picked up a pencil. He jotted some numbers into a notebook and counted off his fingers, sticking the end of his pencil into his mouth. 'That's ten gold coins.'

'Ten? That's a bit steep.'

'There are other shops that sell these items, Miss.' Mackay picked up the box.

'No, wait. How about five?'

'Ten.'

'Five more than covers it.'

'Ten.'

'Six?'

'Ten.'

'Seven.'

'Ten.'

'Seven,' Andra growled.

'Nine.'

'Eight.'

'Nine.'

'Eight.'

'Eight.' Mackay stuck out a grubby hand. Andra stared at it and swallowed hard. Gingerly she took it in her own and they shook once. Andra gave Mackay the coins, shaking her head.

'Did you rip Del off like this?'

'Oh no, you don't rip Del off. Or she'll rip something off.' Mackay grinned. 'Del had a special discount. Did you know her? You should have said, I would have given you the same.' Andra glared at him and snatched up the box. She turned to leave. There was one last thing to do from Del's list. 'Say hello to Del for me,' Mackay called after her.

*

Tabitha was trying to ignore the warmth of Markkus's hand on her back as he escorted her out of the tavern.

'Commander Markkus Kern?'

Markkus and Tabitha stopped. Five of the city guard stood in the doorway of the tavern.

'Yes?'

'You're to come with us, sir. By order of King Rupert.'

Tabitha felt Markkus's hand twitch. She leaned back against him. No. No, don't go.

'Right.' Markkus positioned himself between the guards and Tabitha. 'Go straight home,' he whispered to her. 'Straight home, don't speak to anyone. Make sure you lock the doors. Everything will be all right. I promise.'

Tabitha couldn't speak. There was a painful lump in her throat. Markkus left her and moved towards the guards. The one who had spoken gave him a dirty look.

'You can come back and visit your whore another time,' he said. The silent drinkers in the tavern looked to Tabitha and her face burned.

Helpless, she watched Markkus leave. He gave her one last glance before disappearing from sight. The drinkers turned back to her and she felt tiny once more. The walls and tables around her looming high above and the stares of the men turning into menacing leers.

Breathing hard, Tabitha rushed out of the tavern and without hesitation ran home. Not stopping until she was through the front door and in her bedroom.

Fifteen

Rupert sat on a chaise lounge in his chambers as Markkus was brought before him. Spearing strawberries onto his claws and popping them into his mouth.

'Markkus,' the king greeted him. 'Leave us.' He gestured to the guards, keeping his gaze on Markkus. The guards behind Markkus left him alone with the king, closing the large doors behind them.

'Your Grace.' Markkus bowed.

There was a silence. Markkus found himself glancing around the room, feeling exposed and alone. His gaze landed on Rupert's sharp teeth.

'How long did you serve my predecessors, Markkus?' Rupert dropped another three strawberries into his mouth and munched, juice dribbling down his chin.

'Including my army career, just over twenty years, Your Grace.'

'And how long have you served me?'

'Since your coronation, Your Grace.'

'And how many dragons did you kill during your time in the army?'

'Your Grace?'

'How many dragons, Markkus.'

'I have never personally killed any dragons, Your Grace.'

'Hmm.' Rupert slid a claw into a plump strawberry

and held it up, studying it. 'Then why did you try to kill me?'

'I'm afraid I don't understand, Your Grace,' Markkus said, going cold.

'Do you not agree with a dragon on the throne? You've kept your peace with it for four years, and however many before that.'

'No, Your Grace-'

'Then perhaps it was more personal?'

'No. I have never intentionally caused my king any harm.'

'Please, Markkus.' Rupert licked the strawberry off his claw and looked down his snout at the man stood before him. 'There was poison in my soup and you tasted it. You are the royal taster, Markkus. It is your job to stop me from being poisoned and yet you allowed me to eat that soup.'

'I did not believe it strong enough to do you any harm, Your Grace.'

'That is not the point!' King Rupert stood and knocked over his strawberries, sending his chaise lounge flying across the room. 'The point, you stupid little man, is that it is your job to inform me if someone wishes to do me harm. Who was it?' Rupert circled Markkus, wrapping his tail round to surround his taster. Markkus didn't respond. He was thinking fast, about Del, about Tabitha and her family, about how much he had to protect. 'Markkus, you know who it was. I know that you know. Now tell me.'

'It was me.' Markkus looked up into the reptilian eye of his king. His heart beat fast, pounding against his ribs. His mouth was dry and tasted of blood. He kept his head high and his eye contact with Rupert steady.

King Rupert studied Markkus, absent-mindedly tapping a claw on the tiled floor.

'You are noble, Markkus. I know who you are. I know what you are. You're a man of honour, a man everyone respects. You're protecting someone.'

'No, Your Grace. It was me. I swear it.'

'Then why? Hmm? Tell me why, Markkus. Why such a respectable war veteran such as yourself would attempt to kill his king?'

'I've heard the rumours, Your Grace.'

'Ah, the rumours.'

'Del Thorburn was a close friend of mine.'

'Yes, Delilah Dragonslayer. And you believed your little friend. Did you have evidence of her stories?'

'Well, no. But she did.'

'Did? But she doesn't anymore. And neither do you.' A smile crept onto Rupert's face and his tail stretched and coiled closer to Markkus's legs. Markkus felt the king's tail brushing against his ankles and he stepped away. The tail followed him and Rupert began to chuckle. 'Your friend is going to die, Markkus. And you, for your treason, will join her fate. Now, tell me who attempted to poison me and I will consider exiling you. I can be merciful, after all.'

'I've told you Your Grace, it was me.' Markkus clasped his trembling hands behind his back and stood tall. His right thigh twitched. His legs trembling as King Rupert's tail coiled around his ankle.

'And I've told you, Markkus,' Rupert hissed, lowering his head close to Markkus's face. 'I know that it wasn't you. Never mind.' He lifted his head high above his taster. 'I'm sure I will find who is responsible, with or without you. One last chance, Markkus?'

'It was me, Your Grace.' Markkus lowered his gaze from his king and looked straight ahead, through Rupert's shining red chest and into nothing. He heard the hiss as Rupert exhaled through his teeth. Markkus closed his eyes and moved to step aside as he felt the rush of the king lowering his jaws. Rupert yanked his tail and Markkus flew backwards, landing with a heavy thump onto his back. Pain rippled up his spine and pushed the air from his lungs. He struggled to get up, gasping for breath as he fell back to the ground. Rupert loomed over him, a smile spreading across his lips.

'It's best if you don't fight it, Markkus. You will be given an honourable funeral. As all our brave veterans are entitled to.'

Markkus caught his breath as his lungs opened again, and gazed up at the king through hazy eyes.

'So it's all true?' he asked.

Rupert laughed, wrapping his tail around Markkus's waist and squeezing.

'Why?' Markkus coughed.

'Why? You would see, if you were to live long enough. Do you know when the last dragon king was? The last true dragon king?'

'King George, less than ten years ago'

'No. No, he was a dragon and he had the throne but he wasn't the true king. Tell me, Markkus, do you see any other dragons in this castle? Any with real power?'

'There are noble dragon families.'

'They have no power. It was stripped from them long ago. Any dragon advisors? Any dragons creating laws?'

'No.'

'No. There have been no dragon advisors in this castle since Hermann the Wise. There has been no dragon with power since the day Hermann the Wise died. Well, that is about to change. You humans, you are arrogant. You think you are all powerful because you have won so many battles. Because you have spread throughout the world. Because you speak of peace so easily? Peace tastes of bile in your mouths and you know nothing, you tiny insect. Dragons are as old as this world and you dare think that you own it? The world is going to change Markkus. It is just a matter of time. But you will not be around to see it, not you or your little dragonslayer friend.' King Rupert opened his mouth wide. Just as his teeth brushed the skin of Markkus's scalp there was a knock at the door.

*

In one fluid motion, Tabitha closed the door of her bedroom. Placing the butcher knife on the floor beside her, she dug out an old backpack from under her bed. It had once belonged to her father who had used it when travelling the world. She grew up listening to his stories. Some raised eyebrows had led her to believe they may not be entirely true. Still, she held on tight to the idea of her father travelling from city to city, learning his trade and having adventures. She had often dreamed of living that life. Lying in bed at night after a long day scrubbing floors at the castle. Or as her mother braided her hair and lectured her on the life of comfort and riches Tabitha could have if only she could find the right husband, and how important it was to stay out of trouble. Well, Tabitha had stayed out of trouble long enough. She rummaged around in the backpack until she found her father's old belt. The leather was brown, and worn soft and smooth. Tabitha slipped it around her waist, fastening it on the hole that her father had created for her. She slid the knife into the belt and practised walking around, checking that the blade didn't cut into her. She wanted to try running but there was no room and no time. She'd soon find out if she could run or not.

Yanking her arms into the sleeves of her coat,

concealing the knife, she crept out of the front door without looking back. She didn't notice her father watching her close the front door. She couldn't know that he had seen the knife protruding under her coat.

She ran to the castle. Forcing herself to walk up to the gate and through the servant entrance, nodding to the guards on duty as if nothing was awry. It gave her a chance to catch her breath. By the time she was outside the servants' door to the king's chambers she was breathing normally despite the fear choking her.

She pushed her ear up to the door and heard Markkus's voice.

'I've told you, Your Grace, it was me.'

'And I've told you, Markkus. I know that it wasn't you.' King Rupert hissed and spat. Tabitha could feel his anger burning through the door and she knew that they were talking about her. She pulled the knife from her belt and held it up, keeping her ear pressed to the door and listening.

At one point she moved the knife into her other hand to wipe her sweaty palms on her trousers. She felt sick with fear as she listened to the conversation. The tone of Rupert's voice turned her bowels to water. She wondered if he held Markkus in a claw already or if he was waiting, moving towards the man, playing with him.

'Dragons are as old as this world,' she heard Rupert hiss. 'And you dare think that you own it? The world is going to change Markkus. It is just a matter of time. But you will not be around to see it, not you or your little dragonslayer friend.'

Tabitha could no longer stand the tension. By the sound of the king's voice, he was ready to pounce if he hadn't already. She lifted the knife in her right hand and found the door handle with her left. There came a knock at the chamber's main door. She stopped and pressed her ear back up against the wood.

'What?' King Rupert boomed. Markkus wheezed as the king squeezed him hard and he heard a crack from his ribcage. The doors opened and a guard peeked through.

'I apologise, Your Grace, but there is someone here to see you.'

'Can't you see I'm busy? Tell them to wait.'

'Yes, Your Grace.' The guard's face disappeared. A second later the doors swung open and Mad Erik Dunn strolled through.

'Your Majesty, I'm afraid I just cannot wait,' he proclaimed, glancing around the room. 'Is she here? Hmm?' He looked up at Markkus, held high in the coils of the king's tail.

'Who are you?' the king growled. 'Who is this?' he snapped at the two guards who were staring wide-eyed at Erik from behind the doors. Rupert turned back to Erik who smiled up at his king.

'Your Majesty, I do beg your pardon, I'm looking for someone.'

'Evidently, they are not here. Now get out before I have you arrested.'

'I was told she would be here.' Erik made a show of looking around the room. He stopped and looked up at the king. 'Can I say, it is an honour to meet you, Your Kinglyship.'

King Rupert blinked down at Erik in a daze before coming to his senses.

'Get him out of here,' he boomed to his guards who sprang to life and surged forward.

'Oh, I suppose I should be leaving?' Erik glanced back at Markkus. 'I was sure my daughter was around here, I must have been mistaken.' The guards took Erik, one at each arm.

'Yes, you must,' King Rupert muttered, loosening his grip on Markkus. Markkus took a deep breath and took note of the sharp pain that spread across the right side of his chest. He took care not to struggle or bring Rupert's attention back to him. He watched Erik out of the corner of his eye, wondering who the man's daughter was. He had a sinking feeling that he knew. The man had curly brown hair and Tabitha's eyes.

'She was headed here you know, but it looks like I beat her. I do that. We're always racing and I always win. One day her legs will grow and she'll beat me but until then her dad will always win the races.'

Tabitha held her breath. Tears fell down her cheeks as she listened to her father. The noise he had caused allowed her to risk opening the door a little. She watched him dragged from the king's chambers, shouting and raving with a big grin on his face. She begged whatever gods were listening for him to be safe. The king's tail coiled around Markkus suspended in the air. The king's full attention was on her father and Tabitha wondered if now was the time to move. Markkus seemed to have the same thought as at that moment he bent his head back to look at the servants' door. They locked eyes.

Markkus's mind swam, considering all options of escape. He had no weapon and he was hanging a good few feet above the ground. The king's grip was loosening all the time. Soon he might be able to slip out but he knew that as soon as he started struggling for freedom the king would realise his mistake. And if he did get free? What then? The king would immediately block off the main door. Markkus remembered the servants' door. He bent his head back as far as it would go, pain gripping his spine, and he looked for the small, wooden door hidden behind the wallpaper. Tabitha looked back at him and Markkus jolted, his head springing forward again. He looked towards the mad man. Erik was just out of the door, throwing Markkus another look, still rambling and grinning. Markkus thought fast, he needed a weapon and he needed it now. His arms were still pinned to his sides, his fingers brushing against a pocket in his trousers. He gave a small jump as something pricked his leg. Easing his fingers into the pocket and pulled out his medal. He nudged the pin until he could grip it between his fingers. As soon as he had it positioned, he dug it into King Rupert's tail in-between two scales.

King Rupert gave a cry and his tail uncoiled. Markkus dropped to the ground and found himself unavailable to move. Blinding pain shuddered through his bones where his spine connected with the tiled floor. His legs refused to respond. His shoulders and neck ached with an intensity that sent his head spinning. He waited for it to clear, watching in horror as Rupert moved around to find him, roaring and spitting. The dragon king's head entered Markkus's vision and he managed to sit up, willing his legs to move.

Tabitha was by his side in a moment, helping to lift him up.

'What're you doin' 'ere?' he managed to say through gritted teeth as his left leg began to move.

Tabitha didn't respond. King Rupert was already upon them. He roared and his head swooped down to her. Tabitha rolled away without thinking and landed back on her feet, surprised at herself. Rupert hesitated only a moment before changing the angle of his neck to follow her. She had landed near his feet. As his sharp teeth approached she held her butcher knife high and plunged it into the nearest toe.

The noise was unbearable as Rupert screamed. The walls shook and the windows along one side of the room shattered. Tabitha held her hands over her ears and ran back to Markkus. Her eyes narrow as shards of glass and debris were flung towards them. Markkus pulled himself to his feet. Tabitha risked removing her hands from her head to drag Markkus through the servants' door.

King Rupert fell silent and held his foot up to inspect the damage. Ten guards ran into the room, swords drawn. The king moved his foot one way and then the other, watching the red blood drip onto the floor. He looked up to find both his taster and the girl gone.

'Find them!' he roared. Having not seen Markkus or Tabitha, all ten guards proceeded to run around in a circle, shouting about which direction to go in. 'Wait.' King Rupert found his chaise lounge and corrected it. Sitting, he brought his foot up again for a closer look. The pounding in his ears quietened, the rage subsiding. This could be fixed. Perhaps there was even an opportunity lurking somewhere. The guards waited with anticipation.

'What of that mad man? Where is he?'

'Your Grace, we sent him away.'

'Well, bring him back. And fetch me Lord Gerard. Now.' King Rupert looked up at the ten motionless guards. Wretched, slow humans. He was becoming increasingly tired of them all. 'Now!'

*

Andra sat at her family's kitchen table, stroking the familiar knot in the wood that she had found faces and shapes in during her childhood. Below her feet she could just make out the sounds of her father working. He would often work late into the evening. The sounds of the bellows and hammer against red metal had often lulled her to sleep as a child.

'Andra?'

Andra looked up at her little brother, stood in the kitchen doorway, rubbing his eye with the back of his hand.

'You should be asleep,' she told him.

'Where's mummy?'

'She's out tonight. She'll be home soon. Can't sleep?' Cayden shook his head. 'Come on.' Andra ushered him back to his bedroom. 'Back to bed.'

She tucked the covers around him and caught herself staring at one of his stuffed toys. It had been hers once, she had carried it everywhere. She had been holding it the first time she'd seen Del come into her father's shop. She'd been holding it when she first saw Del on parade.

'Are you happy to be home?'

'Hmm? What's that?' Andra tore her gaze away and looked into the large blue eyes of her brother.

'It's just that you don't seem happy.'

'Of course I'm happy.' She ruffled his blonde shaggy hair. 'I'm always happy to be home. It's hard being out on the road, you know. I miss mum and dad and you and this house.'

'Why are you sad then?'

'It's complicated.'

Cayden gave her a look. It was the look he gave her when their parents couldn't see. It meant that he knew more than he was letting on. Andra sighed.

'What's your first memory, Cay?'

Cayden squinted his eyes and thought hard about this.

'I remember us playing in the road and a horse was galloping towards us and you had to pick me up and we fell over together and it hurt.'

'Really? That's your first memory?'

Cayden shrugged.

'Okay. Well, do you remember the Great War?'

Cayden shook his head.

'No. Why would you, you were a baby when it ended. Do you know much about the Great War?'

'Dad had lots of work but lots of people went hungry.'

'Yes. Well, the Great War was about people from another land fighting with us. They wanted our land and our homes, so we had to defend ourselves.'

'Why did they want our homes?'

'Because quite a few grown-ups measure their power and own importance by how much stuff they have and land is expensive. It's all about power. The more land they own, the more power they have. And some people think that if they own the land that we live on, it means they own us.'

Cayden's eyes widened.

'So King George, do you know about King George?'

'He was a dragon like King Rupert.'

'He agreed that we should go to war. All the able-bodied men joined the royal army away from their families. It was very scary for everyone. Some men never made it back home. Towards the end of the war, women had to join the army to make up the numbers.'

'Like mummy?'

'Well, mummies didn't join because they had their

children to look after. Their fathers had already gone to war, you see. But mum could have gone, as dad was still here making weapons for the soldiers based in the city. Thankfully mum didn't go. Anyway, King George had his royal army, but it didn't seem enough. So he added a few of the dragonslayer companies. One of the companies had a woman for a captain. Her name is Del Thorburn.'

Cayden nodded.

'You talk about her a lot.'

'Yes. I used to watch her on parade. I wanted to be like her. She's why I'm a dragonslayer. She led King George's dragonslayer company into battle. Sadly, King George died soon after without having any children and before the war ended. We voted King Tobyias to take the throne. Do you remember him?'

'Of course.'

Andra smiled.

'Of course. Now before King George died, Del was just obeying the orders that his generals gave her. Her company was part of the royal army. But King Tobyias made her an advisor and gave her an army. She was good at what she did. She won every battle they sent her into. And so, we won the Great War.'

'Hurray!' Cayden nearly jumped out of bed. Andra caught and steadied him.

'But then,' she continued, her voice low as if she were telling a ghost story. Cayden settled and listened. 'King Tobyias caught a fever and died. He was young when he died and it was a great shock to everyone. There were riots. His queen consort went missing and there was no heir. Big arguments broke out about who should have the throne. Our shop was broken into a few times but dad mostly saw the thieves off. Then Rupert came from Seracombe and proclaimed that he would be our king. Of course, he had to be voted in. Everyone remembered King George and how good he had been. Dragons can live for an awfully long time so I suppose that's why everyone voted for Rupert. They wanted peace and they wanted it for a long time. So Rupert became king. Del stayed working in the castle but then she saw things. Or she said she saw things.'

'What sort of things?'

'Bad things. And when King Rupert heard what she was saying about him, he sent her away.'

'And now she's back.'

'Now she's back. And she shouldn't be and I'm afraid that she's going to die.'

Cayden lay back against the pillows and yawned.

'She won't die.'

'Oh? What makes you so sure?'

'She lived through all those battles. Nothing can kill her.' Cayden closed his eyes. Andra kissed him on the forehead.

'I hope you're right. Night little brother.' She stood to leave.

'Andra?'

'Hmm?'

'Petey said today that we didn't always have dragons in the city or as kings and queens. He said people like you used to kill them whether they were good or bad.'

'That was a very, very long time ago. Things have changed a lot since then. For the better.'

'How?'

'That was the Old War. That's another story, Cay. For another time.'

Sixteen

Del made sure no one was looking and then planted a soft kiss on Shadow's nose. She laughed as the horse lifted his lip as if to kiss her back. Her guard appeared from around the corner and she gave Shadow a final pat on the neck.

'Done yet?' Strangles had grown impatient, or perhaps he was having a bad night. Bored of watching his prisoner fuss over the small farm horse, he had ambled out of the stable block and out of sight for a full ten minutes. Del could have easily escaped. She held the boy in contempt.

'All done.' She gave a forced smile, walking over to him. 'You can take me back now.' The boy sighed. 'Do you want to become a dragonslayer, or is the prison guard life the one for you?' Del asked.

'I am a dragonslayer. This is just temporary.'

'Not if you continue like this, mark my words.' Del strode ahead of the boy and into the building. She made her way towards the cells but stopped at the doorway. Lord Gerard swept down the stairs followed by Ami and three dragonslayers, including Andra. Gerard glanced at Del and then caught sight of Private Strangles as he ambled round the corner. Gerard grabbed him by his collar.

'What is she doing out unguarded?'

'My Lord, I-'

'She is not to be left alone,' Gerard hissed before

storming out of the academy.

'What's going on?' Del asked the dragonslayers. She recognised one of them who avoided her gaze. With a raised eyebrow, Del turned to Andra.

'The king has requested our presence,' Andra whispered, giving Del a meaningful glance. 'There's been an attack on his life.'

Del's world stopped for just a moment. She gave a small nod and walked through the door leading down to the cells. Strangles rushed to follow her, running down the stone steps. Del appeared from under the staircase as he rounded the corner and she punched him in the jaw. Strangles stumbled backwards, hitting his head on the cold stone floor and remaining there.

'Sorry,' Del muttered. She retrieved his sword and pistol, and counted to ten before jogging up the stairs. The foyer of the building was empty, Gerard and his captains had left. On the balls of her feet, Del made her way to the stable block and found Shadow's bridle. He whickered, happy to see her again so soon. With a smile she slid the bridle on and opened his stable door. The little horse trotted out of the stable block with her jogging beside. Once out in the open Del swung onto Shadow's bare back and urged him forward into a canter. His hooves clattered over the cobbles as they made their way up to the castle.

*

Tabitha wanted to get out of the castle and fast. She knew the guards would soon be on them but she felt sick with worry for her father. Markkus overtook her as she hesitated, torn. He pulled her down a flight of stairs off one corridor. They took a right when she felt they should have gone left and plunged into darkness. Markkus stopped to light a torch that sat in a hoop on the wall.

'Where are we going? We need to get out of here.' She tried to pull Markkus back but he was a lot bigger and stronger than her. Markkus led the way through the dark corridor and in the light from the torch Tabitha saw it was more of a tunnel. 'Where are we?'

'We need to keep out of sight of the guards. This is an old passageway, built before their time. Chances are they don't know about it.' Markkus looked back into Tabitha's large, scared eyes. 'It'll lead us into Old Town,' he added.

Tabitha walked just behind Markkus, following him through the tunnel. The sound of dripping echoed around them. The torch flame flickered although she could feel nothing but the stuffy warm air around them.

'Did you know that man?' Markkus asked after the silence grew too heavy.

'He's my father.'

Markkus looked down her. 'I'm sure he's fine.'

Tabitha could have laughed.

'What are you doing here? I told you to go home,' Markkus said.

'I did go home but I knew what the king was going to do. I couldn't let him...' Tabitha drifted off, unable to think of a way to finish that sentence without compromising herself. It wasn't that she had feelings for Markkus, but, well, she couldn't think of another reason why she didn't want him to die.

'I'll take you straight home when we get out of here.' Markkus decided out loud. 'Then I'll look for your father.'

Tabitha stopped, breathing hard.

'My mother. What if the guards recognised me? I know some of them. They eat in the kitchen with us at times.'

'Then they're probably fond of you. I wouldn't worry.' Markkus didn't sound too sure of himself but what choice did she have? Tabitha followed him, mind whirring.

*

Del trotted up to the castle gates. Outside the main doors stood Gerard's coach, Andra's mare and another two horses. Royal guards held their reins. With a tut, Del turned Shadow. They trotted back the way they came and ducked into a wynd off to the right. The alley was not built for horses. Shadow lifted his head with a snort as he became surrounded by leaning walls. Del gave his neck a stroke and urged him on. She turned him round a tight corner. Trotting up another narrow path along the frontage of houses, following the line of the castle wall above them. Shadow's pounding hooves echoed as they came out onto a main road. He shook his head, happy to be back in the open, and sped up as Del pointed him at the castle. She would need more weapons. The private's pistol would only do so much damage, she thought, as a couple dived out of her way, shouting. Had Andra bought her supplies? They'd be at her home. But she didn't know if she had time to retrieve them. There would be weapons in the castle, she would just have to make do. Shadow slowed to a halt near a large circular drain that came out of the wall to her left. She dismounted and looked around.

'Excuse me, sir.' She beckoned to a nearby man stood outside his grocers, stacking apples into a crate. He gave her a wary look. 'I will pay you three silver coins to look after this horse. No one is to take him. I'll be back as soon as I can.' At the mention of coinage, the man nodded, his eyes brightening. 'If anyone takes him or if anything happens to him, I will kill you,' Del added, completely serious. The man deflated a little but muttered an acceptance. Del thrust the reins into his hands and whispered a few reassuring words to Shadow. The little horse's ears pricked forward to her and followed her as she made her way to the grated drain. He pawed at the ground, eager to follow. The grocer frowned at the horse, tightening his grip on the reins but keeping him at arm's length.

Del pulled the grate open and it squealed on its rusted hinges. After some exertion the grate opened enough for her to squeeze through. She entered the tunnel and bumped into someone. Heart pounding, hand reaching instinctively for the stolen pistol, Del looked up and into familiar eyes.

'Markkus,' she breathed, looking behind him to a tired looking girl with red eyes.

'Del, what're you doing here?' Markkus peered around Del out onto the streets.

'The king summoned Gerard and a handful of his captains. Someone attempted to assassinate the king.' Del looked accusingly at Markkus and the girl behind him looked down at the ground. Markkus gave a loud laugh.

'Try the other way around. Tabitha, here, and her father saved my life today.' Markkus smiled down at Tabitha who blushed. Del watched, bemused.

'My father,' Tabitha said, as if remembering. She tried to push past Markkus and Del but Markkus held her back.

'Your father?' Del asked.

'He stormed into the king's chambers,' Markkus told her. 'I think he thought Tabitha was in trouble.'

'He's always thought there was something going on at the castle,' Tabitha murmured.

'Right well, you two can't go back to the castle. I suggest you take her home, Markkus. I'll look for your father.'

'No, I must look for him.' Tabitha stepped forward but, again, Markkus stopped her.

'Del's right. I'll take you home. She'll find him. Have you escaped?' Markkus turned to Del.

'How can you tell?' Del smiled. 'They won't know I'm gone. I'll be back in my cell before they realise anything is amiss.'

'You could just run,' Markkus offered.

'Since when have I ever just ran?'

Tabitha watched the two talking and was sharply reminded of her age. She sank back into the shadows, a sickness swelling inside her.

'I have to finish this. If I don't do it, someone else might try.' Del looked pointedly at Tabitha and anger replaced the nauseated feeling. She curled her hands into fists, digging her nails into her palms to keep herself from saying something childish.

Del walked back into the murky darkness of evening. The shopkeeper looked at her with surprise as she took back Shadow's reins.

'Back so soon?'

'Change of plan.' Del swung herself up onto Shadow's back. 'Tabitha. Your father, what does he look like?'

'Oh, 'er father's Erik Dunn the Mad. Everyone knows that,' the shopkeeper exclaimed before looking back up at Del hoping to see more coin.

'Erik Dunn the Mad. That should narrow it down,' Del muttered, wheeling Shadow round and urging him into a trot.

'Oi! What about my money?'

Del turned on Shadow's back and looked at Markkus.

'Three silver coins,' she shouted to him.

Markkus frowned and looked down at the shopkeeper's expectant grin. Digging into his pockets, he pulled out the coins and counted them into the shopkeeper's hand.

'Come on, let's get you home.' Markkus placed an arm around Tabitha's shoulder and turned her. Tabitha struggled a little. 'She'll find him. She will.'

*

Del and Shadow came back the way they had come. Shadow's ears pinned back against his skull as they trotted down the wynd and he kicked up his back heels as they reached the main road. Del glanced up at the doors to the castle through the gates. Gerard's coach and the horses were still there. She rode Shadow down the road away from the castle and towards the academy. Pulling the knot from her hair, she kept her head down, allowing her hair to cover her face. Shadow picked his way around the pedestrians and carts travelling to and from market. The king's guards marched in small groups, armed. There were too many, it was obvious something was going on. It was sure to be the talk of the city by now. Once they reached a distance where the castle was still just within sight, Del slowed Shadow and dismounted. Keeping her face close to his neck, she looked around. Shadow thrust his nose into her hand and she stroked it as she thought through her situation. Just how was she going to find someone she'd never met before? She watched a group of five guards march past her, down the road and turn off to the right. They were looking for someone. Another group of six marched past her, up the road, bearing left and down towards the valley surrounding the castle on its hill. She watched each of them and wondered which group to follow.

Del ran her hand down Shadow's neck. She was going about this all wrong.

'Okay,' she breathed to herself. If she were escaping from the king, where would she go? She tried to forget about the hidden tunnels. Chances were Erik wouldn't know about those. He'd go somewhere busy, where he could blend in. Del led Shadow down the road, his hooves clopping on the cobbles. He'd go, Del thought, somewhere he felt safe. Del couldn't second guess that aspect but she had known enough men in her time. She had worked side by side with a whole army of them. She stopped and tied Shadow to a nearby post.

'Stay here. If anyone tries to steal you, stomp on them,' she whispered. Shadow's ears flicked towards her and his lips pulled at her fingers. She paused, overcome with affection for the small horse and the thought of never seeing him again. Then she pulled herself together and marched into the tavern.

The warmth hit her in the face and she breathed in as old, happy memories flooded back to her. Taverns were like an old friend, each one similar enough to bring up the same memories. Her first drink as a dragonslayer, sat in a dark corner giggling with the other few academy girls watching the men watching them. Eating with Markkus and discussing tactics and politics. Even the day she had discovered King Rupert's secret and she had sat at the bar drowning in her own miserable thoughts over a pint or five of ale. Del looked around and smiled. She walked over to the bar and leaned on the sticky wood. The barman wandered over, looking her up and down, assessing her wealth and drunken state.

'What can I getcha?'

'I'm looking for someone.' Del turned and leaned across the bar to him so that she could keep her voice down.

'We get lots of someones in here. Who wants to know?' The barman planted both of his large, meaty hands on the bar and looked down at Del.

'A friend.'

'Oh yeah?' The barman's eyebrows knitted together to form one giant hairy slug. 'I'm looking for a man named Erik. Erik the Mad.'

'Funny that.' The barman sniffed. 'So are the king's guards.'

'Do I look like a royal guard?'

'No.' The barman ran his eyes over Del's body once more. 'So why're you lookin' for 'im?'

'I need to know he's safe. Do you know where he is?'

'He may have been 'ere, but he ain't anymore.'

'Where did he go?'

'I don't know.'

Del tapped her fingernails on the bar. The barman's eyed flicked down to them.

'You don't know, or you don't remember?'

'My memory could do with a jog.' The barman shrugged.

'And then you might be able to tell me his whereabouts?'

'Depends on the jog.'

Del sighed and reached into her pockets before remembering that she was an escaped prisoner and had nothing.

'Well, I don't have a jog right now, but I can owe you.'

The barman expelled air through his closed lips, his slug eyebrow separating and jumping up his forehead.

'You must have somethin'.'

'I'm a dragonslayer. I will pay you back, my word on my honour.'

'Honour don't mean squat around 'ere, darlin'. Anyway, you don't look much like a dragonslayer.'

'Well, I'm not, I mean, I haven't…I-'

'Run into a spot of bother, have you?' The barman leaned back and looked out of the grubby windows. 'Nice horse you 'ave there. It ain't a dragonslayer horse, but it's nice.'

'He's not on offer,' Del said quietly, thinking.

'Evening Davey,' came a voice from her right.

Del started and looked beside her at Venkell. The two stared wide-eyed at one another.

'Evening Ven, what can I getcha?'

'You. What are you doing…how did you get out?'

'Oh, it's a funny story.' Del stood upright and eyed the door. Venkell positioned himself between Del and her escape route.

'I don't know how you did it, but I'm going to take you back. Now.'

'Wait.' Del held up her hands. Venkell hesitated. 'Aren't you wondering,' Del asked. 'Why I haven't left the city? I've obviously escaped.'

'Go on then.'

'I'm looking for someone.'

Venkell rolled his eyes and approached Del. Del jumped back and opened her mouth to speak when a yell blasted through the tavern. Every conversation, every murmur and slurp of drink stopped and the tavern fell into a thick, apprehensive silence.

Seventeen

'Did you know? All this time?'
Markkus slowed a little at Tabitha's voice.
   'About the king?'
Markkus stole glances back at her as she nodded. Her eyes red from the tears held back yet she seemed determined and tall.
   'I never knew for sure. I didn't know, I guess.' Would it be wrong to take her hand? He felt sure he should be holding onto her, urging her to go faster, but touching her seemed too much. 'I guess I didn't want to believe Del.'
   'But you did. All this time?'
   Markkus stopped and turned on Tabitha, looking into her large brown eyes.
   'I didn't know,' he told her. 'I had suspicions, sure. I wondered, at times. But I never saw anything. Not like Del did. Of course I should have trusted her. Of course, if I had seen something then I would have done something.'
   'What would you have done?' Tabitha continued walking, overtaking him and forcing him to follow.
   'I...I don't know.'
   'Would you have tried to kill him?'
   Markkus smiled.
   'That was brave of you.'
   Now it was Tabitha who glanced back at him.
   'It was stupid.'

'Sometimes they are the same thing.' Markkus reached forward and took Tabitha's cold hand in his, giving it a small squeeze before letting go.

Tabitha led Markkus up to the front door of her family's home, glancing back at him before opening it. She had mixed feelings and no time to untangle them. Her father was missing, the king was killing people, and now Markkus was following her up to her house and into her home, where her mother was waiting. Tabitha swallowed against her dry mouth. Her feelings for Markkus were just as tangled. Before he had been a comforting presence but distant and unreachable. Now he had spoken to her, wrapped his arm around her shoulder, defended her. Now he was inexplicably real. More importantly, he was about to meet her mother.

The house was cold, but it was often cold. Her mother stood in the kitchen, stirring a broth in a large pot with a wooden spoon.

'Erik? Is that you?' she called.

'No, it's me,' Tabitha replied without thinking.

'Tabitha? Where's your father? Where have you been?' her mother stopped when she caught sight of Markkus.

'This is my mother, Milly. Mum, this is Markkus. He works in the castle. He's the royal taster.'

'A pleasure to meet you,' said Markkus.

Tabitha's mother gave Markkus a small, undecided curtsey and a confused smile, and looked to her daughter.

'You didn't tell me you were bringing a guest home tonight.' She raised an eyebrow at Tabitha. Oh no. Tabitha gave her mother a small gesture to try and stop her. 'It's wonderful to meet you Markkus. Although I'm afraid Tabitha is very quiet about those she works with. I didn't catch your family name?'

'Kern. Markkus Kern.'

'Kern.' Milly frowned but only showed it for a second before she smiled politely at Markkus. 'Have I heard that name before?'

Markkus looked to Tabitha.

'He was a commander in the Great War,' Tabitha said, meeting Markkus's eye.

'A commander!' Milly breathed, satisfied. Tabitha chewed on her lower lip. She needed to stop this. Her mother was only confusing things further and yet she felt a sense of joy at her mother's acceptance.

'Yes. Mrs Dunn, I'm afraid this isn't a social visit.'

Milly's smile faded and she looked at Tabitha. Tabitha opened her mouth, now was the time to tell her mother everything. Milly and Markkus watched her but no words came. She closed her mouth.

'Maybe we should sit down,' Markkus offered, placing his hand on the small of Tabitha's back. He removed it quickly but not before Milly had noticed.

'I apologise for the mess, I wasn't expecting company. Can I get you anything?' Milly showed Markkus to a chair. He sat, wincing.

'No, thank you.'

Tabitha's mother gave her a meaningful glance as Tabitha sat in a chair in the corner, close to the window. She peered out, hoping to see her father come strolling around the corner, whistling, hands deep in his pockets.

'Please, sit,' Markkus offered. With a slight bluster, Milly sat opposite and began wringing her hands in her lap. 'Perhaps I should start from the beginning.'

Tabitha listened but didn't turn into the room. Instead she stared out of the window watching for any sign of her father or Del, or the king's guard.

*

Del followed Venkell as the dragonslayer drew his pistol and ran out of the tavern, following the sound of the scream. Del stayed close to Venkell. Among so many of the king's guard, this man had become her lifeline. Shadow's ears where pinned back against his head and he stomped his feet. Del watched him for a moment and then pulled at Venkell's sleeve.

'This way,' she called, moving to lead the way. Venkell snatched at her arm, digging his fingers in.

'You're a prisoner,' he hissed at her. 'You will stay close to me. Don't leave my side. Once I've figured out what's happening, I'm taking you straight back to your cell. Lord Gerard will hear of this, mark my words.'

Del said nothing. Venkell led her down the road at a run. Del slowed and stopped at a door leading into a tall town house, holding her breath to listen. Venkell, realising she had stopped, turned back to her. She gestured towards the house. There came a scream followed by raised voices. Del stepped back, keeping her head down, to allow the armed Venkell to take the lead. Venkell kicked at the door which shook but didn't open. He kicked it again.

'I can help, you know.'

'I don't need your help.'

'Nevertheless.' She took a step back and kicked at the door. Relenting, Venkell grunted. They both took a step back, kicking simultaneously. The wooden door swung open with a loud crack. Venkell held up his pistol and advanced into the house. Del followed, looking around for a weapon. Another cry, weaker this time. Venkell and Del ran through the empty house and out into the backyard.

There he was. At least, Del assumed it was him. It was hard to tell as the afternoons light began to fade. He wore a long, old, brown coat which flapped in the breeze as three of the king's guard held him. There was a distinct look of Tabitha about him. Blood splattered his face and down his front, and his eye was beginning to swell. Del clenched her jaw and frowned, her hands balling into fists. She opened her mouth to speak but remembered she had no authority. She turned to Venkell who ignored her.

'What's going on here?' he asked. He lowered his pistol and glared at each of the guards in turn.

'Royal business, sir. Nothing to worry yourself about.'

'Royal business? It looks like you're beating a man. Is that royal business?'

'I suggest you leave, sir.' One of the guards approached them.

'I am a dragonslayer.' Venkell's voice was getting lower and forceful. Del smiled, maybe she had misjudged him.

'This isn't dragonslayer business,' the guard replied gruffly.

'Well, it is now.'

'Why does the king want him?' Del asked. The guard looked at her, narrowing his eyes as if trying to work out why she seemed familiar, but he made no response. He nodded to his colleagues. They hefted Erik up and dragged him towards a back gate. 'Where are you taking him?' Del made to follow but Venkell held her back.

'No. You're coming with me. Whatever they're after, they've got it. Come on.'

Del glared at Venkell. He was a strange one, she just couldn't make him out.

'It doesn't bother you that they were beating him?'

'I'm sure they do it quite often when I can't hear.'

'That doesn't make it right. What about that man's family?'

'What about them?'

'Venkell, they're taking him to the king. Right now. What do you think will happen to him?'

'They'll stick him in prison, which is where you should be.'

'No. They won't. He'll disappear, just like all the others. Never to be heard of again.' Del paused to let this sink in. 'I know this man's daughter. I told her I'd find him.'

'You did find him.' Venkell sounded uncertain.

'I can't go back to her and tell her he's dead.'

'You won't. He won't be dead and you'll be in prison. Come on.' He grabbed Del's sleeve.

'Please don't make me fight you. I have to get him back. Then I'll go back to my cell. My word on my honour.'

'Your honour?' Venkell laughed and spat onto the ground. 'Your honour means nothing. You've committed treason and turned rogue. I thank you for helping us with that dragon, but I don't believe for a moment that was your first dragon kill since you were kicked out of this city. What gave you that right? You knew the law as well as any of us, but you think you're above it. Swanning around, playing with that farm animal of yours. Piss on your honour, Del Thorburn. You made a mockery of us. You're going nowhere but your cell.'

The words stung, so Del didn't dwell on them. The thought of Erik getting dragged closer to the castle with every wasted minute was too much to bear. She pushed Venkell with enough force to unbalance him. Venkell fell backwards, landing heavy on his back. Del placed her foot on his wrist and pressed down until he released his pistol.

'What are you doing?'

'Taking your weapons,' said Del, reaching down for Venkell's sword. He grabbed her shirt and yanked to the side, pulling her over. She tumbled onto the floor. Venkell made it to his feet, drew his sword and pointed it at Del. Del scrambled up and aimed Venkell and Strangle's pistols.

'I don't need the sword and I'm wasting time.'

As Venkell opened his mouth, Del darted back into the house. Slamming doors behind her, she flew out of the front door. She ran full speed, feet pounding and twisting painfully on the cobbles. Reaching Shadow, she undid his tether in one movement, swinging up onto his back. He pulled his head up and snorted, more annoyed than shocked. Nothing Del did shocked him much anymore. Del urged him on and he broke into a canter, his hooves clattering as Del pushed him faster towards the castle.

*

'So, the king has been eating people and you found out about this and tried to poison him, and your father went to save you and now he's in danger?'

Tabitha bit her bottom lip and nodded.

'You poisoned the king?' Milly repeated. 'Why, Tabitha? You had such a bright future.'

'Mum, I mop floors. All day, every day. I clean windows and polish brass and get shouted at by the chefs and made to carry huge bowls of soup. People who start off where I am end up bossing people like me about. It's not a bright future.'

'You were supposed to meet someone,' her mother murmured, tears filling her eyes. Tabitha felt burning tears of her own and forced them back. She moved over to her mother and embraced her. Markkus sat back awkwardly.

'The only boys I've met are kitchen staff, or stable staff. They all boss me around and get me into trouble.'

'That just means they like you.' Milly dismissed her daughter's complaint with a flick of her wrist.

'Actually, that's true. Boys can be mean to girls they like,' Markkus said. He shrugged as Tabitha looked at him. 'Don't ask me why.'

'Anyway, not those boys. You were supposed to meet someone…noble.'

'I'm invisible to them,' Tabitha told her mother. She sat on the floor next to Milly and curled her feet up beneath her, trying to ignore Markkus. Her mother looked up at him.

'Is my husband going to die?'

Tabitha stared hard at the floor, wondering why she had set all of this in motion. She could feel Markkus's eyes on her and looked up, meeting his gaze. He flinched away as if guilty.

'Del is looking for him,' Markkus told Milly. 'If she finds him before the king then he will live.' What if she doesn't? Tabitha couldn't bring herself to ask the question. She felt sick and empty. This was her fault. Her father could be dead right now and it would be her fault. How could she have been so stupid? She stood clumsily.

'Tabitha? Are you all right?' Markkus stood with some effort and held his arms out towards her but she waved her hand at him. She rushed out into the back yard, making it outside before her body doubled over and her stomach emptied its meagre contents.

Markkus stood looking in the direction Tabitha had disappeared, concern etched into his face. Tabitha's mother stroked a frayed thread on her apron, glancing up at Markkus.

'Are you married, Mr Kern?' she asked, her voice flat. Shocked, Markkus looked down at her.

'No.'

'You are a lot older than my daughter.'

Markkus couldn't deny it. He remained silent, struggling to find words in response. 'But you seem to care for her.'

'I do.' He looked back to the door, listening to the soft sounds of Tabitha retching.

'As a father would his daughter?'

Markkus reeled and searched Milly's eyes. The answer almost left his mouth before he had time to think but now was not the time for rash responses. Neither was it the time for this conversation. She was coming to terms with the news of her husband. She looked at him, appraising him. But behind the gaze he could see her subconscious working through what they had told her. He considered lying to her, trying to work out what answer she wanted to hear.

After a long pause, he said, 'No.' The faintest hint of a smile touched her lips and then vanished. Markkus wasn't sure what to make of it. He was breathing hard, his skin prickling as if with heat, but he didn't regret his answer. He didn't know what he had expected. Perhaps for Milly to shout at him, to scream and throw him from the house. Instead, she leaned back in her chair and played with the frayed thread on her apron.

'When will I know about my husband?' she murmured. 'When will I know?'

Markkus relaxed and crouched in front of her.

Tabitha appeared back at the door, her eyes watery, wiping at her mouth. Markkus looked away from her, resisting the urge to take her in his arms. Instead he looked up at Milly's distant eyes.

'Soon,' he soothed. 'Del will have found him.' Oh please, he thought, let Del have found him.

Eighteen

Del sneaked into the castle, pushing thoughts of Shadow left tied outside out of her mind. She had to take the long way and so she ran. Taking no care in hiding the sound of her echoing footsteps, she ran flat out into the wide corridor towards the king's chambers. It was a guess. The king was just as likely to be in his throne room or even the gardens, but every kill Del knew of had occurred in his chambers. When she reached the large double doors, she slowed and eyed the two guards stood on either side. She didn't recognise either of them. For a fleeting moment she wondered how many of the guards from two years before were still in post, or still alive. One guard lowered his bayonet and aimed it at her.

'Where's the king?' Del asked as she fought for breath. The guards seemed uncertain, turning to look at one another. 'Oh for crying out loud, is he in there?' A guard opened his mouth to speak. 'Yes? Is that a yes?' The guard closed his mouth.

A scream forced its way through the gaps in the doors and echoed around the corridor.

'That's a yes, isn't it,' Del mumbled, pointing her pistols at the guard aiming his bayonet. 'Move.'

'You can't go in there,' he said, although his voice didn't carry any conviction.

'Move, or I will shoot you.'

The guard hesitated and then lowered his bayonet.

'What're you doin'? Shoot her,' the other guard urged.

'You do it.'

Del glared at both of them.

'I don't have time for this.' She stepped towards the double doors.

'Guards!' King Rupert's voice boomed just as Del reached out to open the doors. A guard pushed her out of the way and popped his head around the door. The other guard grabbed Del's arms and pinned them behind her back. Del strained to hear the king's words. 'Fetch the doctor,' Rupert ordered with a smack of his lips. Bile rose in Del's throat.

'Okay, all right, okay.' She shrugged out of the guard's grip as the door shut and one guard sent a messenger to the doctor. 'I'll go. Fine.' She made a show of straightening her shirt.

'I'll escort you out.' The guard gave a defiant nod.

'No, no. I know the way,' Del said.

'No, no. I'll show you out.' The guard held her arm and led her down the corridor. Del mumbled something. 'What was that?'

'Nothing. Just don't know why everyone wants to put up a fight today.'

'Everyone? Been drinkin' have we?'

Del shook her head and slowed her pace as they reached the corner. The guard began to drag her. 'Come on. Ain't got all day.'

'Then I wouldn't want to keep you.' Del gave him one last chance.

'It's my job, miss.'

Once round the corner Del threw all her weight forward and then sideways, forcing the guard to crash against the wall. Shaken, he let go of her and she smashed her elbow into his head. The man crumpled onto the floor. 'Sorry,' she whispered. She peered around the corner as the castle's doctor and three young men entered the king's chambers from the opposite corridor. She moved back towards the doors.

'Hey.' The remaining guard lowered his bayonet. Del aimed a pistol at his groin.

'Don't make me do to you what I did to your friend.'

The guard lowered his weapon.

'I just want to see what's going on, that's all. Are you going to let me?' The guard looked down at the pistol and nodded. 'Good.' Pistol still aimed at the guard's delicate area, Del peered around the door. The doctor had his back to her but she recognised him as Rotterdam, the same royal doctor who had served during the Great War. He was crouching, studying something on the ground. King Rupert mused happily to himself, scratching a claw through the thick puddle of blood on the tiled floor next to the doctor and licking it clean. Erik's head and chest were visible. His breathing was shallow and his eyes closed.

'I want him kept alive.'

'Your Grace, he has lost a lot of blood.'

'Then you must fix it,' Rupert said matter-of-factly.

The doctor stood and bowed, making the rest of Erik's body visible. Del pulled herself away from the door and fought the urge to vomit, gripping her stomach and gulping in air. The guard watched her, alarmed that she might be out of control but still had the pistol well aimed.

'What is it?' he asked, attempting to move out of the way of her firearm. Del spat a foul taste onto the floor and wiped her mouth on her sleeve.

'Don't move,' she whispered, her voice trembling. Her tone made the guard rip his attention away from the pistol.

'What is it?' he repeated.

'His legs.' Del felt the tears burning her eyes. 'He's ripped his legs off.'

'The king has no legs?'

'He's ripped his legs off.' Del didn't know what to do, her mind span and with it her stomach, swirling and tipping one way and then the other. The guard said nothing, at least Del didn't hear anything. As she fought against her body's reaction, the door opened in her face. She stayed behind, trying hard to listen to any words spoken.

Doctor Rotterdam and his three colleagues emerged, carrying Erik between them. The guard caught sight of Erik's shortened body and the blood left behind, and his skin turned bright white.

'What was that? Why?' he muttered, bewildered. Del watched as the doctor's team carried Erik down the corridor and round the corner.

'Guard?' The king's voice sounded through the open doors.

'No. Don't go in there,' Del whispered, pushing the door shut while keeping out of sight. She gestured for the guard to close the remaining door. 'If you go inside, he will kill you. Close the door and run. Run home. Now. Your friend is just round the corner. He's fine. Take him with you.'

Del didn't wait for a response. Still shaking, her knees wobbling, she started after the royal doctor and Erik.

*

It was getting dark. Tabitha looked out the window, her cheeks stained with tears, sipping at a cup of water that Markkus had brought her. Her mother hadn't moved, she stared down at her lap. Markkus paced. Tabitha wasn't sure which was worse.

'Please,' she said finally. 'Please, stop it.'

'She should-' Markkus stopped himself and sat in a chair, wincing, a hand pressed against his ribs. She should be back by now, Tabitha finished silently. She stared hard down the road, willing for Del or her father to materialise. A man walked around the corner and Tabitha's heart leapt. She slumped when it turned out to be the man who lit the lamps. He stopped at each lamp, touching his torch to them and walked whistling past their house.

'I shouldn't have sent you there,' Tabitha's mother whispered, almost inaudible. 'I should have let you work in a tavern. This wouldn't have happened if you'd gone to work in the tavern.'

Tabitha and Markkus exchanged a look.

'It isn't anyone's fault,' Markkus told them. Milly shook her head.

'I don't care if you marry a wealthy man,' she choked, her chin creasing as the sobs started. 'I just want you to be happy. I just wanted you to have a better life.' She began to cry and Tabitha moved over, wrapping her arms tight around her mother.

'I know,' she soothed, kissing her mother's cheek. 'Please. It's not your fault.' It's mine, she thought.

*

Del entered the empty royal infirmary. Like the prison, it was a building off to the side of the main keep. She walked along the long wall lined with beds to the end of the hall where large double doors led to the surgery. She pushed through the doors unnoticed. The ceiling was high enough to allow a medium sized dragon to walk though. White washed walls and metal instruments sparkled in the light from so many lamps. The windows were useless and so dirty that Del could barely see the glow of street lamps through them. The doctor and his juniors were working on Erik who lay on a narrow wooden table. A junior was feeling Erik's pulse at his wrist while the other two bustled about him. The doctor was looking at the space where Erik's legs should have been. A junior placed bandages down and another brought an iron rod. The doctor turned as Del moved in closer and she stopped, her stomach feeling as if it would come up her throat.

'Please,' she murmured. 'Please, don't stop. Save him.'

The doctor turned back to his patient, clicking his tongue in thought.

'Heat it up.'

The junior disappeared with the iron.

'How are you, Del?'

'I've been better.' Del stepped closer to Doctor Rotterdam, a man she had known a little during her career. He had a shock of grey hair and tired, wise eyes. His hands were old and wrinkled but moved quickly with an expert touch. The corners of his mouth pulled down from his constant frowning. She wondered how many times he had seen this happen.

'We'd heard you were back. Busy day for you tomorrow, isn't it? I wouldn't have thought you'd be walking around the castle.'

'This man's daughter asked me to look for him.'

'I see. Well, it isn't looking good.'

'Can you save him?'

'We can but try.'

'You've known all this time, haven't you? Does it

sit well with you, doctor? What the king does.'

'Of course not.'

'Then why are you here?'

Rotterdam sighed and sagged.

'Do you want this man to live?'

'Yes.'

'That's why I'm here.'

His junior reappeared with the iron, now red hot.

'Hold him,' the doctor said. 'We may need your help too, as you're here dragonslayer.'

Del rolled up her sleeves.

'What are you doing?'

'The wounds must be cauterised before he bleeds out. I've numbed his pain but he'll still feel it and then there's the smell. Help to hold him down.'

Del blew out her cheeks and moved to Erik's side, putting her arms across his chest. He was conscious, just, and mumbling something under his breath. She strained to make out the words but his voice slurred.

'It's the pain medication,' a junior told her, approaching from the other side and leaning across Erik's chest. 'You'll have to use all your strength and weight.'

Del nodded and fought the temptation to look back at the doctor, to the bloody holes in Erik's torso and the glowing red iron.

'Here we go,' said Rotterdam. Del leaned all her weight onto Erik, grasping his shirt in her fists. There was a hissing noise and Erik gasped, wide-eyed and with an almighty cry he tried to sit up. The doctor and juniors talked quickly to one another but Del heard none of them. She buried her head in Erik's chest as she fought to keep him still and block out his screams. The stench of burning flesh crept to her nose and made her eyes water. It felt like hours passed as the tears trickled down her cheeks and dampened Erik's clothing. Her muscles ached and strained from the effort of keeping him still.

Erik began to calm. His breath coming out in short, fast whimpers. Del eased herself up and risked looking at his face. His eyes closed and his head fell to the side.

'He's fainted. It's good, it'll make the rest easy. We have to be quick.'

Del straightened and hastily brushed the tears and snot from her face.

'Look, I'm not supposed to be here.'

'You don't say,' Rotterdam muttered, brandishing the iron onto the other hole in Erik's torso. Del watched in shock. All that agony and torment, all those screams and the stench, just for the one leg. She thanked the gods that Erik had passed out.

'But I can't let the king keep this man.'

'The king has authority over us all. I'm sure this man did something bad enough to justify his suffering.'

'His only crime was to save Markkus Kern's life. Just like you did once. He thought his daughter was in trouble. Is that enough to earn having his legs ripped off? To be kept alive to suffer more in place of Markkus?'

Rotterdam glanced up at Del.

'That may as well be, but I serve my king.' He placed the freshly heated iron rod onto Erik's other wound. It sizzled and the stench in the room grew worse. Erik murmured, fitfully turning his head.

'To what end? Let me take this man. I'll take him to his family and they can leave here. The blame doesn't have to fall on you.'

'This man is no fit state to go anywhere.'

'That won't stop the king having him summoned back to rip something else off,' Del murmured, in case

Erik could hear. 'Please. You can help to stop this madness.'

'I remember why you were exiled, you know. I remember the things you said, the trouble you caused.'

'At least I acted, at least I tried to do something. It may not have got me far, but I did what I could at the time.'

'And now you're back.' Rotterdam raised an eyebrow at Del as he gave the iron rod to a junior. 'Now you're back and in the castle despite your public execution being tomorrow?'

Del bristled.

'I'm sure the king has more in store for me. This poor man is just a game to him.'

'Yes, he'll be planning something much worse for you.'

'What does he have on you?' Del asked. The doctor looked away. 'On all of you? Did he tell you these jobs would keep your families safe? Is that it?' Rotterdam didn't respond. He took a prepared solution from another junior and began to clean the blood from around Erik's wounds. 'You're doing such a good job of keeping him alive, doctor. Why not make sure he stays alive long after you've treated him?'

'Does the dragonslayer have a plan?' Rotterdam mused.

'Yes.'

'I won't ask what it is.'

'I wouldn't tell you if you did. You don't need to know. All you do need know is that if you give this man over to me that you will live long into old age.'

Rotterdam smiled and held up a wrinkly hand.

'I already have, young lady. What else can you offer me?'

Del sucked in air through her teeth.

'That your families will be safe and that you won't end up like poor Erik. There'll be no good doctor to stitch you back together.'

The doctor hesitated, his eyes glazing. He plopped the dirtied gauze into the tray of solution and passed it back to the junior.

'Very good. When I am done, you may take him. I am not responsible for whether he lives or dies when he leaves my surgery, that onus will lie with you. And if you fail in your plan, if the king learns that I had a part to play in this, then I will ensure that you do suffer that fate worse than death. You think the king can be cruel? He doesn't have the equipment that I do.'

Del bit her lip and nodded.

'Understood. Thank you.'

Rotterdam moved to Erik's head and lifted his eyelids in turn, gazing at his eyes. Placing fingers on Erik's wrist, he cocked his head to the side.

'You'll have to wait until I'm finished and he will need strict medications. He's suffering from shock and that could kill him.'

'Just tell me what he needs.'

Nineteen

Tabitha's eyes were beginning to droop. She hadn't moved from the window but the lamps shed little light and it was now too dark to see the road. The last person to walk past had been over an hour ago. She watched a city fox trot down the road towards the city centre, no doubt to the butchers to raid the bins for scraps.

She must have fallen asleep because she hadn't seen anyone approach when there was a loud and hurried knock on the door. Tabitha leapt to her feet before her eyes were open. Markkus stood, holding the back of his chair to steady himself, and rubbed his eyes. Milly didn't seem to hear, still stroking the frayed thread on her apron, staring at nothing. Tabitha, trying to ignore her stiff legs, made her way to the door, glancing back to Markkus as he followed.

'Do you think it's...' she trailed off.

Markkus took a deep breath and reached past Tabitha to open the door. Del and a grey haired man stood outside in the darkness, holding Erik between them. Shadow stood in the road. Tabitha looked to the little horse while her mind processed the sight of her father. The gap between his torso and the floor, the pale colour of his skin, the sheen of sweat, the half open eyes. Her mind seemed to shut down, incapable of thought, and with it went her strength. Without a word, she fell to her knees.

Markkus stared at the space where Erik's legs should have been. His own missing lower leg throbbed at the sight. He felt Tabitha fall beside him. Instinctively, his hand moved out to her but only brushed against her hair.

'What happened?' he murmured.

'We need to lay him down,' Doctor Rotterdam replied. Markkus moved forward then hesitated, unsure whether to replace the old man or the woman. He moved over to Doctor Rotterdam, knowing exactly what kind of reception Del would give him. Rotterdam stepped aside and traded positions with Markkus, allowing him to take his share of Erik's weight. The doctor helped Tabitha to her feet.

'Remember, he needs a lot of rest and I suggest you move him as far away from this city as possible.'

'Don't worry. That won't be a problem,' said Del. As Rotterdam left, Tabitha led the way into the house and to her parent's room where Markkus and Del lay Erik on the bed. He mumbled something before slipping back into unconsciousness.

'What happened?' Markkus turned to Del as Tabitha fussed over her father's pillows.

'The king found him before I did.' Del placed a hand on Tabitha's shoulder. 'I'm so sorry. I know nothing will make this right but the king will pay for what he's done.'

Tabitha didn't appear to hear her. She stroked the sheets covering her father.

'She's in shock,' Markkus whispered to Del.

'She's not the only one,' Del murmured. 'Rotterdam gave me instructions. What to do to keep him settled.' She thrust her hand into a pocket, 'And pain medication.'

'They need to leave the city,' Markkus suggested.

'No, they don't. They just need to stay safe until I can do what needs to be done. If I don't succeed, that's when you need to get them out. Quick.'

Markkus agreed, crossing his arms and watching Tabitha as she looked over her father's sleeping, broken body. Her cheeks were wet although he couldn't see any tears. He dug his nails into his arms, fighting the conflicting emotions building. Del glanced out of the window at the night sky. 'I should be getting back. They must be roaming the streets looking for me by now. I'll write down the doctor's orders. Can you stay with them?'

Markkus nodded without hesitation. Leaving for the night hadn't crossed his mind, it was unthinkable. Del squeezed his arm in gratitude. She rubbed Tabitha's shoulder as she passed.

'He'll be ok,' Del murmured to her. 'He can still live a good life.' Tabitha gave a subtle shudder. As Del left, Markkus tried to shake off the feeling of helplessness that she had left behind. Del had tried and failed, now it was his turn. He took a deep breath, turning his attention back to Tabitha. He expected her to look younger but instead she seemed taller, older, her features darkened, her whole body trembling.

'She's right, you know,' he said, moving close to her but feeling unable to touch her the way Del had. Tabitha kept her eyes fixed on her father, her chest heaving with each breath. 'He will be all right.'

Tabitha shook her head, unable to speak. 'Doctor Rotterdam fixed me up too, and I made a full recovery. I'll help him, Tabitha. I'm here, whatever you need.' Tabitha flinched as his fingertips brushed against her shoulder and he withdrew sharply. She looked up at him, her brown eyes shimmering with unspent tears, her lips shivering. She nodded, her face crumpling as the tears began to fall, and moved into Markkus's arms. Markkus held her, her face against his chest, his nose and mouth in her hair. He closed his eyes and breathed her in, silently urging her to stop shaking, to stop crying.

They stayed like that for a few moments, as Tabitha failed to hold back the sobs, her fingers grasping at Markkus's clothes, her tears soaking through his shirt. He didn't know what else to say or do. More than anything, he wanted to march to the castle and kill the king but he didn't want to leave Tabitha. Alarmed, he realised he didn't want to let her go. Immediately, he dropped his arms. Seemingly unaware, she stepped back and wiped the tears from her cheeks and eyes. Sniffing, she looked back to her father.

Markkus tore his gaze from her and back to Erik. Her mother was still in the kitchen, he thought, still worrying at her apron.

'Tabitha. I know this is a shock but your mother needs to know. She's only in the next room. Would you like me to tell her?'

Tabitha focused on Markkus and took a deep breath. There was a wet stain on his shirt but she couldn't feel embarrassment for it. Her body was numb, her mind and thoughts were too chaotic. Even the embrace, which had immediately given some degree of comfort, had felt distant. She could still feel the pressure of his large hands on her back and waist, as if they had left imprints. It didn't feel like she had imagined, like she wanted it to. King Rupert had taken that away from her, just as he had taken her father's legs. Her mind swam with thoughts of blame and anger, but she couldn't put them together into anything coherent.

Markkus was right. Her mother needed to know, she

was only in the next room. It was Tabitha's responsibility to inform her mother. This was her fault. She had put Markkus and her family in danger. She was the reason her father was teetering on the edge of death. The reason that an assassin was trying kill Markkus. So it stood to reason that it was also her responsibility to find the solution.

'No,' she said, barely audible. 'No, I should tell her.' She walked into the next room, unaware of her legs moving. Markkus followed.

Milly sat in her chair staring, unblinking, down at her hands in her lap. Tabitha crouched in front of her and took hold of her hands.

'Mum?' Her mother stirred and met her eyes. 'Mum, dad's home.'

'He is?' Her mother brightened.

'Yes, mum. But something's happened.'

'He's alive?'

'Yes, mum. But…' Tabitha struggled. How could she put this into words when she couldn't bring herself to think about it. 'But.' She looked up at Markkus. He pulled up a chair and sat opposite Milly, leaning towards her.

'Something has happened to your husband, Mrs Dunn,' he started. 'Unfortunately, the guards took him to the king before my friend could find him. I'm afraid the king…well. Your husband is fine but I'm afraid he won't be able to walk again.'

Milly lifted her eyes to Markkus.

'What?'

Tabitha wanted to speak but tears spilled down her cheeks as she opened her mouth. Her throat closing with a choking tightness.

'Your husband has lost both of his legs,' Markkus told her in a soft voice. Milly's lower lip quivered.

'What?'

*

No one seemed to notice Del as she made her way back to the Dragonslayer Academy. She spent too long settling Shadow, burying her face in his neck as he pulled at his hay. The events of that night replayed in her mind. Searching for Erik, meeting Venkell, riding hard to the castle. The sight of Erik's broken body, of the blood, the stench of his cooking flesh. Of Tabitha's expression as her world fell apart. She dissected the memories as she removed Shadow's bridle. That's when it dawned on her that this would be the last time she would see her plucky little horse. Refusing to cry, Del pushed all thoughts of the king, Erik and Tabitha from her mind. She spoke to Shadow as she took her time brushing him down.

'Do you remember when we first met?' she asked, smiling as she ran the brush over his belly. 'You were so thin. I could see your ribs and your spine. You looked so dejected. Now look at you.' She ran her hand over his round stomach, counting his invisible ribs beneath her fingers. 'You are the best horse I ever had,' she whispered to him, stroking his cheek. 'You are the bravest, most sensible, warmest horse. Any dragonslayer should be proud to ride you.' Her nose burned as she held back the tears. 'I don't know what will become of you,' she told him. 'I don't know who will care for you. I don't have any control over that. But I hope, with every part of me, that you end up with someone who loves you as much as I do. Who appreciates you as much as I do. Who will keep you fed and happy.' Del pushed her face into his mane. 'I'm sorry I brought you here, little country horse.' He would probably never leave the city if she failed. She wrapped her arms around his neck. 'I will come back for you,' she told him. 'This isn't goodbye. Not really. I will be back.' Her chest ached at the thought of never seeing him again. He snuffled at her, pulling at her shirt and lifting his lips to her. She smiled and rubbed his nose, kissing it before rubbing his small ears the way she had done every day for two years.

Some drunken dragonslayer, returning from a night in a tavern, had left the door unlocked. Del slipped in and made her way down the stairs to her cell. Stopping at the open cell door, she looked unseeing at the pile of straw on the ground, reliving the night again.

Could she have gotten there faster? Could she have stopped the king? Every way Del looked at it, she kept arriving at the same answers. She didn't want to believe it, but she knew she had pushed Shadow hard, she had run fast and still she had been too late.

There was a bitter taste in her mouth, making her lips curl. Lifting up one hand, she watched her fingers tremble as her body began to relax and shock took over.

For the first time in a long time, she was becoming overwhelmed. Real doubt surfaced, the reality hitting her like a wall. She clenched her eyes shut, forcing back the tears, fighting to keep control.

'You came back.'

Del span round to face Lord Gerard, sat on a chair opposite her cell door. How long had he been there? How much she had given away?

'Of course,' she said warily.

'I wasn't sure if you would. Did you find what you were looking for?'

'Yes.'

'Making final preparations for tomorrow?'

'Just a little errand to find someone.' She gave a slow smile, her composure regained, as Gerard's grin faltered.

'Who?'

'Someone I had to make peace with.' Del waved away the questions and made her way into her cell. She swung the door closed on herself.

'And you came back?'

'Of course.'

'Why not run?'

'Why do you think?' Del sat cross-legged on the straw and stared up at Gerard.

'The king will crush you, should you try anything,' he murmured.

'Yes. As far as I'm aware it is illegal for a dragon to crush a human. But then, as the Head of the Dragonslayer Order, I'm sure you're already aware of that. What will happen when our king crushes me, my Lord? Will you avenge me?'

'Maybe Captain Ferrer will.'

Del stiffened.

'I know she wants to help you, any fool can see that. Do you really think she'll be safe? Even after you die?'

'What have you done to her?'

'Me? Oh, I won't do anything. Not without orders from my king. And then there's your old pal Commander Kern. Another soul you've brought into this wretched affair.'

Del broke eye contact and stared hard at the floor.

'I'm sorry that it has come to this,' came Gerard's softened voice. Del looked back up and saw that he meant it.

'It's not too late,' she told him. 'You could still stop this.'

Gerard shook his head and then paused, as if giving

it serious consideration.

'No. No.' He seemed to remember himself. 'We have witnesses that claim you slew a dragon. You have turned rogue. The punishment is death.'

'That's not what I meant,' Del murmured. 'You know that.'

'That's all there is to it.' Although he was no longer talking to Del.

'This is your chance, my Lord,' Del told him. 'Your chance to show the city who you really are. To do the right thing. Please.'

Gerard grimaced as if there were a foul smell in the air, and then he sneered.

'I never thought you one for desperate ploys,' he said, holding his head up. He walked up the stairs, slamming the door shut and leaving Del in an unlocked cell and darkness. For a moment she watched the empty space he had occupied, gritting her teeth. She lay back on the straw and curled up. Her hands trembled in the little light coming through the window. Del finally relaxed, letting the sobs out. Closing her eyes, she wondered when Rupert would realise his latest toy had disappeared.

*

Tabitha and Markkus watched over Erik as he slept. Markkus checked his wounds and Tabitha held his hand, monitoring his temperature. She remained close to her mother who had fallen asleep curled up on the bed like a child, cuddled up to her husband. Markkus sat in a chair at the foot of the bed, his legs stretched out in front of him, arms crossed. His chin dropped to rest on his chest and soon a soft snore emerged. Tabitha sat on the edge of her parent's bed and watched him.

This man for whom she had felt awe, this man who confused her feelings. Now she looked at him and saw the man who protected her, the man who stayed behind to help her family. Tabitha watched Markkus drift off to sleep with a growing warmth of love and affection. The memory of King Rupert holding Markkus burned in her. She looked down at the flat space where her father's legs should have been beneath the sheets. Unable to stay still any longer, she stood and moved through the dark house to her own bedroom. It was cold and she shivered as she looked around. No, she thought, this wouldn't do.

She moved back to the kitchen and found a small sharp knife. She had left her stolen butcher knife in the king's chambers. How could she have been so stupid, she thought, fresh tears pricking her sore, tired eyes. To think that a butcher knife would do any good against a dragon king. The most it had done was serve as a distraction for them to escape. She was thankful for that but now she needed something more. Del said that she would sort the problem but Tabitha couldn't help but think she would get there too late. How could Del sit in her cell when she could kill the king whenever she liked? Just as she had walked into the castle and found her father, ruined and near death. Del had been too late for him. Tabitha couldn't afford to let her make the same mistake twice.

She strode out of the house, slamming the door shut behind her without thinking, waking Markkus with a jolt.

Twenty

The sun peaked over the horizon down by the docks as Andra walked through the stable block. She stopped at the door to her horse's stable and watched the chestnut, clucking her tongue. The horse moved over and poked her large dark red nose into Andra's hands, hoping for a treat. She munched on the carrot she found there as Andra rubbed her ears.

'She came back then.'

'What?' Andra ran a hand down her mare's neck and glanced at Venkell.

'Del. She came back.'

'Yes. I heard Lord Gerard was waiting for her at the cells.'

'And that's it?'

'What more is there? She's being executed today.'

Venkell reached out to stroke the horse's neck.

'You don't sound upset. You like her, don't you?'

'I never thought I'd get to meet her,' murmured Andra.

'So now you can take her down from that pedestal.' Venkell moved past Andra to check on his own horse. Andra glared at his back.

'Why did you become a dragonslayer, Ven?'

Venkell shrugged.

'My father was one. I wanted to join the army, like my grandfather, but he wouldn't hear of it.'

Andra shared a look with her mare. That explained a

lot.

'You're a good captain.' Venkell was watching her out of the corner of his eye as he moved back to her side. Andra tried to ignore it, rubbing her horse's nose.

'Del's the reason I joined, you know. I used to watch her, in my father's shop, on parade. I'd stand in the crowds and listen to the stories.'

'You're twice the dragonslayer she is,' Venkell told her, sidling closer. Andra stiffened and moved away.

'No I'm not. But one day I hope to be close to what she is.'

'Are you going to the execution?'

'Maybe. Are you?'

Venkell scoured Andra with his eyes. He made her feel naked. She turned her back to him, unable to decide if she liked it or not.

'Haven't decided yet. I hope you're not planning anything stupid.' Venkell stepped closer, his breath on her bare neck, sending shivers through her. She closed her eyes for a moment before facing him.

'Like what?'

'Like helping Del. I do hope you haven't been listening to her. She'll get you into trouble, Andra.'

'Don't you ever have doubts?'

Venkell breathed her in, not responding. 'About our orders? About the king?'

Venkell hesitated.

'Sometimes.'

'And?'

'It doesn't make her right. It certainly doesn't mean you should put your life in danger for her. She's not worth it, Andra. You have so much going for you, so much to give. Don't throw it away because of a childhood hero gone bad.' He gave her one last look and then moved passed her, out of the stable block and out of view.

Andra rubbed her sweating palms on her trousers and mentally shook herself. Her mare had grown bored and moved back to her hay. With a sigh Andra walked over to Shadow's stable. The little cob immediately stuck his head out and snuffled her pockets and shirt. With a laugh, Andra gave Shadow a gentle pat.

'I bet you'd help her too, if you could, wouldn't you Shadow,' she murmured, so that no one else could hear. Finding no food on Andra's person, Shadow pulled at the fabric of her sleeves between his lips.

*

During the night Tabitha had found an old sword, rusted and blunt, round the back of the Ferrer's smithy in Old Town. As dawn reached over the city, Tabitha hid in the shadows of the wynd going through people's rubbish. Unable to find anything to sharpen the blade, she sat outside the shop to wait for the blacksmith to wake. Tabitha watched the sun shine on her toes as the street began to fill with those excited by the prospect of a hanging. The skin on her face was tight from the dried tears and dirt from digging around in the bins with the foxes. There were no thoughts, only a calm silence that filled her mind. The shop door opened and a large man stood looking down at her. She squinted up at him.

'Yes?' Ferrer looked from Tabitha's swollen eyes to the rusted sword in her hand.

'How much will it cost to have this sharpened?' Tabitha asked. The blacksmith eyed the sword.

'Is that one of mine? Could have sworn I put something like that out back for smelting a couple of days ago.'

'I found it,' Tabitha answered. There was no

inflection in her voice. Ferrer's brow creased but his eyes softened. He nodded.

'What'd you want it sharpened for?'

'Protection.'

'A big sword like that? For protection?'

'He hurt my father.'

'Ah, revenge? Revenge is something best left to people with only half a mind, my girl. I suggest you forget about it and go home to your father.'

Tabitha shook her head.

'He'll die if I don't do this.'

'Right then,' Ferrer said, looking Tabitha up and down. 'In that case, we'd best get it sharpened. Come on in.'

*

Del dreamed of blood and screams. She woke with a start as a dragon's angry roar echoed through her skull, fading as she remembered where she was. Pale early morning sunshine poured through the small window of her cell. She could hear the birds singing and horse hooves clopping and cart wheels turning down the cobbled streets. She was alone. There was no plate of breakfast and no guard keeping watch. Del hugged her knees and waited, wondering how Erik was. How Tabitha was feeling. She even considered the looks that Markkus had been giving Tabitha. Anything to take her mind off what she was waiting for.

The door opened and Lord Gerard, in full uniform, walked regally down the steps.

'It's time. A little earlier than planned, although I'm sure you have nothing better to do. King Rupert requests your presence before we take you before your public.' He walked back up leaving Private Strangles behind. Del had wondered how the king would play this. It surprised her that he wished to see her before the execution. She had expected to be cut down from the gallows, barely alive, and dragged to him. Strangles opened her cell door and pulled her to her feet. The private bound her wrists in thick rope behind her back and pushed her out of the cell and towards the stairs. Del took a deep breath. Today was the day.

*

Markkus didn't feel able to leave Milly and Erik but he was restless. He had to get to the castle before Del's hanging began, but mostly he found himself worrying over Tabitha and her whereabouts. He repeated under his breath that she wouldn't be stupid enough to go back to the castle. But he didn't believe it. He paced around the small house, looking in on Erik and Milly from time to time. Husband and wife still lay on the bed asleep. Milly had woken long enough to cry a fresh wave of tears over her husband's broken body before drifting off to sleep again, her arm draped over her husband's chest.

Markkus began to gently clean Erik's wounds. The actions and smell of the medication brought back sharp memories. His missing right calf ached in response. Erik woke and gave Markkus a small smile, placing an arm around his wife and drawing her close.

'Tabitha?' he asked with a croak. Markkus held a cup of water up to Erik's lips. Erik gulped two mouthfuls.

'Tabitha's fine.'

'Where is she?' Erik blinked his heavy eyelids.

'She's...out.'

'She's okay?'

'She's fine. She won't be back for a while yet. But I have to pop out. I won't be long. Will you two be okay?'

Erik looked sideways at his sleeping wife.

'You'll come back?'

'Of course.' Markkus nodded.

Erik gave a small nod.

'Look after my daughter. They're all I have, you know.'

Markkus waited until it seemed Erik had drifted to sleep again before backing out of the room. He left, jogging as fast as his numb right thigh would carry him to his own house.

*

Ferrer offered the sparkling sword to Tabitha. It hardly resembled the weapon she had found but the shape and weight were the same.

'Now. I want you to think long and hard before you make your next move.'

'How much do I owe you for the sword?' she asked.

'No, you found this sword, it's yours.'

'What about the sharpening? And you cleaned it.' Although she suspected it was a completely different blade. The blacksmith studied her, his head to one side, and sighed before bending to look her in the eye.

'Now you listen to me,' he murmured. 'Whatever you're planning to do, however you want to take your revenge, it won't be worth it. You have your sword, you have your protection. Now go home to your family and look after your father.'

'My mother can do that.'

'And she'll need your help.' His voice was soothing. Tabitha bit the inside of her cheek hard to stop the tears that were threatening to ruin her rage. 'Go home.'

Tabitha blinked. Markkus had told her to go home. If she had listened to him, he would be dead now and her father would still be at the mercy of the king.

'Thank you,' she said.

Ferrer straightened.

'You remind me of my daughter, you know,' he mused. 'She's a dragonslayer, a captain. Bloody strong willed. She was just like you when she was young. Listen, don't tell people I go around sharpening swords for free.'

Tabitha left the shop and lifted the sword in front of her, feeling its weight. It was still heavy and she wondered how she would wield it. That was a thought for another time. Tabitha set off towards the castle, carrying her dragonslayer weapon.

*

Markkus opened the small wardrobe in his bedroom and rummaged through his belongings. Pulling out boxes and old clothes, and chucking them on the floor behind him with urgency. There, leaning against the wooden back was his old sword still in its scabbard. Next to it was an ornate silver box. Pulling both out, he lay the sword on the bed. Inside the box was a pistol and selection of bullets. He checked the pistol, feeling its weight and rubbing his thumb over a smudge left by his finger prints. It was clean, immaculate even. He loaded a bullet into the chamber and placed the pistol down. He slid the sword from the scabbard with care. The metal glinted in the morning sunshine that shone through his bedroom window. Replacing the sword, he unhooked his old commander uniform and ran his fingers down one of the sleeves. There was no time to stop and think, no time to reminisce. The more time went past, the more certain he became that Tabitha would be at the castle. His confidence in Del, a skilled dragonslayer, confronting the king was shaky at best. The idea of Tabitha in that position nauseated him. Placing his uniform on the bed, he lifted his shirt over his head, knowing he would have to be quick.

*

Lord Gerard pushed against the cushion at his back as his carriage bounced towards the castle. He hadn't been too surprised when Andra politely declined joining him in taking Del to see the king. If the women were planning something, Gerard thought the captain would need to stay close to Del. It hadn't gone past his noticing that Andra and Del had spent a considerable amount of time together, particularly in the stable block. Gerard shook his head. Del's relationship with that little farm horse was fascinating. What could have happened to her out in the wild for her to want such a creature? Not that it mattered, not after today. He wondered briefly how much Shadow would fetch.

Gerard had never doubted Del's claims about the king. He often considered, usually late at night after too many brandies, why he didn't act upon her suspicions. There was no hard evidence against the king. Gerard had not seen anything untoward himself and he was loyal to the crown. That was his excuse but he knew it wasn't his reason. He wouldn't admit his reason for never defending Del. He would let the king do what he wanted with her and then this would all be over. He did not doubt that Del would try something but he also knew that it wouldn't matter. Just one person was no match against a dragon, the whole of the king's guard and an order of dragonslayers. Whatever their skill level. No one would dare accuse the king of such things after Del was gone. Rumour would spread and fear with it. Gerard settled back and tried to act as if that would make him happy.

In the prison coach behind Lord Gerard's carriage sat Del, one knee bouncing. Did Andra know they were moving? They hadn't had much chance to speak since Del had given her a list of supplies, and Del would need her if this was to work. She closed her eyes, listening to her own strained breath. Trying not to think of Andra, or Shadow or the Dunn family and instead fighting the urge to cry and vomit.

The prison coach stopped and a guard led Del down the steps and towards the castle. She counted the thirty guards around the forecourt. Behind her she could hear the sound of a hammer against wood as her gallows were prepared. The shouts and calls of market sellers drifted on the breeze. A crowd would be gathering.

Lord Gerard walked in behind her.

'This seems an unprecedented number of guards. Should I be flattered?'

'Apparently there have been some security issues,' Gerard said. Del kept her head high, her mind spinning. Andra was nowhere in sight. She needed a backup plan. Each of the guards carried a weapon. She hoped the security level would continue as they walked up the steep pathway, into the main keep and towards the throne room.

The guard holding Del stopped her outside the throne room doors. Gerard stood by her side.

'I don't know if you are planning something,' he whispered. Del's heart thudded against her ribs. She watched Gerard, wondering if he was about to come through for her. 'But you would be dead before you could draw a weapon. Look at all these guards.'

Del scowled.

The throne room doors opened and Lord Gerard strode inside. The guard pushed Del after him. She could feel her pulse in her throat as she walked and she swallowed hard to dislodge it. Their footsteps echoed around the vast room. Rupert sat curled on his throne, the tip of his tail tapping against the floor. They stopped before him and Gerard bowed. Rupert ignored him, his glare fixed on Del.

'Leave us,' he boomed. The mass of guards filed out of the throne room, leaving only Del and Gerard standing before the king. Del watched them go. She watched their swords and pistols and bayonets leave the room and the doors close behind them. She looked up at the king who gave her a slimy smile.

'Good morning, Delilah Dragonslayer.'

'Good morning, Your Grace.' Del curtsied.

'Please excuse the number of guards. It appears there is a thief in our midst and I couldn't afford anything to go awry today.'

'Of course not, Your Grace.'

'No, I plan on enjoying myself today. I wonder.' Rupert leaned in towards Del and Gerard. 'If you had anything to do with the theft?'

'Your Grace, I've been locked in a cell since the day I re-entered the city. How could it have been me?'

Gerard glanced sideways at Del but said nothing. It would not do to show himself up before the king.

'Never mind. I still had fun.'

'As I'm sure you do with all your toys, Your Grace.'

Rupert looked down his long nose at Del.

'Lord Gerard. Leave us.'

Gerard bowed and hesitated, as if he would speak. He glanced at Del. 'I said leave us,' Rupert snarled. Del stared at Gerard. Say something, she urged, say anything. He gave her a long look and then turned and left. Rupert kept his gaze on Del as the doors closed behind Lord Gerard. Del twisted her wrists in their rope bonds. A heavy silence filled the vacuous room. The sound of her own breathing was too loud in her head and her mouth was dry. The enormity of King Rupert and being alone with him made it hard to breath.

'What to do with you,' Rupert mused, sitting back in his throne. 'My people want a public execution. You hear that? They welcome your death. But then, where is the fun for me? You have caused me so much trouble, Delilah Dragonslayer. It seems that a simple hanging is too good for you.'

'If you eat me now, your people will be upset.'

Rupert scratched at his chin with a single claw and grinned, showing off each of his pearly sharp teeth.

'Do you think that is my plan, foolish human? I know you stole my toy,' King Rupert hissed. 'I was looking forward to playing with him this morning. Imagine my disappointment to find him gone. So I shall have to play with you in his place. My people will not care of the condition you turn up to your own hanging in. They only wish to see someone die. They will watch you hang, and just before you take your last breath you shall be cut down and declared dead. Don't think that you will die a quick death, Delilah Dragonslayer. You will be dead to the people but you will survive within my infirmary. A win-win situation, don't you think?'

'Except for me.'

'Well, unfortunately for you, your opinion doesn't count.' King Rupert slid off his throne and stood tall over Del. She backed up a few paces so she could keep his teeth and his tail in her sights, twisting her wrists against the rope. 'This won't hurt a bit.' Rupert lowered his head. Del backed up and thought fast. She had to keep him talking. The longer he spoke, the more time she had.

*

Tabitha entered the castle through the staff doors at the back. She moved swiftly, avoiding any of her colleagues. Through the servant quarters, past the kitchen and into the narrow service corridors, she ran towards the king's chambers. Pressing her ear against the door, she listened for any sign of life in the rooms beyond. Silence. She eased the door open, cringing at the smallest of creaks from the hinges. The room was empty. He would be in the throne room. She continued along the service passageway. Without breaking step, she entered the main corridor and headed towards the throne room. Stunned by the presence of so many guards, her step faltered. She walked right up to the doors, daring any guard to stop her. Lord Gerard stood outside the doors at a strange angle, somewhere between listening in to the conversation inside the throne room and respectfully ignoring it. Tabitha could hear the king shouting and growling beyond the doors. She recognised Gerard, everyone knew him. A nobleman, an aristocrat, the Lord of the Fourth Corner of Drummbek and the Head of the Dragonslayer Order. Like the king, he was not known for his kindness.

'Is Del in there?' she asked. Lord Gerard looked at her in shock, looking down his nose at her small stature and large sword held in both hands. He blinked as if attempting to rid a memory from his eyes.

'And what exactly are you?' he asked. The closest guards, five or six of them, began to surround her.

'My name is Tabitha and the king tried to kill my father.' Instead of surprise at how steady her voice was, Tabitha just felt numb, as if watching the exchange from a great height.

Lord Gerard raised his eyebrows.

'Did he now? Well, you'd be a fool to try anything, but then this place is full of fools. I suggest you leave, girl.'

'I'm not leaving.'

Gerard looked Tabitha up and down.

'Go home.'

Tabitha gritted her teeth, her knuckles turning white as she gripped her sword.

'Doesn't it concern you,' a deep voice sounded from behind Tabitha. 'That the king will replace you all soon? He has been questioning his staff's loyalty recently. I should know.' They all turned, Tabitha, Gerard and all of the guards, to Markkus. He stood in a uniform of red and gold, a battle uniform. Instead of medals there were hints of mud and blood that no amount of washing could remove. In his belt were his pistol and his scabbard holding his sword. Tabitha remembered to breathe, succumbing to a wave of relief and warmth at the sight of him. There was a glint in his eye, something that called to her. It was a look learned on the battlefield. Rather than scare her, it made her want to stand beside him, knowing no harm would befall her as long as he was there. 'I am Commander Markkus Kern, the king's royal taster, and the king tried to kill me. I suggest that if you do not wish to have the same fate that you leave now.' Markkus drew his sword.

*

'Don't you want to know how I did it?' Del asked. Rupert paused.

'Did what?'

'Rescued the poor man you were mutilating. Last night.'

'Ha! It was you.'

'You ever doubted?' Del allowed herself a smile, surreptitiously pulling at her bonds.

'I don't care how you did it. You bribed the guards, you bribed the doctor. Whatever. I have a new toy now. A better toy.' Rupert licked his teeth.

'It doesn't bother you that people in your court are no longer loyal?'

'I will deal with them once I have dealt with you.'

Del shook her head.

'It's all falling apart around you and there's nothing you can do to stop it. You can't kill everyone, so how will killing me help?'

'It will make me feel better,' Rupert growled.

Del tutted.

'All falling apart and nothing you can do.' She was close to the doors now and her bonds were loosening. Hoping help was waiting behind those doors, she drew breath to keep Rupert talking. The dragon lunged forward with a growl that vibrated through her insides. One mighty claw settled on her chest and pushed her back. She landed heavily, the ropes around her wrists giving way. She instinctively reached out to break her fall but too late. Pain rang through her spine and ribs, her head banging on the floor. Rupert held her there, pinned beneath his foot, her head and legs protruding from between his claws. Her hands gripped the nearest claw, pushing at it. Del gasped for breath as Rupert loomed over her.

'Do you know what I did to him, Delilah Dragonslayer?' he snarled. Del struggled. 'Do you? I ripped his legs off. It was easy. Like pulling the wings from a fly. Your human children do that so easily. Pull limbs off a creature smaller than themselves without any consideration for the pain they feel. Why shouldn't I? Just for my own amusement, I ripped his legs off, one by one and listened to the agony. The screams and yells that didn't do what he was feeling justice. Is he still alive? If he is I doubt he will last much longer. Shock has a funny way of killing humans. You are so weak. Is it any surprise that your time is soon to come to an end?'

*

The guards left, some dropping their weapons and running, as Markkus changed his stance, ready to fight any who challenged him. Perhaps they recognised him, or maybe his words had resonated with them. Either way, there was hardly a second thought given to the decision to leave. Lord Gerard looked around the now empty space.

'A war veteran and a slip of a girl. What are you planning to do? Kill the king? Neither of you know the first thing about taking down a dragon, never mind a dragon king.'

Markkus aimed his sword at Gerard.

'How about some pointers then?'

'Not necessary.' Andra ran past Markkus, Tabitha and Gerard, and planted her ear against the doors to the throne room.

'What the hell is going on?' Gerard demanded. Andra was holding the handles to a large bag which she carefully set down.

'I'm late. That's what's going on.'

'Captain Ferrer, I will have your title for this. You'll be exiled, if you're not executed. This is treason! Stand down at once.'

Tabitha did a double take at Andra at the sound of her name.

'Del is going to be killed. Right here, right now. She was one of your best.' Andra turned on Gerard. 'Don't you care?'

'Our duty is to the king. Del has committed treason.'

'She accused the king of a true crime and has served a punishment for it.'

'And then she turned rogue,' Gerard cried with exasperation. 'Kings breath, Andra, this has to happen. It is the law.'

Andra stared Gerard in the eye. Before she could make a move, Markkus pushed her out of the way and, with a grunt, took a swing at Gerard. Lord Gerard fell back, his head hitting the floor and falling to the side. Markkus turned to Andra who stared at him with wide eyes.

'You didn't have to do that.'

'Del is in there, yes? Without a weapon? We don't have time for you two to argue.'

'No. I have her weapons.' Andra turned to the doors.

'Fine.' Markkus pushed Andra aside once more and slid through the doors.

'Markkus!' Tabitha rushed forward but Andra caught her arm.

'And who are you?' asked Andra. Tabitha ignored her, struggling against her grip.

Twenty-One

Del tilted her head back to look at Markkus from her position on the floor, beneath Rupert's claws.

'Markkus, you've returned,' Rupert purred. 'There really was no need to dress up, although I appreciate the thought.' The king shifted his weight, making Del whimper as the pressure around her ribs and stomach tightened.

'Your Grace, I would like to offer my resignation.'

'I do not accept.' King Rupert swung at Markkus with his tail. Markkus managed to dodge it somehow, but his old and fresh wounds were obvious. He stumbled, making an easy target of himself. Del pushed against Rupert's foot.

'Markkus,' she called, reaching out to him. Markkus lifted his sword and chopping neatly through the tip of Rupert's tail as it swung towards him. The king roared and sat back, freeing Del. Markkus grabbed Del's wrist and dragged her into the corridor. Andra slammed the doors shut and barred them, jamming a discarded bayonet through the handles.

'That won't hold him.' Andra turned to help Del to her feet.

'We need to create some distance,' Del said, her ribs aching and tender with each breath. 'We need a bit more time.' She glanced at Markkus and Tabitha. They were here now, so she might as well make use of them. 'Tabitha, there are service corridors around here, yes?

Too narrow for a dragon of his size if I remember correctly?'

Tabitha nodded.

'Take us to one.'

Tabitha led them at a run towards the door she had originally come through. She led them in and back towards the king's chambers and the kitchens. In the middle of the dark corridor, Del stopped them.

'Right. Did you bring it all?' she asked Andra. Andra placed her bag on the floor, crouched and opened it. Del turned to Markkus and Tabitha. 'I don't want to know why you're both here. I can guess. I don't want any of you involved. This is my fight. But it is nice to know you have my back.' She smiled at Markkus. 'Just like old times.'

'He tried to kill my father.' Tabitha's voice was small in the narrow corridor. 'I want to be a part of this.'

'And you will be, if I fail,' Del told her, looking down at Tabitha's sword. She glanced at Markkus's sword. 'But not with those weapons.'

'Dragonslayers fight with swords,' Tabitha said.

'Yes, but you don't bring a dragon down with swords. Swords alone make for a dangerous and bloody fight. A dragon can kill you before you can blink if it wants. The only reason we're still alive' - Del gestured to herself and Markkus - 'is because Rupert wants to play. We need to act fast, he won't be in the mood to play anymore.'

'So what then? If not swords.'

'Explosives.' Del smiled. Andra stood and handed her the bag and a box of matches. Del peaked inside the bag. 'Good. Thank you. How was Mackay?'

'Creepy.'

'Yes. I should have warned you about that.' There

was a crashing from the other side of the wall. 'He's looking for us. Tabitha, what is the nearest room from here?'

'The king's chambers.'

'Good, take me there. Markkus, may I borrow your sword? Then you must all promise to stay behind. Running away would be better. No one interferes. I will not risk more lives. Okay?'

Tabitha led them to the door of the king's private chambers and stopped before the steps leading up to the door. Del looked past her. She ached, every part of her hurt. Then there was the exhaustion. She could feel the last two years creeping up on her but the adrenaline kept her upright, kept her moving. Just a few more pushes, she told herself. It was nearly over.

'What can I do?' Tabitha asked.

'Honestly? Go home. Look after your parents. But if you won't, then do whatever Andra says.' Del smiled at Tabitha and squeezed her shoulder. 'You're very brave, everything you've done has been brave. But no one expects you to be a part of this fight.' Del turned away and opened the door, the light from the empty room filling the narrow, dank corridor. Del stepped inside and closed the door so that she was alone. On light feet she made her way through the first of the chambers and into the adjoining room on the right to the king's large bed. Crouching, she emptied the bag of explosives, setting them under the foot of the bed. She ran a trail of gunpowder from the explosives to the servants' door, keeping close to the line of the walls and various pieces of furniture in an attempt to keep the gunpowder hidden. She gripped the box of matches and waited.

Behind the closed servants' door were Andra, Markkus and Tabitha, listening, waiting. They wouldn't run without her, she had no doubt. The crashing and wailing of the king rumbled throughout the castle. The noise grew as the king approached and Del tried to ignore the guilty thought of anyone getting caught in his rampage. Now was the time for action and she had waited long enough to do this. She focused on the memory of the tears and anguish of those who had lost loved ones. The deaths she could have and should have prevented. Of Erik with his missing legs lying in a pool of his own thick blood, of Tabitha's reaction. That this king, this dragon, had almost killed Markkus. Del stood tall, feeling every ache of her ribs and lungs protesting, and drew Markkus's sword.

The door smashed inwards sending wooden shards and splinters across the room. Del shielded her face with her arm. When she lowered it, King Rupert stood in the doorway. There was a trail of blood behind him, leaking still from his damaged tail. Three bodies of royal guards crumpled in a heap just behind him. Use it, Del thought as she ripped her attention back to the king, use it so they didn't die for nothing.

'You're going to be late for your execution, Delilah Dragonslayer,' Rupert rumbled. His eyes flashed gold as he stormed into the room. Del ducked away from his claws and rolled towards the bed. Rupert followed her. He swung his tail and made contact with Del, hitting her in the stomach and sending her flying. She smacked into the wall on the far side, winded, dropping her sword. Rupert stomped over to her as she climbed onto all fours, struggling to regain her breath. 'I have waited so long for this.' Rupert opened his mouth wide. Del was struggling with the matches Andra had given her. She didn't want to waste them but now struck one and hoped. It caught immediately and she jammed it between two of Rupert's teeth as his jaws came to meet her. The stench of rotten flesh and blood on his breath filled her nostrils and mouth before she could roll underneath him. Rupert lifted his head in shock at the sudden burning against his gums. He scratched with a claw, trying to dislodge the match which fell to the ground, spent. Del was on her feet, bent double, and running back towards the nearest wall and line of gunpowder. Rupert stomped a curled claw in front of her. She moved to the right to avoid it and kept running. With a laugh, Rupert swiped with his claw and sent her crashing into the servants' door.

Andra, Markkus and Tabitha jumped back as the door shook.

'We have to help her,' Markkus said. 'He'll kill her.'

'Give her time. He's strong and she's alone, it was always going to be hard.'

'Hard? It's impossible. She needs help.' Markkus moved to open the door. Andra stopped him.

'Not. Yet.'

Tabitha watched and stood close to Markkus as he backed away from the door. He smelt musty, likely the uniform that had been hanging unused for so long. There was a tang of sweat and adrenaline mixed in there too and Tabitha couldn't help but draw herself closer to him.

Del fought to pick herself up before Rupert made his next move. She dug out the box of matches. There were three left, three chances to set the explosives alight. Rupert was by the bed and making his way over to her. Perhaps she was wrong, perhaps he still wanted to play.

'Why kill people? That's what I don't understand,' she tried, ignoring the pain in her legs as she tried to get them under her. 'Why eat them?'

'Because they tasted good.'

The bluntness of his response made Del's stomach churn.

'But you're a king.'

'I'm a dragon. Older than human existence. I watched you being born.'

'No you didn't. Your ancestors, maybe. But not you. You're not that much older than me.'

'And still plenty more centuries left in me. You don't even have another day left in you.' Rupert grinned, flashing his sharp teeth at her.

'Centuries ahead of you and still so much to learn. You've shamed your ancestors.'

Rupert roared and flicked his tail to Del just as she struck a match. Blood splattered up the wall as his broken tail sang through the air. He knocked Del in the head, sending her sprawling to the floor, the match extinguished and lost.

Rupert paused as there was sudden noise behind the small wooden door nearby. He often forgot that door existed. He knew the maids came and went and that they didn't use the same door as him, but still, he had never given it much thought. Now he stared at it as it shook and voices from behind became clear. A man and woman arguing, the distinct low pitch of Markkus being one of them. Rupert waited, licking his teeth and feeling the throb in the tip of his tail. The time to end this was coming. The more his tail hurt, the less he wanted to play. No, there was still time. Rupert had all the time he wanted. He was so close that not even Delilah Dragonslayer could change the course of events that would follow. The thought made him rumble and eased the pain in his poor tail.

That little door opened and Markkus stormed in. He

looked to Del and then up at Rupert.

'Markkus. You shouldn't have come back.'

Markkus didn't respond. He walked towards the king, his eyes hard. Rupert would have backed away if the man hadn't been so small. 'What do you hope to gain from this, Markkus? Hmm? Is this about Delilah Dragonslayer? Ah, the complexity of the human relationship. Tell me, why would a woman like her want an old, tired man like you?'

Tabitha nearly said something at that as she ran out behind Markkus's distraction to help Del sit up.

'You don't deserve to be our king,' Markkus growled, holding up his pistol and aiming it at Rupert's head. Rupert laughed.

'And just what are you going to do with that antique? You have no idea how to kill a dragon, do you?'

'There's always a first.'

'Yes, well, not for you. And for slicing my tail I will reserve a special punishment for you once I have finished with Delilah Dragonslayer.' Rupert glanced at Tabitha, squatting beside Del. 'And you. You must be the one who is handy with poison, hmm?' he mused. 'I'll give you something,' he told them. 'You humans have a way of surviving. For weak, insignificant creatures you have mastered longevity surprisingly well. But, like the great monsters of old, your time is coming to an end. We dragons were there at the beginning. We have seen it all. We will be there at the end. It is only a matter of time and now that time is drawing near.'

Del stiffened under Tabitha's arms.

'Now, Tabitha,' Andra hissed from the doorway.

Tabitha struck a match but it didn't catch. She tried again. Rupert grinned.

'Fire? Fighting a dragon with fire? That can only mean one thing. I wonder where you've hidden them, Delilah Dragonslayer.' Rupert lifted up an ornamental chest of drawers and sent them flying to the wall behind Del and Tabitha. They ducked, shielding their heads as the drawers smashed. 'No, not under here.'

Del, still dizzy and shaken, growled.

'Don't call me Delilah.' She took the box of matches from Tabitha and roared as she struck at the match. It split in half from the force but a flame licked the end. Del threw it to the ground and the gunpowder trail lit up. It would take time for the flame to find the explosives. Del, sick with rage, took up Markkus's sword from the floor and charged at Rupert. Rupert backed up a couple of steps towards the bed. The king yowled in pain as Markkus fired his pistol, catching Rupert on his neck.

Tabitha watched. She didn't feel able to do anything else. She watched these two humans attacking the dragon and something inside her shifted. Was that, she thought, was she actually feeling pity for him?

'Stop,' she breathed. If Rupert died now then the deaths would stop and she would have vengeance for her father. Then what? The anger would remain, just as the blacksmith had said. How would the city move on? How would the dragons react to such violence? 'Stop!' she shouted. She ran back towards Andra. 'Stop them.'

'What?'

'Stop them!'

'He's been killing people, this is what we do.'

'Not like this.' Tabitha's words all came at once, her breathing coming in short gasps. 'If they kill him like this they are no better than him. What will happen? With the other dragons? There will be war.' Tabitha looked hard into Andra's eyes. 'Don't they realise that?'

Andra looked over Tabitha's shoulder at Del, Markkus and Rupert. She only paused to think for a second but it seemed much longer to Tabitha. Andra looked to her right.

'We need to get out of here. Now.' She gestured to the line of spent gunpowder. Tabitha's bowels loosened at the sight of the flame licking so close to the explosives. 'We need to stop them and run.' Andra unsheathed her own sword and ran into the room.

'You have to stop,' Tabitha shouted, following. 'You have to stop.'

Del glanced over her shoulder at the sound to see Andra and Tabitha running into the room. She looked at the explosives. It was too late to stop them.

'Cover!' she yelled. She ran to Tabitha, grabbing her around the waist and yanking her back to the servants' door. Andra pulled at Markkus, ducking away from Rupert's tail.

'Stop! We have to go. Now.'

Markkus withdrew and allowed Andra to lead him to the servants' door. As they ran through King Rupert followed, smashing through the wall, brick and plaster cascading around him. Coughing, they ran through the corridor.

Rupert watched them, waiting for the cloud of debris he had created to lift before following. His shoulders and spine smashed against the brick walls and the plastered ceiling. The corridor collapsed around him as he ran. He felt the weight of the castle around him, it bore down on him making his skin and bones ache, but his rage made him move on. The iron taste of blood filled his mouth and the only thought that turned and twisted and screamed in his mind was that Del had to die. If only he could kill her, then everything would be all right. He should have killed her himself the day he exiled her. The castle ripped apart as he followed them until the vibrations and noise of a smothered boom made him stop. The walls and floor rippled around him, coursing up through his legs, around his body and down his spine. He roared in pain as flame burst through the debris behind him. The ceiling in front of him collapsed and he was engulfed.

Del and Tabitha ran. Tabitha couldn't feel her legs anymore but she could feel Del's grip on her wrist, pulling her onwards. She was aware of pounding footsteps behind and hoped they belonged to Markkus. They ran straight out of the servants' corridor, into the main castle and out through the front door. Once in the forecourt they slowed and stopped. Next to them, the carriage horses that had pulled Gerard and Del to the castle lifted their heads high. Tabitha bent over, hands on her knees as she fought for breath. As the explosion shook the hilltop the horses reared and snorted, the whites of their eyes showing. One tore itself from its harness and galloped out of the forecourt. Guards backed away, dropping the reins of the horses, muttering under their breath. Del was scanning the forecourt as Tabitha turned away to stare at the main castle doors.

Markkus and Andra stumbled out and down the steps. Tabitha grinned, relief coursing through her. The two approached fast, faces dirty and breathing hard.

'Everyone all right?' Del asked. They all nodded. 'Good.'

Tabitha straightened and looked straight into Del's eyes.

'You shouldn't have done that.'

Del watched her curiously.

Tabitha continued, 'If you've killed him you will be no better than him. It may start a war. There has to be another way.'

'Of course there is,' Del told her. 'You don't think I tried every other way? I didn't attempt to kill Rupert when I first discovered what he was doing. I approached Lord Gerard, the most powerful of all the dragonslayers. I beseeched help from those who could. I approached the High Circle. They all ignored me. This is the last resort and this is what it has come to. There is no other way now. The king will kill and he will keep killing. Something bigger is going on here. Did you hear what he said?' she asked Andra who frowned. 'Someone's protecting him and there will be no end to it.'

Tabitha shrunk back. So Del understood it all. She knew what she was doing and she was willing to start a war.

'Where is he?' asked Markkus, looking back to the castle.

'Maybe he's dead.' Del shrugged. She walked over to a bench against the far wall, opposite the castle doors, and sat. Tabitha watched Markkus and Andra.

'Is that it?'

'No,' said Andra. 'You two should get to safety. I'm going to get my men.'

'Del has sent a message to the High Circle,' Markkus told Andra.

'I know.' Andra looked shocked. 'I'm the one who sent it.'

'No.' Markkus's brow furrowed. 'I sent an assassin to her and he took the message.'

'Charles the assassin?' Tabitha whispered.

'Yes. I paid him twice what the king offered to kill

me.'

'So two messages have gone to the High Circle and there's been no response.' Andra's shoulders sagged. 'Del was right. This is all we have.' She looked up to the forecourt entrance. On the left the top of the gallows peaked over the wall. 'I'll get my men and we finish this now.'

Andra strode towards the crowd of people outside the forecourt gathering for the execution and drawn closer by the explosions. Tabitha drew in a deep breath. It should be over by now, she thought, what more could she do? She looked up at Markkus who winked at her. Just for a moment the world seemed a little better.

*

The crowd was growing outside the castle gates. Next to the castle walls sat the gallows, freshly sanded and varnished. Temporary market stalls surrounded the crowd, the owners bellowing their latest bargains above the din. Johnny made his way through the mass of people. He was looking up at the gallows but he was thinking about the sausages in buns that he'd just walked past.

Hangings in Drummbek were not uncommon. The city was brimming with life, and therefore death. There were more than enough people in the city who turned to killing, whether on purpose or by accident. It hardly mattered which. The penalty for murder was death, usually by hanging. It had been a long time since there had been a hanging for the charge of treason or of a dragonslayer turning rogue. Or for a person whose name was so well known throughout the households of Drummbek. Here was someone who encapsulated all three. Such a thing had become unheard of. This was a great event in Drummbek. Del had long ago earned a heroic status with the lower classes who had claimed her as their own. As such, most of Old Town had turned out for her execution. Some may have believed she deserved it but many just wanted an excuse to eat questionable meat in a bun and get drunk.

Johnny had known Del. Not as well as Markkus, but he had met her and worked with her during the Great War. Here were so many people laughing and joking, even excited about the prospect of seeing her die. He wasn't going to offer any support, even if that meant not buying a sausage in a bun.

He looked above the crowds, searching for the Head of the Dragonslayer Order's carriage, the prison coach, Markkus. The sight of any would have done but Johnny could see none of them. He made his way towards the gallows. Facing the crowds, he searched each face for some familiarity.

*

Tabitha sat close to Markkus and watched as smoke spiralled up into the sky. Half of the castle had collapsed and as they sat in silence, a small part of roof caved in.

'Do you think he's dead?' Tabitha asked.

'Only one way to find out.' Del stood as the sound of hoof beats filled the air and echoed around the forecourt. They all turned to watch Andra hurry back into the forecourt on foot and not looking best pleased. Lord Gerard, astride his black charger, trotted into the forecourt followed by what looked like the entire Dragonslayer Order of Drummbek. There were just over a hundred of them, all dressed in full uniform. They rode large, toned horses with nostrils flaring and springs in their steps. They pulled up to a halt in the centre of the forecourt, the horses throwing up their heads and snorting. Markkus and Tabitha remained sitting. Tabitha's heart quickened. She had only seen so many uniformed, mounted dragonslayers at the parades or at large celebrations. At the end of the Great War and at the king's coronation. She glanced at Markkus. Had he ever seen anything like this?

Del hung back, nervous to approach when she was so vastly outnumbered. Andra reached her and turned to stand defiant by her side. Something that Del found immediate comfort in. Lord Gerard gave Del a cold look as he dismounted. Dropping the reins of his horse, he marched towards the steps leading to the main castle doors. There, he turned on the nearest, scattered royal guards.

'Men. Your king is in there. Are you just going to leave him?'

The guards were hesitant and Del didn't blame them. She watched as they mumbled to one another, gesturing to their colleagues. They shuffled together and made their way into the ruins of the castle. Gerard climbed the still standing steps to the castle entrance and turned back to his companies.

'Dragonslayers!' he called. A hushed silence fell upon the forecourt. 'Make this space ready.' Each of the dragonslayers turned their horses. They positioned themselves in a circle around the forecourt leaving only the main entrance clear. They drew their swords and pointed them towards the circle centre. Del's world seemed to spin. She looked up to the sky.

'Can't be,' she murmured. Markkus and Tabitha followed her gaze.

'What? What is it?' Markkus stood, leaving Tabitha on the bench. Del didn't respond. She turned, searching, leaning to see around the castle turrets.

The ground shuddered beneath their feet. The dragonslayers looked straight ahead, expressionless. To Del the loud booming was like a familiar friend. The noise from the gathering crowds outside the forecourt rose. Some shouted, someone screamed. There was another thud and a large green and gold dragon swooped in above them, flying over the castle and hovering. The ground shuddered with each beat of the great wings. A silence fell on the crowds waiting outside the castle. Each dragonslayer raised their swords as one to point towards the sky and bowed their heads. The dragon lowered, landing delicately in the centre of the forecourt. Del flustered a little as she became light headed. Everything seemed too bright, but here was hope. She moved as if to sit down and then straightened, moving a hand back to lean on Andra.

'Who's that?' Markkus whispered.

'The Lady Gaia,' Del breathed. Coming to her senses as she voiced the name, she dropped to her knee and bowed low to the dragon. Andra, beside her, did the same.

'Should we bow?' Tabitha hissed to Markkus.

'No, I don't think so. We're not dragonslayers.'

Lady Gaia walked towards the castle entrance. She surveyed the ruins of the castle and sniffed the air. She was a little smaller than Rupert. Her green body shone in the sunshine, reflecting back a golden sheen. There were gold sweeps under her eyes and a gold trim lined her ears. Her polished claws sparkled in the weak sunlight, and golden rings adorned her long tail. Lord Gerard bowed low before her.

'Lord Gerard of the Fourth Corner of Drummbek.' Her voice was like silk. 'I am glad to see that you received my message. I understand there have been accusations towards King Rupert of Drummbek. Accusations made by a dragonslayer.'

Del felt herself redden. The walls around the forecourt seemed to bend and flex as she breathed but some part of her mind was still working.

'Fetch Tabitha's father. Gods, I hope he's still alive,' she whispered to Markkus. 'Quickly. Hurry. Now.'

Twenty-Two

Markkus didn't question Del. He gestured to Tabitha and they walked behind the dragonslayers and out of the forecourt. No one tried to stop them. Once outside, Markkus turned to Tabitha, trying to put the noise of the crowds behind him.

'I have a chair on wheels. You go home and prepare your father. I'll get the chair. Quickly now.'

'Wait. I don't want-'

'-Your father is proof of what the king's been up to.' Markkus's brow creased. He assumed that was Del's plan. It was risky. Would Erik's mind cope? It may be too soon to face him with another dragon. But what other choice was there. Tabitha frowned but nodded and ran towards Black Bull Lane and her parents.

Markkus ran and jogged to his home over the bridge. In a cupboard behind his front door was a chair. It was an ordinary wooden chair with wheels fitted to each leg and two handles on the back. A gift from Ferrer the blacksmith when Markkus had returned from war split, burned and broken. The original cushions still sat on the seat. Markkus rolled it out and unburdened it of the bags and boxes thrown onto it over the years. He hoped it would still hold the weight of a man. It had been a faithful friend until he had learned to be independent on his new leg. He lifted the chair, holding the back under one arm, and returned to the streets. He would have to be quick but his arms and legs were already tiring from the weight of the chair. Despite switching it to his other arm, it wasn't long before that too became unmanageable. He stopped and placed the chair down on its wheels. Pushing it along, he strained to control it as it bounced over the uneven road.

Just around the corner from his front door was a line of horses and shining black cabs queuing along the edge of the street waiting for fares. Markkus walked up to the horse harnessed to the cab at the head of the line.

'Excuse me?'

The driver stood on the opposite side of the horse, stroking the animal's cheek. He peered at Markkus from underneath his horse's neck.

'Yes mate, where can I drop you?' He walked around his horse and stopped when he saw the chair. 'Oh no, sorry mate. Don't have room for that. What is that?'

'A chair on wheels. You're sure? It's an emergency.' The cab driver licked his lips and exhaled in a whistle. 'I can't. But I know a man who could.' He placed two fingers in his mouth and gave a shrill whistle. His horse bobbed its head at the noise, its eyes wide and nostrils flared, and he gave it a swift, comforting pat on the rump. A small boy in a smart cap appeared at their side.

'Yes, uncle?'

'Go get your daddy and his cart, will ya? This man and his chair need a lift. It's an emergency.' The man raised an eyebrow at the boy. The boy looked over at the chair suspiciously. 'Emergency, Sid. You know what that means? It means now.' The cab driver gave his nephew a kick on the behind sending him scurrying to his father. 'Won't be a tick.' The cab driver grinned at Markkus. 'So, not life and death I hope?'

'I hope not.'

'Good, good. You're not going to the execution

today? Been an explosion up at the castle. Did you hear it? I was hoping you might want to be going in that direction. See, I have to wait for a fare before I can see it for myself.'

'Actually, I was just there.'

'Were you now? So you know what's going on?'

'Not…no,' Markkus stuttered.

'Shame. One of my mate's just got back from there. There was one hell of a crowd anyway, on accounts of the hanging, but now the roads are just filling up. Are you headed back? You might have some trouble.'

'I need to go to Old Town first.'

'Ah well, that shouldn't be a problem. Did you see, by the way? The dragon coming in to the castle? Bet it's come to see the king. Whereabouts in Old Town do you want?'

'Black Bull Lane. And then to the castle. Through the crowds if possible.'

The cab driver stared at Markkus.

'Will ya now?'

Markkus nodded.

'So you're involved then? Or just fancy taking your old granny sightseeing?'

Markkus glared at the man.

'How much will it be?'

'Ten silver pieces normally. But to go through the crowds right up to the castle gates, with everything that's going on? That'll be two gold.'

'One gold.'

'No, mate, you didn't hear me right. Two. Horses could get spooked, deliveries lost. Remember, it's not me taking you. It's me brother. He delivers fruit and veg round the city. Have to factor in cost of tenderin' and possible damage to his cart.'

Markkus blinked. This was a savvy cab driver. A

large cart laden with barrels and pulled by two heavy chestnut horses pulled up. Markkus glanced up at the driver, who appeared to be a larger version of the cab driver, and was staring at the chair on wheels.

'Fine, two.' Markkus dug his hands into his pockets and counted the money into the cab driver's hands.

'Sid, help this gentleman get his chair up.' The cab driver moved to give his brother half of the gold as the boy helped Markkus lift the chair onto the back of the cart. Markkus sat beside it, his weary limbs and cracked ribs complaining. Soon they were moving, the cart tumbling along and Markkus grimacing with each bounce.

*

Johnny had watched with interest as the dragonslayers pushed through the crowds into the castle forecourt. He'd marvelled along with the crowd at the arrival of the strange green dragon. Whatever was going to happen today, he doubted it would happen where the crowd could see. He smiled to himself. Del would not hang today, he was sure of that now. He was also satisfied that he now knew where Markkus was. Indeed, he had watched his old army commander leave the forecourt with a girl. They had separated. She had run down the road away from the castle and Markkus had hurried away in the direction of New Town. Johnny had considered following him but got the feeling he would hold his old buddy up. He turned to the direction in which the girl had disappeared but she was lost in the crowds. Frustrated, Johnny turned and looked up at the gallows. The castle gate was now blocked by the city guard. The press from the crowd now so strong that they forced those guarding the gallows to move to the gate. Johnny decided to test his luck. He placed a foot on the first step of the gallows and waited. No one scolded him. There were no shouts or bellows. He climbed the first few steps and waited again. Nothing. No one had noticed. Using the platform of the gallows, Johnny found a foothold in the old castle wall. He clambered up and peered over the top. The castle was near to ruins, rubble and stone piled in a heap. It was a shocking sight for someone who had grown up with the view of that castle, to see it so easily demolished. Johnny looked down into the castle forecourt at the array of dragonslayers on their horses and the elegant green dragon shining with gold. There, behind the dragon, was Del.

*

'Is the dragonslayer making the accusations here, Lord Gerard?' the Lady Gaia asked.

'Yes, my Lady. Please excuse the crowds outside the castle gate, she is due to be hanged imminently. She is also the cause for the destruction of the castle. King Rupert is still inside. I have sent his guards to look for him. With your permission I will dispatch some of my own men.'

'No need. I'm sure his guards are capable. Where is this dragonslayer, Lord Gerard?'

'Behind you, my Lady.' The Lady Gaia's head swivelled round as she sought out Del, still by the bench. Del stood tall, hands clasped behind her back. She stared straight ahead. Focusing on controlling her breathing and ignoring the sweat beading on her forehead.

'Hello, Del Dragonslayer.'

'It is good to see you again, my Lady.' Del bowed.

'I remember when I last saw you, Del, and the accusations you made against King Rupert. Am I to understand that these still stand?'

'Yes, my Lady. King Rupert has been eating people.' The words sounded stupid leaving Del's mouth, despite the amount of times she had uttered them in the past. She cleared her throat and focused on standing tall.

'That is a dangerous accusation, Del Dragonslayer. It was then and it is now. Your message did not mention evidence. I hope that you have not brought me all this way with nothing to show me?'

'My Lady, unfortunately my first witness disappeared.' Del risked glancing up at the Lady Gaia.

'Your witness was eaten?'

'I have no evidence of that, my Lady. But his wife was.'

'Do you have any other evidence?'

'Yes, my Lady.'

'Which is?'

'On their way, my Lady.' Del shifted her position.

'On their way?'

'Yes, my Lady. I was not informed that you would be joining us.'

'You sent me two messages to come along with the date and time of your hanging.'

'Yes, my Lady, but I could not be certain that you would believe me.'

The dragon smiled showing off a row of pearly white razored teeth.

'Belief, Del Dragonslayer, is an interesting concept. I am yet to believe you. But you have piqued my curiosity.' The Lady Gaia gave a small sigh and settled into a sitting position. 'It has been a long journey. May I request a drink?'

'Of course, my Lady.' Lord Gerard jumped to

attention. 'Of course.' He hissed something at the nearest dragonslayer. 'What would you like, my Lady?'

'Just water.'

The dragonslayer and his horse trotted out of the forecourt. Del listened to the crowd as the dragonslayer appeared among them, heading towards the academy to fetch the second most ornate dragon tableware, the first being in the ruined castle. The Lady Gaia studied Del.

'I remember you well. You haven't changed a great deal since our last meeting.' She no longer raised her voice so that everyone could hear. 'But oh, the shock of seeing you when you were first exiled and you brought your concerns to the High Council. I remember. Gone was the proud, smart dragonslayer we once knew. You still had that fire though. I found your claims curious then. I have heard the rumours since.'

Del said nothing, not trusting herself to say anything uncontentious.

'I understand that no one responded to you after you brought forward your concerns?'

'No, my Lady.'

'I apologise for that. How long have you been a dragonslayer?'

'Twenty three years, my Lady.'

'And how many of those did you spend in exile?'

'Two.'

The Lady Gaia nodded.

'I understand that you are one of the best.'

'I don't know about that, my Lady.'

The Lady Gaia stood and turned to Gerard.

'I like her, Lord Gerard.'

'Yes, my Lady.'

A cart drove through the waiting crowds surrounding the forecourt entrance. Del listened to the rumbling of the expectant crowds outside. She wondered how many out there were friends. How many would have been sad to watch her die. There were gasps from beyond the castle walls as the Lady Gaia stood and the people waiting outside caught a glimpse of her. Del hoped the city guard would hold them back. It was a fair bet that none of them knew who the Lady Gaia was and if this were to get out of control it could become embarrassing.

The small cart held a large bowl, in silver with embedded rubies, filled with water. The cart, led by two smart ponies, stopped before the Lady Gaia. One of the ponies rolled its eyes at the dragon and began to worry. The other stood steadfast and gave it enough courage to stop it bolting.

The Lady Gaia lifted the bowl to her lips and drank.

'When is your evidence getting here, Del Dragonslayer?'

Del looked to the main entrance.

'Soon, my Lady,' she hoped.

*

Johnny gave a small smile, watching the dragon drink from the large bowl and speak to Del. His smile faded when someone pulled on his trouser leg. He looked down.

'And just what do you think you're doing?'

Johnny slid down the wall back onto the gallows platform.

'Sorry. I was only looking. I'm an old friend of-'

'I don't care if you're an old friend of Hermann the Wise, you're not allowed up there. Get down now. If I see you up there again I'll arrest you.' Inspector Monterey visibly resisted waggling a finger at Johnny.

Instead, he opened his arms, herding Johnny down to the ground and into the crowd. Johnny watched the inspector return to his men at the castle gates. Well, he thought, that was that.

As Johnny turned away he heard the inspector shouting. Looking over his shoulder, Johnny watched a cart trundle through the crowd at a fast paced trot. The two thickset horses pulling the cart threw up their heads, snorting and dancing. The cart rushed towards the castle gates and through, scattering the city guard. Inspector Monterey ran after them shouting. Johnny caught a glimpse of Markkus hanging on to the back of the cart.

*

There were a few moments of awkward silence before the cart rolled into the forecourt. The large man driving swore under his breath but only loud enough for those nearby to hear. Inspector Monterey followed them in at a run.

'I'm sorry, my Lord. They pushed through, they-'

'It's okay, Inspector. I requested them,' Del called. Monterey turned to Lord Gerard who gave a swift nod. The inspector's gaze landed on the Lady Gaia for just a moment too long before he bowed and returned to hold back the crowd. Del moved to the back of the cart. Markkus dropped to his feet with a groan. There was Tabitha standing, holding onto the handles of a chair upon which Erik sat. He was on cushions with a blanket over the space where his legs should have been. His torso strapped to the back of the chair to keep him in place. It was a joint effort between the three to lower him to the ground. Tabitha wheeled him around the cart to face the dragon under Del's instruction.

'Good idea, the chair,' Del whispered to Markkus.

Markkus thanked the driver who gladly turned around and fled the forecourt.

The Lady Gaia looked down at Tabitha and Erik who both stared up at the dragon.

'My Lady,' Del said loud enough for all to hear. 'May I introduce Tabitha Dunn, a maid under royal employment in the castle, and her father, Erik Dunn. Tabitha, Erik, this is the Lady Gaia-'

'Hello Tabitha and Erik Dunn,' the Lady Gaia interrupted, rolling the names around on her tongue. 'Do you know who I am?

Tabitha and Erik shook their heads. Erik looked better than when Del had last seen him though he was still ghostly pale. His eyes were narrow slits as he squinted against the light and his hands gripped the blanket so tight that his knuckles were white. His cracked lips parted as he breathed and there were dark bags under his sunken eyes. Tabitha gripped the handles of the chair, not daring to let her father go. 'I am the oldest dragon in the world and I sit on the High Circle of Seracombe.' The Lady Gaia grinned, showing off her sparkling teeth. Erik flinched, pulling his blanket higher as if to hide behind it. The Lady Gaia dropped her lips. She studied him a little before continuing. 'I am here because Del Dragonslayer has made some serious accusations about King Rupert of Drummbek. She said that you have seen first-hand certain behaviour from your king?'

Tabitha nodded.

'Yes,' she replied with a small voice. The Lady Gaia turned to Del.

'Continue.'

Del bowed her head.

'My Lady, I don't have a witness of the king eating people but-'

'You do,' Tabitha interrupted in a small voice. Del looked to her. 'I happened to come across the king's chambers as I went about my duties and I saw...' Tabitha drifted off.

'You saw?' the Lady Gaia prompted. Del stared at Tabitha wide-eyed, fighting the urge to hug the girl.

'Blood. I heard a scream and then I saw King Rupert...eating her.' Tabitha's voice quivered. Markkus stepped forward and placed a hand on her shoulder. The Lady Gaia's eyes flicked to him.

'My Lady. This is Commander Markkus Kern, the royal taster. King Rupert recently tried to kill him.'

'It's true, my Lady,' Markkus said, loud and strong enough for all the dragonslayers to hear. 'Erik, here, interrupted the act by storming into the room. He thought Tabitha was in there and in danger, my Lady. It was enough of a distraction for the king to release me. He saved my life.' The Lady Gaia looked down at Erik.

'Unfortunately, the king went after Erik, my Lady,' Del continued. She moved forward and took hold of the blanket. 'Can I show her, Erik? Everything will be okay. I promise nothing bad will happen to you,' she told him. After a moment Erik nodded and released the blanket from his grasp. With slow movements, Del removed it from his lower half.

A low noise filled the forecourt at the sight of Erik's missing legs and the cauterised wounds. The dragonslayers broke from their regulated positions to gasp and murmur to one another. The Lady Gaia's eyes widened. She brought her head down to Erik's level.

'Erik Dunn, did King Rupert do this to you?' Erik's lower lip began to quiver.

'Ripped them. Held me up and then it hurt. Pain like I've never known.' Tears filled his eyes. 'But I didn't say anything. He can't have her, you know. Never.'

The Lady Gaia looked up at Del and Markkus.

'He means me. He was trying to save me.' Tabitha swallowed hard on a sob. The Lady Gaia nodded.

'Replace the blanket,' she said sadly. She grew tall and turned back to the castle. 'Where is King Rupert? I would speak to him. You set off explosives?' She turned to Del. Del nodded. 'Then you better hope he is alive. I believe he may be guilty of murder, let us hope that you are not.' Del looked down at the ground and took a shaky breath. 'Where are the guards? Find the king.' The Lady Gaia walked over to the castle and gazed over the ruins. Guards were picking their way through as best they could. One waved. The Lady Gaia strode through the ruins towards the guard. Stretching out her wings and casting long shadows, she leaned over the rubble. Picking up lumps of brick and rock in her claws and placing them to the side. King Rupert lifted his head and upon sight of the Lady Gaia, flinched and lowered it once more.

'King Rupert. Can you move?' The Lady Gaia asked.

Rupert hesitated. This was a dream. A vision. An hallucination. She couldn't be here. Not now. The world swayed. He became aware of the chill breeze against his cuts and scrapes, making them sting. He was awake.

'Yes, my Lady.' Rupert fought off the debris that covered him, opening his wings. The guards around him tried to escape the king's body and the rubble falling from him. Rupert gazed around the forecourt as he picked his way through the debris and around the still standing walls and turrets. It was not over yet. There had to be an opportunity here, but his mind was swimming. Each thought was an effort to form.

'Ensure the guards are safe,' the Lady Gaia said to

the nearest dragonslayer. Five dragonslayers dismounted and moved into the ruins to pull out the guards. 'King Rupert. You are accused of murder, of eating humans and of dismembering this poor gentleman. What is your response to this?'

Rupert glanced around, trying to catch up with what he had missed. His gaze settled on Del.

'You,' he hissed. 'She tried to blow me up. Arrest her!' He pointed a claw at Del who stiffened.

'No, Rupert,' the Lady Gaia scolded. 'Answer my question. Have you or have you not been killing and eating humans?'

King Rupert looked the Lady Gaia in the eye.

'You of all the dragons should understand,' he told her. 'You, of all the dragons. Bigger things are coming.'

'Did you rip the legs from this man?' The Lady Gaia pointed to Erik who gave a sharp cry. Tabitha moved to hug her father, speaking soft words to him.

'They are insects,' Rupert hissed. 'This is just the beginning.'

'Of what, Rupert?'

'You know exactly what,' Rupert boomed. It had been a long shot, expecting any kind of loyalty from her. She would see, in the end, that he was right. Doubt had no place in his mind, although he conceded that now was not the time he had planned for. Before the Lady Gaia could respond, he opened his wings and beat them, heart pounding.

The force of the wind Rupert's wings created threw Del and Andra backwards. Markkus dived to create a barrier between Erik and Rupert. Dragonslayers fell from their horses as their mounts reared and stumbled. King Rupert lifted into the air. He beat his wings and rose higher, taking off above the castle.

'King Rupert, return at once. Your fleeing is a sign of your guilt,' the Lady Gaia called above the din. With an earth rattling growl, she opened her wings and lifted into the air. Picking up speed, she followed King Rupert. They climbed higher and higher, and were soon red and green dots in the sky. The crowd beyond the castle entrance shouted and screamed at the spectacle.

'What will happen?' Tabitha asked, stroking her father's shoulder.

'I don't know,' Del said. She wrung her hands, watching the dragons and straining to keep her eyes on the Lady Gaia. Willing the dragon to catch up with Rupert and to survive.

There was a boom that shook the foundations of the forecourt walls. Horses squealed and some fell to the ground. Del's hearing became muffled and a loud, shrill ring pierced through her.

*

Johnny and the near silent crowd watched King Rupert and the green dragon lift into the air. A hush had fallen over the city as all eyes looked up at their monarch, soaring away from this strange dragon. Johnny looked around him, at the expectant faces. Who was this green dragon? What in the king's breath was going on? He was sure he couldn't be the only one to feel so frustrated at having none of the answers. A boom shook the ground beneath his feet. Some in the crowd fell to their knees. Johnny kept his balance although his hands moved instinctively to his ears.

The red dot fell from the sky, growing larger. The body of King Rupert hit the ground just outside the city walls.

Twenty-Three

The day the king fell from the sky. It would be the talk of the city for weeks. Rupert had landed on a field of crops. The Lady Gaia ensured the farmer in question received compensation. Rupert was not killed by the fall, although reports told of some broken bones and a torn wing. The Lady Gaia had taken him away. There was to be a trial before the High Council. Soon Drummbek often spoke in hushed tones of the king's execution in Seracombe.

The Lady Gaia promised Tabitha and Milly compensation for the loss of Erik's legs and the wages he once brought into the home. Tabitha and her mother accepted but a depression still descended upon their house. Erik no longer spoke in coherent sentences. Doctor Rotterdam told them that his mind was trying to cope with the situation and that it wasn't coping well. Tabitha's mother grew silent and dazed.

Markkus visited every day since the king fell from the sky. Tabitha opened the door to him.

'How is he?'

'He's fine, I guess. He's eating and today seems to be a happy day.'

'He's doing well, it'll just take time.'

Tabitha nodded.

'And your mother?'

'The same. She ate last night but not today.' Tabitha shrugged. She had cried her tears and no more would come.

'And how are you managing?'

'I got the job at the local tavern. Where dad used to go. I guess they took pity on me. It's good of you to keep visiting. Would you like to see him?'

Markkus followed Tabitha inside and waited in the small family room. Tabitha smiled as she fetched her father. She enjoyed Markkus's visits, more than she cared to admit. She didn't feel like the same Tabitha that had once been nervous of stealing glances of the royal taster. She felt older, wiser, and, dare she admit, happier. Despite her father's health, despite her mother's. That spark of happiness often came riddled with guilt, but still it flickered and grew. Her father beamed as she helped him into the wheeled chair, and placed his hand on her cheek. Markkus had allowed him to keep the chair in the hope that he would never need it again himself.

'Good morning, Erik,' said Markkus as Erik and Tabitha appeared at the door. 'How are you today?'

'Good morning, soldier,' Erik snapped back happily. 'You're back from war.'

'Yes, Erik. I'm back.' Markkus smiled. Erik's happiness was contagious, no matter how dire the situation.

'Good. And when will you be wedding my daughter?'

'Dad!' Tabitha rushed forward and poured her father a drink. 'Drink?' she offered Markkus. He nodded and took the cup from her hands.

'I'm afraid I won't be marrying your daughter, Erik,' Markkus told him, giving Tabitha a fleeting glance.

'Don't be silly. It's obvious you care for her. And you're not getting any younger. Look at her! She's beautiful and she loves you. You'd be a fool not to marry her.'

Tabitha's cheeks burned.

'It's just his way of coping,' she said, partly to Markkus, partly to herself. Markkus laughed it off but his gaze lingered on Tabitha a little longer than Tabitha would have considered normal.

'Maybe when she's older, Erik.'

'Ah yes, perhaps she is a little young.' Erik looked Tabitha up and down.

'And I'm afraid this will be my last visit.'

'What?' Tabitha nearly shouted.

'Off to war again?'

'Yes, Erik. I'm afraid so.'

'Sad day. Make sure you come back for my daughter.'

'Of course, Erik.'

'Where are you going?' Tabitha asked.

'To war, darling, pay attention.' Erik patted his daughter's hand.

'I'm going to visit family in Arisdon.'

'Arisdon?'

'It's not that far away.'

'When are you going?' Tabitha didn't care that her tone was close to a whine.

'Tonight.'

'Why?'

Markkus gave her a sad smile. He gestured to her and they walked away from Erik.

'I have to get out of this city, Tabitha. Just for a while. I will be back, I promise.'

'But without you, I-'

'You'll be fine.' Markkus waited until she looked up into his eyes. 'You're strong and clever and you can do whatever you want.'

'But I want you to stay. I don't think I can do this

alone,' she murmured.

'You can. I haven't been doing anything. It's all you. I will be back and I can't wait to see what you'll have become.' Markkus placed a kiss on her forehead and went back to Erik. Tabitha watched him in disbelief. The warmth of his lips lingered on her skin and she paused, not wanting to lose the sensation. Markkus said his goodbyes and left, hunched over against the cold. He turned to look back just before he was out of sight. Tabitha and Erik watched from the front door. Tabitha hugging herself and attempting a weak wave as Markkus turned. Erik looked up at his daughter.

'Lovely man. Don't worry, love. He'll be back when the war is over.'

Tabitha tried to smile for her father and fought the urge to run away to her room and cry.

'By the time he returns from war, you'll be a woman. Ready for marriage and children. Now is your time. What do you want to do, Tabby?'

Tabitha stared down at her father.

*

Andra stopped in front of Ami's desk. Ami looked up and gave a curt smile.

'Captain Ferrer.' She moved to open the door to the Head of the Dragonslayer Order's office. Poking her head around, she uttered some muffled words before returning to her desk. 'You may enter,' she told Andra.

Andra straightened her clothing, took a deep breath and walked past Ami into the office.

Lord Gerard was gone, missing since the day that King Rupert fell. The whispers floating around the city told of him taking his own life by the docks, his body washing out to sea. Or that he had fled the city with as much of the king's gold as he could carry. Others told that he now dwelled under the city, living off scraps. A strange sadness came over Andra at not seeing him seated in the chair behind the grand desk.

'You wished to see me, sir?' she said.

'Ah, Captain Ferrer isn't it? Yes, do come in.' The man sat in the chair seemed friendly enough. His cheeks were burnt red from years spent outside in his youth and suckling on a bottle through his middle age. General Early had fought in the Great War. Upon coming home, he had locked himself in his great mansion within New Town. He was not a dragonslayer but since Lord Gerard had abolished the rank of general within the Order, there was no one else suitable to take his place. 'Please, take a seat. I understand you played a key part in the recent drama at the castle?'

'Yes, sir.'

'And that you lead a company of dragonslayers? Seconded by a certain Sergeant Venkell?'

'Yes, sir.'

'I fear I must tell you that Dante Venkell has asked to be considered for promotion. If successful, which I believe he will be, he will be leaving your company to become a captain.'

'Oh.' Andra deflated. She tried to shake the feeling off. 'He certainly deserves a promotion. I will help in any way I can.'

'Yes, you will be required to attend a meeting or two to give a report on his character and qualities.'

Andra nodded. Venkell's promotion was long overdue, but it was a change she didn't look forward to.

'Can I ask, sir? What will become of Del?'

'You haven't heard? As the throne is now vacant the High Council ordered her release as of yesterday. She has been pardoned of her original treason, due to her being bang on about young King Rupert. And she has been pardoned of being a rogue due to her heroic actions of protecting the people of Drummbek. I offered her a position in the academy and put in a good word to the High Council, but she refused.' Early leaned forward on his desk and smiled. 'I hope to make some changes to this academy, Captain Ferrer. The first being the reintroduction of the rank of general. Ridiculous not having any and I need a panel of advisors. And I would hope that my dragonslayers would take advantage of this. Especially certain captains who have been so involved in high profile cases. Please, let me know if you have any bright ideas or any issues.'

*

'You're leaving?' Del stood at Markkus's front door. She moved out of his way as he walked past carrying a box. He hefted it onto the cart already half laden with his belongings.

'Yes. To Arisdon. I have family there.'

'Liar. Where're you really going?'

Markkus smiled and shrugged.

'Anywhere but here. I need to get away.'

'I know the feeling. What about Tabitha?'

'What about her?'

'Please. I saw how you looked at her. How you protected her.'

'She's a child and I'm an old man.'

'She's no child, Markkus. She's a woman and she'll be more woman before you know it. You'll miss your chance with her.'

'She's too young. She doesn't know what she wants. She certainly doesn't want an old man.'

'You're wrong. Think about that before you leave.'

Del walked over to Markkus, went up on tip toe and kissed his cheek. 'Look after yourself.'

'What are you going to do?'

'Me? I'm going to find out what Rupert was on about when he said this was just the beginning. I've heard too many dragons use the words "matter of time" lately.'

'Del, he was obviously insane. Don't go on a fool's errand.'

Del shrugged.

'Maybe I'll see you on your travels. I hope I will see you again.'

'Stay alive and I'm sure you will.'

They looked at one another fondly. Del went to leave, allowing herself one glance back to see Markkus continuing to pack.

*

'Hello?' Tabitha croaked, pushing open the door to the Dragonslayer Academy. She cleared her throat. 'Hello?'

'Hello, love. Can I help?' An elderly woman in an apron appeared from her right.

'Oh, yes. I want to become a dragonslayer.'

The woman looked Tabitha up and down.

'Up the stairs, fourth floor, left and then first left.'

'Thank you.' Tabitha walked up the stairs, looking at each portrait that dotted the wall as she went. The old woman watched her and smiled before returning to her work.

There came a knock at the door. With a sigh, the old woman turned back and opened it.

'Yes?' She looked the man on the doorstep up and down.

'Hello. Who do I speak to about joining the academy?'

The old woman smiled.

'Up the stairs, dear. Fourth floor, left and first left.' She opened the door further to let him in.

'Thank you.' Johnny walked into the academy. He took a moment to let the grandeur of the building sink in and then he trotted up the stairs. The old woman shook her head and walked away from the door, for fear of any other visitors.

*

Tabitha reached Ami's desk.

'Excuse me?'

Ami looked up with a smile which immediately faded.

'Yes?'

'I want to become a dragonslayer.'

Ami wrinkled her nose and sneered at Tabitha.

'There are fees to enroll.'

'That shouldn't be a problem.' Tabitha produced a large piece of paper which held the stamp and signature of the Lady Gaia.

*

Del smiled as she read through her pardon once more. Her thumb stroked the Lady Gaia's signature. Carefully she folded the pardon and slipped it into her back pocket. Shadow's neigh greeted her as she made her way into the academy stables. Del rubbed his ears, unable to keep the grin from her face.

'Del! As I live and breathe.'

'Smith!' Del beamed at the elderly man and moved

to embrace him. The two held each other for a moment before Smith patted her back.

'I heard you were back, dear. How have you been?'

'Better now, thank you. Where have you been?'

'Ah, in bed I'm afraid.'

Del raised an eyebrow.

'And what have you been getting up to?'

Smith laughed which broke into a hacking cough.

'Oh, I wish,' he breathed. 'I wish. My lungs.' He tapped his chest. 'Are not so good.'

'I'm sorry to hear that.'

Smith waved Del's concern away.

'I'm fine. Strong as a cart horse. Speaking of which, I hear that this fine specimen belongs to you?' Smith reached up a trembling hand and gave Shadow a soft pat on the cheek. Shadow snorted.

'That he is. Shadow is his name.'

'You named him?'

'Yes. Well, his old owner named him.'

Smith stared at Del.

'Never thought I'd see the day when you would name your horse.'

'He's not your average dragonslayer horse,' Del said, running her fingers through Shadow's mane.

'No. So, you've finally realised what an asset a good horse can be?'

'Definitely.'

'I remember the first time you sat on one of our horses,' Smith murmured. 'I'm glad you've found what I was always telling you about.'

'Me too.'

'Would you like him readied?' a stable boy asked from behind Del.

'Please,' she told him. 'With saddlebags. We're leaving today.' The stable boy bowed his head and went to fetch Shadow's saddle.

'You're leaving?' Smith asked.

'I'm afraid so.'

'I heard you've been given a pardon.'

'Wow, word gets around quick doesn't it? Yes, by the Lady Gaia no less. You heard about King Rupert? It sounds like you may have missed everything.'

'Oh I heard. I heard.' Smith winked at her.

'Never miss a thing, do you?' Del chuckled. 'Not even from your sick bed.'

'You did a good thing, Del Thorburn, Protector of the City. You were always destined for great things. Knew it the moment I saw you as a small, scared young woman. Will you be coming back?'

'I hope so.'

'Well, don't leave it too long, Del.' Smith grabbed her hand and squeezed it. 'Off you go, leaving just as I get well enough to venture outside. You come and see me again before I die.'

'Don't talk like that. I'll see you soon.'

'If not in this life, in the next aye?'

'Promise.' After a moment's pause, Del hugged Smith again. Smith gave Shadow one last look.

'A fine horse,' he said. Del gave a sad smile as she watched him walk away and disappear into the tack room at the far end of the stable block. She stepped outside and breathed in the damp air. It was going to rain.

'Thought I might find you here. You're off already? Where are you going?' Andra asked, approaching from the academy.

'Travelling. Just while everything settles down.'

'You're going after the dragons, aren't you?'

Del smiled.

'So that's it? We go through one wild ride together

and now you can read my mind. Rupert said it was just a matter of time. We've both heard other dragons saying that. You said you saw it written in other captains' reports. Something's going on and I want to know what. What else am I going to do?'

'Settle down and take on Early's job offer? Become Head of the Dragonslayer Order and fight for king and city?'

'That does sound like a nice life.' Del sighed wistfully. 'Maybe when I return.' She studied Andra. 'I never wanted to be a dragonslayer, you know.'

'No? What did you want to be?'

Del looked up at the sky.

'I don't know. I wanted to be me. I wanted to go to the city. I had a fool's notion that I would find myself here. You could say I just fell into the academy.'

'No one just falls into it,' Andra said. 'You ended up here for a reason. I don't think you're done yet. Do you have enough money to keep you going? Don't you need a job?'

'I'm a widow, remember. My husband was a wealthy man.'

'I feel like you didn't tell me the whole story about that.'

'Ah, but you know enough.' Del grinned, patting Andra on the arm. Andra shook her head, smiling.

'So why keep doing it? If you never wanted to.'

'One thing I learned, about finding myself, is that you've got to do what you're good at.' Del stretched her back as Andra watched her.

'I don't think you're right,' she murmured. 'Do what you enjoy.'

'Are you doing what you enjoy, Andra?'

Andra thought about this.

'Yes. I always wanted to be a dragonslayer, ever

since I first saw you on parade. Your clothes were muddy and stained, and you walked out of time and you just didn't care. And there you were. I thought, there is a woman who is her own boss. There is a woman who is in control of her life.'

'That's what you wanted?'

'I wanted to be me.'

The women smiled at each other.

'Captain Andra Ferrer, the Dragonslayer.' Del's smile fell. 'I've been doing this job a long time, you know. It isn't about what you enjoy or even what you're good at, Andra. It's important, don't get me wrong. But it's not truly about that.'

A stable boy led Shadow out and handed Del the reins. Thanking the boy, she mounted Shadow in one easy motion. 'It's about survival. Thank you for your help, Andra. It's been something of a strained pleasure. One day I hope that we can meet again under nicer circumstances.'

Andra nodded.

'It's been an honour to finally meet you properly.'

'Oh, don't. Thank your father again for my new weapons. The sword's a beauty. Oh, and next time I see you I want hear you've been promoted.' Del winked at Andra and clicked her tongue at Shadow. Dragonslayer and horse trotted under the archway, out of the academy and towards the city gate.

***

Despite Our Enemies

Book Two in the Last War Trilogy is coming Spring 2017.

Acknowledgments

This book wouldn't be possible without the three most important people in my life (I love you).

Along with the job where I had nothing to do for the first week, the filmmakers who inspire me when I'm too tired to think, Julia the designer who inadvertently made me do my best Kermit the Frog impression when I opened her email, friends past and present who read my stories even when we haven't spoken in years, and the English teachers and History teacher who encouraged me.

Want more?

You can find out more about J E Nice at www.jenice.co.uk.

It doesn't take much to get updates and access to all the goodies that J E Nice showers on her supporters.
Simply put in your email address at
 www.jenice.co.uk/updates

Made in the USA
Charleston, SC
28 August 2016